MW00769768

Philippa HOLDS Court

CLAVERING CHRONICLES 2

JENNIE GOUTET

ISBN 978-1-4003-2456-9
Copyright © 2021 by Jennie Goutet

Cover design by Shaela Odd at Blue Water Books
Edited by Jolene Perry, Ranée Clark and Arielle Bailey

Published August 2021

Dedicated to my dear friend, Emma Le Noan,
without whom I might never have discovered the delight
of reading Georgette Heyer. Thank you for supporting me
in life and fiction.

CHAPTER ONE

London, 1819

*P*hilippa Clavering removed her straw poke bonnet with red ribbons and handed the item to the butler, following it with her ivory cloak made of light wool. It had been two years since she'd laid eyes on the well-lit corridor of her brother's townhouse, and she brightened at its familiarity. A sense of contentment lifted her spirits for the first time since she'd arrived in London.

"Sir Lucius and Lady Clavering are in the nursery, miss." Briggs gave a smile of welcome and draped Philippa's cloak over his arm.

Her maid untied her own bonnet as she moved forward. "I'll be in the kitchen, miss, for when you need me."

"That will be fine. We won't be staying long." No mother of a newborn would appreciate an extended visit, and Philippa was not about to impose one on her sister-in-law. Besides that, her friend Susan had sent word that morning requesting Philippa to come to Carnaby Street as soon as she could do so.

"I'll announce myself." With a nod to the butler, Philippa turned and climbed the stairs to the nursery and opened the door. Inside, an intrepid beam of early spring sun poked through the sheer curtains and traveled across the gold-accented white room, coming to rest on the face of an infant of some weeks, who was nestled in the protective arms of his proud and weary mother. Lucius was seated in a chair nearby.

Philippa exchanged a wordless smile with Selena Clavering and came to her sister-in-law's side, kneeling beside the sleeping baby, who jerked suddenly as if plagued by a bad dream.

"How he does scowl at one," Philippa observed, tucking her finger under her sleeping nephew's limp hand. Adopting an innocent expression, she turned wide eyes upon her brother. "He is your very portrait, Lucius."

A chuckle escaped Selena, and she sent Philippa an amused glance before turning her gaze back to the object of her adoration. Selena had the ability to share in one's humor, an unexpected and much-valued commodity in a sister-in-law, Philippa found.

"He will need the scowl to keep his future sisters in their place," Lucius replied, stifling a yawn. Philippa had never seen her brother like this. For Lucius to appear in company—even in the company of a younger sister—unshaven and wearing no cravat, slouched back in his chair with one arm thrown over its side, showed more clearly than all else how the arrival of his heir had overturned Lucius's carefully planned existence. Not that falling for Selena hadn't already done that, but at least with Selena's addition to his life, Lucius had still managed to dress himself.

Philippa pursed her lips, caressing the tiny fingers of her nephew. "I highly doubt any future niece of mine will be frightened away by a mere scowl."

"Not if I have any say in the matter," Selena murmured, peeking at Lucius from the corner of her eye, her lips upturned. Philippa observed with satisfaction the unspoken affection that passed between the couple. Coming from a family that did not hold matrimonial—nor filial—bonds to be of great value, Lucius had done very well for himself in marrying Selena. The propensity to invest his heart in the well-being of his family, a hitherto dormant trait in Lucius, had been coaxed into being by the addition of a wife, and now son, to his life.

Philippa tucked the blanket over the leg of the sleeping baby, who startled at the sound of carriage wheels over the cobblestones underneath the window. Though still asleep, the baby's arms remained frozen in alarm midair, and Philippa laughed as Selena soothed him and gently pressed his hands back into place.

"Fear not, Hugh," his mother said. "It is just the sights and sounds of London. You will soon grow accustomed to it."

"That begs the question," Philippa said. "Although I am vastly pleased to see you both here, why did you come to London so soon after Hugh's arrival?" She swiveled to look at Lucius. "I had thought you would stay at Mardley. I could get nothing out of Maria."

"That is because I do not confide in Maria—which you know very well," Lucius replied, turning his sardonic gaze on Philippa. There was no great love between Lucius and their oldest sister, Maria Holbeck. "I have some interest in a committee being drawn up in the Commons to discuss repealing a bill that—without leading into politics too complicated for you to understand—keeps the bread prices too high for the laborers to afford."

Ignoring his insinuation that she was too dull to grasp the rudimentary concepts of a parliamentary bill, Philippa peered at him in surprise. "Are you thinking of putting your name up for election?" It would be unthinkable for Lucius to stir himself in such a way.

Her brother put the notion to rout with a withering look. "I get enough encouragement from Holbeck should I ever wish for such a thing—which I don't. I am merely interested in this one committee, but I did not like to leave Selena behind."

"Had I known you would be here for the Season, I would have insisted you sponsor me," Philippa said in a teasing tone. "You all but gave me your word to do so last year, after having left me to endure my first Season with Maria as guide. A mere honeymoon was your very poor excuse."

"Yes, minx. And you all but promised me you would be married after one Season, and consider, if you will, what came of *that* promise." Lucius stood. "I must ready myself to go out. Selena, I insist you hand the baby off to Nurse for a few hours this afternoon so you may sleep. Give me your word."

"I'll give you my hand, my dear, so you may kiss it." Selena extended her hand, and Lucius took it in his own, kissing his wife on the lips, before walking off without another word spared for Philippa.

Lucius's reminder of Philippa's failure to procure a husband in her first Season did not bother her. In truth, she was in no rush to be married. If anything, Philippa rather thought she might find her husband tucked away in some village, either at Lucius and Selena's house in St. Albans or where her mother lived, newly remarried, in Watford. The sobering truth, however, was that as little as she relished the idea of rushing headlong into the married state, none of the alternatives that lay before her were ideal.

She did not feel she could impose upon her brother in such a way as to take up permanent residence with him, although she suspected Selena would welcome her in their home. And living with Philippa's mother did not inspire more enthusiasm than living with Maria. Their mother was just as self-centered and, unfortunately, a great deal less practical. Nor did Philippa have any strong attachment to her younger brother and sisters. This, she supposed, did not say anything very flattering about her sense of family obligations, but given that her siblings were still in the nursery and spent more time with their nurse than with Philippa, she could not claim to hold them in any real affection. As a whole, Philippa's home life left much to be desired, but she was not foolish enough to think that marriage was the remedy.

When the door closed behind Lucius, Selena met Philippa's gaze. "All jesting aside, I am sorry we could not sponsor you this Season. It was the very thing I wished to do."

Philippa smiled and shook her head. "I was merely teasing Lucius. Of course you cannot host me when Master Hugh is in need of you. I will do very well with Maria and Charles, as I did last year. I must simply agree to everything she says and then do whatever I wish."

Selena laughed. "Does she never notice that you haven't done *precisely* what she requests?"

"'Commands' is what you mean to say. I'll wager she does notice, but when she sees that her scolds fall on deaf ears, she convinces herself that what I've chosen to do is precisely what she'd had in mind. She persuades Mama to think the same thing, so all around, I am thought to be a very well-behaved girl."

"You *are* a very well-behaved girl," Selena replied instantly and glanced down as Hugh made motions as though to wake. "You simply possess strong opinions for a young woman"—she raised her expressive eyes to Philippa's—"which I happen to value, as you know. Perhaps you don't so much need a guiding hand as you do a listening ear. And if it comes from someone who has spent more years in the *ton* and can navigate its gossip, all the better."

"Maria firmly believes I need a guiding hand, as does Lucius. But I assure you, I can manage the gossip and every other challenge a London Season might toss my way." Philippa saw that Selena wished to sit up, and she stood to tuck the cushions more firmly behind her.

"Well, I wouldn't dream of offering an opinion my husband does not share," Selena murmured, a smile hovering on her lips. "Is that not so, Master Hugh? Your father is right about everything."

"Do not think it, Hugh. That is a faradiddle if ever I heard one," Philippa countered, wiggling her nephew's foot under the blanket. "I must be off. Truly, I came only to see how Hugh had grown in the three weeks since I've seen him. You have grander things to attend to than my silly concerns."

"Where are you off to?" Selena lifted the baby so he was against her chest, his head tucked into her neck.

"I have promised to visit Susan Blythefield. She sent a note around this morning, saying she is full of news and I must come at once."

Selena knit her brows. "Do you have someone accompanying you? Do not say you will go on your own, for it is one thing to visit your brother with no one in attendance, and it is quite another thing to go to a strange home unaccompanied."

Hugh began to squirm in Selena's arms, making small grunts of dissatisfaction as Philippa picked up her cloth reticule. "Do not worry about me. I have Fernsby, who is enjoying a comfortable gossip in the kitchen with the other maids until I call for her. You must have Hugh fed before he begins to wail."

"Yes, my little man. You will be fed." Selena laid him back down on her lap and began to untie the string that held the neckline of her shift closed. She glanced up at Philippa, who had paused on her way to the door. "Do not give me that shocked look, my dear. I did not wish for a wet nurse, and even were I to hand my baby over to someone else for his feeds, I still could not be brought into fashion. Give my regards to your sister."

Philippa smiled. Her nephew would grow into a happy, robust boy with such parents as Lucius and Selena. "I am sure Maria would have me extend her regards as well."

At the door, she recalled just how little regard her sister actually *had* for Selena, and she turned back to find Selena looking at her in amusement. Philippa curled her lips into a wicked smirk. "Most civilly."

***

The ride from her brother's townhouse to that of her friend took a full half hour. Two carriages had crossed paths in front of hers, locking wheels on the road and causing one of the carriage wheels to come loose. Philippa, traveling behind the unfortunate vehicle, had no trouble hearing the disdainful shouts that included the words *cow-handed* and *cod's head* and the embarrassed defense that volleyed back. She laid one gloved hand over the other in the carriage and waited.

It was not as though she were in any rush. After visiting Susan, Philippa would simply return to the Holbecks' house, where she was spending her second London *Season*. Once she entered those hallowed doors, she would resume the mantle of dutiful little sister who was too innocent to know her own mind and should therefore trust her brother-in-law on the subject of marriage—especially where it concerned the undesirable attentions of Theodore Thackery. Presumptuous, arrogant man with no heart.

However, Philippa *did* know her own mind—and had a pretty fair idea of how the minds of others worked, too. That was precisely what lent such satisfaction to helping her friends with *their* matches instead of being led meekly into a trap set for her own. At least her intentions were pure.

Susan scarcely permitted the butler to admit Philippa and Fernsby before flying out of the drawing room and taking her friend by the hands. Susan's eyes were brimming with excitement, and Philippa allowed herself to be led into the somber drawing room, only extricating her hands from Susan's to remove her bonnet once the door was closed. Although Susan could at times be silly, Philippa was unlikely to find someone more loyal or sweet.

"My dear Susan," she said, laughing. "What can be so exciting? The Season has only just begun. Surely you have not received a proposal already!"

She had meant it as a jest, but Susan's eyes widened. "How did you know?"

Philippa paused in the act of removing her gloves. It was awfully sudden but perhaps not impossible? "Could it be … Mr. Evans?"

A look of confusion crossed Susan's features, and she shook her head. "I know Mr. Evans is a friend of yours, but he has not shown any marked interest in me."

Philippa refrained from uttering a protest. Matthew had not shown interest in Susan because he was paralyzed by shyness. Furthermore, he had not yet come to London to pursue Susan in earnest, which he would need to do if he wanted his suit to prosper. Susan could not find one more worthy than Matthew Evans—a man Philippa had known since she was a girl.

She knit her brows. *Who else could have proposed?* "Not Mr. Browne, I should hope." Susan's letters since last Season had been filled with the better-to-be-forgotten Ambrose Browne, who had raised all Susan's hopes with a determined pursuit before turning his attentions elsewhere—and without a word of explanation.

When Susan shook her head again, Philippa breathed a quiet sigh of relief. She was, however, no closer to being enlightened as to who this mystery man could be.

"But you have been in London a mere week before me. Surely a man could not have engaged your affections in so short a time. How did this come about?"

"It was love at first sight." Susan plopped herself on the sofa and pulled Philippa down next to her. "Christopher told me it could only be that or Mr. Merrick wouldn't have made such a cake out of himself." Her dreamy gaze moved to the ceiling.

"Christopher? Do you mean your brother Christopher?" Philippa prompted, squeezing Susan's hands to draw her attention. This was flighty behavior, even for Susan.

"Yes. Christopher knows Mr. Merrick from White's." Susan sighed and brought her gaze back to Philippa. "I was coming out of Hookham's when Mr. Merrick crossed paths with me. He just stopped and put his hand on his heart like *so*…" She demonstrated, her pale face serious.

"A speaking gesture to be sure," Philippa offered when she saw that her friend expected a reaction. Susan had drifted again in her reverie, so Philippa summoned her patience and nudged Susan's knee. "You must tell me more. Had you met him last Season? Mr. Merrick's name is not familiar. What look has he?"

"He has the look of an angel," Susan breathed.

"A paragon, then," Philippa replied dryly, rapidly losing patience at the dearth of information that was actually useful. She would never be so foolish as to fall for a man over a mere gesture. It would have to be a man she could respect—and one who respected her in return. "In one week, he has had time to secure your affection and speak to your father for your hand? He must be determined indeed."

She pulled back to examine Susan, who'd cast her gaze downward. Although she and Susan had grown close, their friendship was not of long date. They'd met at the end of last year's Season when Matthew Evans begged Philippa to make the young woman's acquaintance. Matthew was the shyest of all her brother George's friends, and Philippa liked him best—enough to call him by his Christian name as she would a brother.

So when quiet, steady Matthew Evans was struck at last by Cupid's arrow, Philippa became determined to help him with his suit. The only problem was that he had been too tongue-tied to do more than request Susan's hand for two dances and had not disclosed to anyone that he was suffering from the pangs of unspoken love until nearly the entire *ton* had left London. It had almost been too late.

After Susan's initial euphoric outburst, she fell unnaturally silent, and Philippa studied her more closely. Susan's look of rapture had been replaced by one of worry. "What is it, Susan?"

"Mr. Merrick has not yet approached my father," Susan confessed. "But Christopher believes Mr. Merrick to possess a respectable fortune and said that any man who could wear such a well-fitted coat could not be half bad. He thinks Father cannot disapprove."

The wheels in Philippa's mind were turning. She could not bear to think that poor Matthew could lose his heart's desire before he'd even had time to win Susan over. "How did your brother know of Mr. Merrick's interest? Did Mr. Merrick speak to him?"

Susan shook her head. "I don't think so. At least, Christopher didn't tell me if Mr. Merrick has *particularly* spoken of me. You see, Christopher had been detained inside Hookham's, and he came upon us on the street before Mr. Merrick took his leave. He said he shouldn't be surprised if Mr. Merrick were to attend the Yardmouth ball tomorrow night. And my mother has positively promised that she will accompany me this time."

Philippa had met Susan's mother briefly on her way to another social cause before their respective families had left town for the summer. An older version of Susan, with a pale complexion and large blue eyes set in the soft folds of her face, Mrs. Blythefield had rather absently approved of Philippa as a correspondent for her daughter. It behooved Philippa, she'd thought at the time, to continue the friendship for Matthew's sake—to make mention of him in her letters and see whether his suit might flourish. And she had rather thought it might, for although she could not rate Susan's intelligence as particularly high, much as she held her in affection, nothing in Susan's letters had led her to believe her friend's heart could be so easily won by a stranger.

The footman brought in the tea service and set it on the table in front of them. Abandoning her dramatic posture for the more serious business of preparing tea, Susan picked up one of the saucers and examined it with a frown. "Tell Mrs. Hart to begin using the red-and-gold set when we have company. This set is too worn to be used outside the family."

She crossed the room to take the tea leaves and sugar out of the broad mahogany cabinet near the wall. Weak beams of sunlight coming through the windows trespassed on the dark wall hangings in the drawing room and fell on Susan as she crossed its path. The rays lit her creamy complexion, translucent eyelids, and rose-tinted lips that gave her an uncommon beauty when paired with her thick amber hair.

Philippa reflected on this new suitor and had to concede that Susan— left prey, as she'd been, to any chancer-by—was not a girl to go unnoticed for long. With a naturally timid disposition and a willingness to defer to those with a stronger nature, Susan would be many men's ideal. Philippa could well believe that the mysterious Mr. Merrick might come up flush against such a creature and have fallen irrevocably head over heels in love. And if Susan's brother were in support of the match, Matthew stood in danger of losing his conquest, which would be a shame since Matthew Evans, plain as he was, would make a devoted husband. What were the chances that the same might be said of Mr. Merrick?

It would not do to abandon the cause too soon.

"He has not approached your father, then," Philippa mused when Susan resumed her seat. So no proposal yet. The case was far from bleak, as she had at first feared. In fact, it appeared the entire match was a fancy on Susan's part and a suggestion on the part of her brother. "Do you think your father will agree?"

Philippa had met the elder Mr. Blythefield once, and he did not appear to be a man overly scrupulous about whom his daughter married, as long as he was not disturbed by an excess of female emotions. At least that was what Philippa gathered by their passing introduction when he'd hurried into the drawing room to fetch paper and had fled just as quickly.

"Christopher said he will speak to our father if the need arises. But if Jack is opposed to the match, my father may listen to him instead." Susan gave a little pout. "It makes no sense that my father would, really, considering Christopher is my father's heir. But Jack generally gets what he wants."

The tea leaves were now steeping, and Susan placed the lid on the teapot as Philippa tried to follow this ambulatory discourse.

"Who is Jack?"

Susan laughed and leaned back, adopting a lounging posture on the settee that Philippa's sister Maria would have pronounced very ill-bred. "Silly. Jack is my older brother. I have written of him. I am certain of it."

"You have written of Christopher, to be sure, but I did not know you had another brother. He is your second oldest brother, then?" Philippa had rarely crossed another name in Susan's letters other than Mr. Browne. She would have remembered a Jack.

"Oh." Lips puckered, Susan breathed out the word. "Yes. He is my older brother, but the second son. I must have forgotten to mention him. Christopher was with me in the country, you see. He was on a repairing lease, and I must say I was not surprised. Christopher is frightfully expensive. Jack was tending to his other property, so I did not see him at all this summer. Then he spent the winter in London, which must be why I made no mention of him."

"I see." Philippa was mildly surprised that Susan would have neglected to mention a second brother at least once in their conversations or in all her letters. But then, he was a second son. She dismissed Jack as a person of interest. Surely his influence with their father must be exaggerated, since what weight could a second son carry to approve or deny his sister's suit?

Philippa accepted a cup of tea and set it in front of her, then selected a small cake to put on her plate. "Present Mr. Merrick to me, then, if you will. I shall be glad to make his acquaintance for your sake." *And perhaps divert it for Matthew's, if this Mr. Merrick should prove an ill choice.* She sipped her tea and smiled. "Let us speak of what you will wear."

"Oh!" The exclamation was somewhat mumbled since Susan had taken a large bite of cake, but she swallowed and proceeded to describe her dress, which would likely be a flattering color but with more bows than Philippa would have permitted on one of her own.

Philippa smiled over her cup, half-listening and mulling over this development in her friend's career. Even if she'd had no interest in the matter for Matthew's sake, Philippa feared Susan would be taken in because of her sweet, trusting nature. She would have to see if this second brother did indeed have any say against a match with Mr. Merrick—a man who apparently claimed a woman's affections without seeking an audience with the young woman's father. Philippa would have to be the voice of reason to keep Susan from doing anything hasty.

She took another sip of tea and nodded to show she was listening. It was a good thing she was able to manage her own affairs. Her brother George was entertaining but flighty, and Lucius and Selena were preoccupied. Maria was overbearing, and her mother could not be relied upon. Among Philippa's own family, she could not think of one upon whom she could depend.

CHAPTER TWO

Jack Blythefield stepped out of the House of Commons following an afternoon of speeches that had gone on at least two hours longer than expected, due to Robert Laine's love of his own voice. On most occasions, Jack left Parliament flanked by other Members looking to be heard on various issues—hardly surprising for a man whom the senior Whigs were considering for the role of Leader of the Opposition.

Today, however, Jack was alone and eager to make his way home quickly. Having accepted an invitation to attend an informal party that evening, hosted by the mother of a handsome woman of sense Jack had set his sights on, he was left with little time. He crossed Parliament Street, dodging both a salt vendor and a phaeton pulled by matched bays, when a familiar—and not entirely welcome—sight met his eyes. Reluctantly, he came to a stop.

"Christopher! I do not suppose you are waiting for me?" Jack could not imagine what could bring his indolent brother so far from his usual haunts, be they the clubs, the gaming hells, or the racetrack.

Christopher turned, stiff in his shirt points, his face revealing the usual mix of irony and laziness. "Why, no, dear brother. I had a friendly game at Cecil's, while you spent hours listening to speeches, trying your best not to fall asleep lest you be caught drooling. And now, let me guess—you are on your way to the Yardmouth ball?"

"Some of us are not content to fribble the day away, gambling each night—or wearing such abominable waistcoats. Are those yellow things … ducks?" Jack directed his gaze ahead to the busy street, hoping to spot an unoccupied hackney even at this hour. "I have an engagement to dine at Mrs. Sommers, and I must flag a hack. Do you accompany me?" A hackney driver saw Jack's lifted hand and pulled over, and Jack negotiated the fare before climbing in.

Christopher climbed in after him. "Why are you not going to Yardmouth's?" He leaned back on the squabs and pressed his boots against the forward-facing seat. "Ah, I see. No need to dance attendance on your political friends and foes. Repealed the Corn Laws, did you?"

"You need not sneer at our bills when you haven't attended Parliament in I don't know how long. That bill has not yet come up for vote." Jack looked down and brushed the brim of his hat. "I've my own reasons for preferring Mrs. Sommers's party."

"I suppose you might if *Miss* Sommers is your object. She's a handsome gel, although a bit stiff for her sex. As for me, I have a previous engagement I cannot miss." He peered at Jack under heavy eyebrows. "Or rather, I should say I *will* not miss. She's a prime article."

Jack shook his head. "Do you think you will ever stop talking about women in such a boorish fashion and at last settle down? Father is right in saying it is time you produced—"

"No more lectures, if you please. I might ask the same of you, by the bye. Why do you not marry if you are such a proponent of the state?"

"Considering how rarely our paths cross, I suppose now is as good a time to tell you as any. I have decided on such a path, as a matter of fact." Jack pushed aside the curtain to peer out the window. They had not much longer to go, and he would need to dress in a hurry.

Christopher turned in his seat to stare at Jack. "*Oh ho!* This is news. And who is the favored lady to take on the Blythefield name? Have you fixed upon Miss Sommers, then?"

Jack crossed his arms on his chest. "Miss Sommers is certainly of interest, but I am not decided upon whom. However, now that I have determined upon this course, I will simply look for the handsomest, quietest, most biddable young woman"—his gaze dropped, and he added with soft cynicism—"with hips wide enough to bear a parcel of heirs without a problem."

"I recommend you lead with that line," Christopher said dryly. "That ought to pique her interest."

Jack had an inclination to laugh, and goodness knew, the urge was rare enough. "Well, we are here, and I have not much time. I do not like to be late." He climbed down from the carriage and handed the fare up to the driver, then headed up the steps with his older brother trailing behind.

Christopher tapped his cane against the road as he strolled. "At times, Jack, I think your godmother's bequest was the worst thing that could have happened to you."

That opinion was not one Jack had thought to hear expressed. His bequest at the death of his godmother two years prior had saved their family from ruin. His godmother could not have been chosen with any hope of material blessing, since she was still wife to a wealthy merchant and mother to two sons at Jack's birth. But Jack had been attached to his godmother, especially after she'd lost her husband to illness and then two sons—one in the war and the other less nobly, as he was killed in a duel of vengeance by an unfaithful woman's husband. With Mrs. Rutland's fortune left to Jack, he was able to pay off most of the family's debts and even set up his own estate near to where his family's lands were.

Jack stopped and looked back, resting his hand on the iron railing. "Why?"

Christopher stopped, too, and pierced Jack with his gaze. "You're in danger of becoming a dead bore."

Annoyance nipped at Jack. It was not as though he'd had any choice in behaving as he did, considering the family he had been blessed with. "And you—you've become so dissipated as to be wholly irresponsible." They stepped through the front door, and Jack dropped his voice. "Between Father's 'investments' and your—"

"Ah, lectures again." Christopher pushed past Jack. "Cut line—I don't know why I said anything."

Susan appeared at the top of the bannister as the sounds of their voices echoed through the stairwell. "Christopher. You *are* here. What a divine stroke of luck." She hurried down the stairs. "Do you go to the Yardmouth ball tonight? Do you think Mr. Merrick will indeed be there?"

Jack stuffed his gloves in the pocket of his cloak. "Who is Mr. Merrick?" He crinkled his eyes in thought. If it was the Merrick he knew from the Commons, lackey to the Parliament-driver, Mr. Thackery, he wasn't so sure he approved.

His sister clasped her hands in a gesture that put Jack on his guard. Drama was likely to follow. She hurried down the stairs. "Mr. Merrick is a *very* respectable gentleman, who has fallen passionately in love with me. Christopher said he is a fine match."

Christopher turned on his heel as though he wished to escape before Jack could question him any further, but Jack would not let him off that easily. "And what makes Mr. Merrick such a worthy catch? Christopher, I had no idea you were so busy matchmaking."

Susan rested her hand on the bannister and, with a voice throbbing with passion, said, "Mr. Merrick has sustained a great *coup de foudre* from the very first time he laid eyes on me."

Christopher turned and met Jack's gaze with an ironic smile. "And he has his coats made at Weston's. What more does a man need to recommend him?"

"You don't owe him money, do you?" Jack asked with sudden suspicion.

"Of course not." Christopher drew back, affronted. "If you must know, I met him at White's. I don't suppose even you could find fault with him. He actually sits in Parliament."

"If he meets at White's, then he's the Tory I was thinking of." Jack would have to look into that affair to make sure his sister was not imposed upon.

Shanks, their butler, advanced in shuffling steps down the corridor to where they stood. He had been in Jack's grandfather's employ, then his father's, and Shanks did not wish to retire—nor could Jack's father bear to pension him off. Jack had been accustomed to taking off his own cloak since his youth. He now handed the item to their butler and added, "I doubt Mr. Merrick and I will see eye to eye on anything."

Susan let out a squeak of protest but was interrupted from speech by the bustle of their mother coming down the corridor, dressed to go out.

"Christopher, Jack, Susan. How delightful to find you all here at once." Mrs. Blythefield had not retained her figure, nor had she aged well. What she possessed in abundance, however, was enthusiasm. "I most particularly wish to invite you to tonight's event. Why, one might say it is providential that you are all here so that you do not miss out on this most extraordinary chance."

Jack and his brother turned to look at the end of the corridor as their father exited the library. With a quick glance at his wife, Mr. Blythefield scurried across into the billiard room. Christopher murmured, "I see Father has discovered a sudden urge to improve his game."

Jack brought his attention back to his mother, highly suspicious. "What extraordinary chance is that, Mother?"

"It is what I am constantly telling your father," Mrs. Blythefield said. "It's a chance to make a real difference in this world. A meeting! I think it high time you saw to your responsibility as is befitting your station in life." She tucked a healthy stack into her reticule of what Jack recognized as the Methodist tracts she had taken up distributing as of late.

"A meeting. The parish orphans again?" Christopher asked, a hint of dread creeping into his voice.

"No, dear. Not tonight. How silly to think we would be visiting orphans in the evening," she replied, a benign smile lighting the wrinkled folds of her face. "I have discovered this charming gathering called The Society for the Suppression of Vice and have made it my objective to join them. Does it not sound thrilling? We are tackling the gin houses next."

"May God preserve us." Christopher turned abruptly to head toward the study.

"Mother, you have forgotten." Susan shook her head at the tracts her mother attempted to hand her. "You are promised at the Yardmouth ball this evening. You are to escort me there."

Their mother lifted her gloved hand to Susan's cheek and gave an affectionate pat. "And so I am. But I cannot go. Jack, you shall have to take her in my place."

Susan clasped her hands together and turned to him. "How splendid, Jack. You had better hurry. You have not long to dress, you know."

"I am otherwise engaged—" Jack began.

His mother kissed him on the cheek. "You are a dear. Your sister cannot miss the opening ball, of course. Here." She pulled a handful of tracts from her reticule. "While you are there, you may hand these out to anyone you please. I will supply you with more when you've run out. Well, I must be off." Mrs. Blythefield waved her hand as she went out the door.

Jack turned to Susan, gripped by a familiar sensation that his well-laid plans were about to be hindered and his evening stolen from him. "Christopher must take you." He cried out after his brother, "Your plans are not fixed, whereas mine cannot be altered. Have the goodness to take Susan."

Christopher called over his shoulder as he entered the study. "Impossible. If I do go, I will not attend until much later. Jack, you will have to accompany Susan."

Susan grabbed Jack's hands impulsively. "Oh, do say you will."

"Emphatically, no!" Jack replied.

***

An hour later, the butler alerted Jack that the carriage had come around to the front, and Jack tapped his foot, waiting. Considering Susan had already been dressed for the Yardmouth ball when he arrived home, he could not imagine what was keeping her. At last, she appeared and smiled beatifically, not troubling to explain her tardiness. Jack helped Susan on with her pelisse before stepping outside and into the carriage.

As they rolled over the packed road, Jack let his gaze wander to the townhouses they passed, some of which were lit with candles inside and others that had not yet been un-shuttered. He wondered if the Sommerses would notice his absence. Likely, since Miss Sommers had seemed to indicate he would be a favored guest. Jack had been looking forward to the chance to further their acquaintance. It was a shame that would have to be delayed. It really was high time he found himself a wife and set up his own establishment so he would not be stuck escorting his sister everywhere. That was something his wife could be doing.

His thoughts having gone in that direction, he turned to Susan and announced, "I have decided to take a wife." He was not accustomed to speaking with such spontaneity, but having told Christopher, he might as well inform each of his family members. Perhaps they would give him a reprieve from their requests for once and the freedom to carry out his mission.

"Excellent." Susan clapped her gloved hands together. "I know just the girl for you."

"Girl." Jack shook his head decisively. It was not a girl he needed, but a woman of sense who could run a household and hold intelligent speech with his political allies but who knew when to step back in submission. "I do not want a *girl* with high flights and fancies and dreams of romance. I want a woman who is rational and quiet and can keep house."

"Oh." Susan's shoulders slumped, and she fingered the strings of her reticule.

Jack had not expected such an easy capitulation. After a moment, his curiosity got the better of him. "And who is this girl?"

Susan's smile returned. "Philippa Clavering. My dearest friend."

Jack spun the black ribbon of his quizzing glass around his finger. "I've never heard of Miss Clavering before. How could she be your dearest friend?"

"Well … we have not known each other prodigiously long, but we have been writing to each other ever since last Season, and we have become quite thick. She is my confidant and knows all about Mr. Browne—"

"I should hope you are not still thinking of Mr. Browne?" Jack turned and studied her with a frown.

"—but I've informed her of my change in affections only this afternoon." Susan went on as if he had not interrupted. "She has already visited me, having only just arrived in London this week. Philippa is an *angel*. You will see."

"Perhaps." Jack did not see any point in elaborating, but the idea began to take root. If this Miss Clavering was anything like his sister in temperament, it might suit, should his interest in Miss Sommers prove unrewarding. Susan was generally a biddable girl. Although, if Miss Clavering were even half as silly, it would not do.

Jack frowned. It was not that he wished to think of his future wife and sister in the same breath, but it would be a convenient thing if they were friends. Then, when he was spending his time in Parliament and at the club, his wife would have someone to talk to. A wife with female friends would not trouble him with an excess of sensibility. It was a matter worth looking into.

"You may introduce her to me. I shall look her over."

"Jack, you say the funniest things," Susan said. "She is not a horse."

He glanced sideways at his sister. Susan was showing unusual spirit, but he let the comment pass.

They were late to the ball, and Jack led Susan to the host and hostess to pay their respects before assessing the other guests gathered around the room. There was no one he needed to speak to that couldn't wait. Susan smoothed the front of her gown and opened and shut her fan until

Jack could bear it no more. He leaned down to murmur, "Susan, you are fidgeting. You must not wear your heart on your sleeve, you know."

Susan inhaled sharply and grabbed his arm. "There is Philippa!" She stood on her toes and lifted her hand until the woman in question smiled in acknowledgment and turned to walk toward them.

Jack was about to tell Susan not to make a cake of herself, but he stopped short at the sight of Miss Clavering, who did, in fact, resemble a celestial being. In terms of appearances, hers could certainly tempt a man to press his suit. Face like an angel, a halo of golden curls, smile as fresh as dew, her waist nipped in most appealingly, but hips ample enough to carry an heir—and even a spare. She was certainly eligible for the post he had in mind. Miss Clavering made her way across the room as Jack prepared himself to honor her with his attention.

Susan spoke the introduction. "Jack, permit me to present you to my friend, Miss Philippa Clavering. Philippa, this is Mr. Jack Blythefield."

Jack bowed. "Your servant." Although he was not a particular fan of dancing, he had decided to unbend enough to ask Miss Clavering to dance a set, as it would be difficult to engage in conversation otherwise. And he needed to assess whether she was as docile as she appeared. If she was, then she might answer very well. Miss Sommers was indeed a handsome woman, but Miss Clavering was nothing short of stunning— the kind of face a man could look at without it spoiling his breakfast.

"Enchanted, Mr. Blythefield," Miss Clavering replied. Her clear voice and answering nod revealed more character than he could perhaps wish for, but with her eyes assessing him, Jack had the bemused sensation of being the one enchanted.

She turned from him and released Jack from her spell, linking her arm through Susan's. "I have been waiting for you for an age." Miss Clavering led his sister away, their heads bent together, and did not spare him another glance.

A surge of irritation welled up in Jack. This woman had missed her opportunity to tempt him to the altar, and she'd had no idea.

CHAPTER THREE

*P*hilippa had been on the lookout for Susan ever since she'd arrived, eager to assess just what kind of rival Mr. Merrick would prove to be. Once Susan had performed the introduction to her brother—Mr. Blythefield was a handsome man, but his severe countenance did not encourage Philippa to linger—she took hold of her friend's arm, weaving through the groups of people congregated on the sidelines to a more spacious place. They halted between two refreshment tables that held bowls of punch chilled with ice. The twang of violins and the more mellow sound of the cellos filled the hall. Brightly-clad couples danced, ducked, and spun between the clusters of people, and the whirling colors caught Philippa's eye.

"It's a sad crush, is it not?" Philippa observed cheerfully. There were enough people for her to have shaken off Maria's overly protective gaze. Her sister did not feel that Philippa's one London Season could possibly have been preparation enough to permit Maria to loosen her watch over Philippa, who might at any moment be pulled into an alcove by a rake bent on seduction. She opened her fan and leaned into Susan. "Well, is Mr. Merrick here?"

Susan was pale, despite the spots of color on her cheeks brought on by the heat. She bit her lip and shook her head. "It doesn't seem so. We arrived late, and if he is not yet come, I begin to fear he will not show at all."

Philippa snapped her fan back and forth with vigor. Much the better. If Mr. Merrick was not here, perhaps it indicated his suit was not serious and Matthew's case not quite so desperate. She would have to tread carefully. Philippa had only mentioned Mr. Evans once or twice in her letters since last Season, and she did not wish to set up Susan's hackles by pushing the match when her heart was not yet engaged. Then again, neither did she wish to let this Mr. Merrick claim such an easy victory.

She squeezed Susan's hand. "If he is a suitor worth his salt, he will be here, for he would not miss an opportunity to see you. However, do not take it to heart if he does not come. A worthy suitor's affections will not wane so easily, and if his do, it is better you should know now. After all, there *are* gentlemen whose hearts can be trusted to remain true, so why throw ours away on the first handsome face?"

Philippa could have happily throttled Matthew for being so shy last Season. If he had been more forthcoming about his feelings, her tenderhearted friend would already be engaged to him and not ripe for the plucking by someone like Mr. Merrick.

Where *was* Matthew Evans anyway? Philippa looked around, not expecting to see him at the ball, for she'd had no word, but was surprised all the same. She thought he would not delay in coming to London with so much at stake.

Philippa's words seemed to have bolstered Susan, though perhaps at cross-purposes, for Susan drew a deep breath and stood straight, smiling at a gentleman who bowed to her in passing. A determined movement to Philippa's left caught her attention, and one glance revealed the form of Mr. Lloyd bearing down upon them—one of Philippa's persistent suitors. His unwelcome interest in her took root at the end of last Season, where he frequently attempted to gain a private audience. He bored her to tears.

Susan drew in a deep breath and clutched Philippa's arm. "He has come. And he has caught sight of me."

"Mr. Evans?" Philippa's head shot head up. She did not know when he'd planned to arrive in London, but his suit would be more successfully performed by him than by her.

"No." Susan turned to her, a slight frown tugging at her features. "Mr. Merrick."

Philippa chastised herself for being so bird-witted as to bring up Matthew just now. It was all Mr. Lloyd's fault for distracting her. She looked around the room for a gentleman she might summon to her side to protect her from Mr. Lloyd's attentions. Susan would not be the slightest deterrent.

"Miss Clavering." The deep voice coming from her right belonged to Mr. Blythefield, who was now standing at Philippa's elbow. She startled at his unexpected nearness and found herself staring into eyes whose blend of browns and greens were as pretty as marble. He gave her a short bow. "I had intended to extend an invitation to dance when we were presented earlier, but I was not given a chance."

Philippa glanced at Susan, who was not paying the least bit of attention to her brother and appeared to be searching for Mr. Merrick, who had not come straight to her side.

"That is very kind of you." Philippa looked up in time to see Mr. Lloyd veer off in a different direction. Mr. Blythefield's arrival had been timely. However, she was not tempted by his cordial tone and stiff demeanor. It was not as though she needed any favors from him. And if Philippa left Susan's side now, she might not have a chance to meet Mr. Merrick.

"*Mm.*" Her lack of immediate acceptance was bordering on incivility. She certainly had no intention of dancing with a man who did not put himself out to please, but she could hardly refuse Mr. Blythefield, unless...

Philippa smiled up at him. "I would be delighted to, but I am occupied at present. May I suggest Miss Percy as a partner for this dance? She is standing near the column there and happens to be free." To ease the snub, Philippa added in a teasing tone, "She makes for lively conversation and will not bore you by expecting an offer at the end of the dance."

Mr. Blythefield pulled back to look at her. "Are you saying *you*, Miss Clavering, would expect a proposal at the end of one dance?"

"From you? Oh, heavens no." Philippa laughed and glanced at him again, but her laughter quickly died away. Never mind that Mr. Blythefield had just the sort of look that attracted her, she was not interested in her friend's brother—or really, attaching herself to any man at present, if she had to own the truth. Her freedom, such that it was, was too valuable.

"Jack, I wish to present you to someone." Susan rested her hand on her brother's arm, breaking a conversation that was quickly growing awkward. "He was coming this way a minute ago but has been drawn into conversation. I am sure he will not tarry."

Mr. Blythefield pulled the focus of his gaze from Philippa and looked about the room. "A prétendant for your hand? It is not that Mr. Browne, is it? The one who ruined a good many of your handkerchiefs and my own besides?" He darted a glance at Philippa and checked himself from further speech.

Philippa was surprised, though it did not appear to rattle Susan from the looks of it. Philippa had not expected Mr. Blythefield to have been aware of his sister's heartbreak. They must have a closer relationship than she'd thought, considering Susan had not even mentioned her brother's existence.

Susan shook her head. "No, you were quite right about him. I have given up entirely on Mr. Browne. Mr. Merrick is here—whom I told you about earlier."

Mr. Blythefield followed her gaze, skimming the crowd until his eyes lit upon the person in question. "Ah, yes. *That* Mr. Merrick—whose political ideas are questionable. I do know him. By all means, you may present him to me. It will save me the trouble of having to seek him out and warn him away."

Susan gasped and scrunched up her face in outrage. "How could you? I thought you cared for my happiness."

Philippa sent Mr. Blythefield a repressive look. "Now, that will do, Mr. Blythefield. You have coaxed your fair-complexioned sister to a depth of feeling that may be speculated upon by everyone assembled tonight. She will not thank you when she has to confront the whispers in the drawing rooms tomorrow."

Philippa curtsied to Mr. Blythefield and linked her elbow through Susan's. "Come. This part of the ballroom has become stifling. I see a corner that promises fresh air near the retiring room."

By the time they'd made slow progress around the crowds lining the dance floor, with Philippa speaking on indifferent topics to distract her friend, Susan's color had resumed its normal hue. Her attention, however, had not shifted from its object. "Jack is so unfeeling."

"Older brothers generally are," Philippa replied, although her mind was busy. How could she turn Mr. Blythefield's disapproval to good account to lessen the sudden attachment Susan felt for Mr. Merrick? "But if what your brother said is true—that Mr. Merrick possesses unpalatable ideas? It is possible that your brother was trying to protect you, and it is not Mr. Merrick's *politics* he objects to."

Susan shook her head. "It is, though. Jack only said that because Mr. Merrick is a Tory and Jack is a Whig. He thinks all Tories have questionable politics."

Philippa raised her eyebrows. Besides the fact she happened to agree with him, this bit of information was useful. If Mr. Blythefield was ready to dismiss a potential suitor simply because he affiliated with the opposite party, her next steps were clear. She needed only to strengthen his disapproval. Perhaps she would pretend toward Tory sympathies as well. Nothing like a contrary opinion to bolster a man's dislike.

"Well, men generally have a much better understanding of political issues than we women," she said mendaciously. "I would not wholly discount your brother's assessment of Mr. Merrick before you lose your heart entirely to him."

Susan was scarcely listening, and her breath was coming in short gasps. "I believe he is coming this way."

He was indeed. Mr. Merrick's brown curls cascaded down to the collar of his bronze-green coat, and his cream-patterned neckcloth hid what was possibly a weak chin. Despite that, he was a handsome man, and as he made his stately way across the floor, he bowed to ladies and acknowledged gentlemen. He seemed to know just what to say to everyone, for he was trailed by a sprinkling of laughter from the people to whom he condescended to spare a few words.

Then the man himself was upon them, and he bowed before the two ladies. "Miss Blythefield, I had hoped I might find you here tonight." He bowed before Philippa. "And you are in such charming company."

Philippa smiled and inclined her head but did not attempt to procure an introduction. Mr. Merrick had great address, and if he had truly lost his heart to Susan, poor Matthew did not stand a chance.

"How do you do, Mr. Merrick?" Susan smiled at him shyly.

When she did not present Philippa to Mr. Merrick, he cleared his throat and glanced Philippa's way. It appeared as though all Susan's thoughts had fled, for she still did not perform the introduction. *She is much too innocent.* It was no wonder Mr. Browne had left her for worthier prey. Mr. Merrick would be given his chance to do the same, if Philippa had any say in the matter. She would ensure he did so before he broke Susan's heart.

When Mr. Merrick received no introduction, he turned back to Susan. "Miss Blythefield, if you've not been spoken for, might I request the honor of this dance for the next set?"

Susan blossomed under his attention, her cheeks growing rosy. "You may." She laid her hand on Mr. Merrick's outstretched arm, and he bowed to Philippa. "Good evening, Miss—"

Susan put her free, gloved hand to her mouth. "I beg your pardon, Mr. Merrick. Please meet my dearest friend, Miss Clavering."

"Miss Clavering." Mr. Merrick puzzled his brows as though in recognition, but he quickly smoothed his reaction and replaced it with a smile. "Will you allow me to escort you to someone, now that I am removing your companion?"

"You are very kind, Mr. Merrick. There is no need, as—" Philippa paused, struck by an idea. Perhaps she would learn more about him if they appeared to share common ground. "My brother-in-law, Mr. Holbeck, has someone he would like me to meet. I will simply return to him."

Mr. Merrick had moved to turn with Susan on his arm, but at Philippa's words, he turned back. "You are related to Charles Holbeck?"

"He is married to my sister. Do you know him, then?"

"As a matter of fact, I do. That must be why..." Mr. Merrick broke off and laid his hand over Susan's. "He and I see eye to eye on quite a number of subjects."

Philippa wondered what he had been about to say. "How wonderful. I see you are a man of sense." The lie sprang easily to her lips. With men she couldn't give two figs for, she'd found it was better to agree with them—they usually left more quickly. Mr. Merrick gave her a lingering glance before leading Susan away to the dance floor.

It was time to find out what Mr. Blythefield thought of his sister's suitor.

The room was growing more crowded, and Philippa was of short stature. She could not see above the shoulders of most of the men there, and Mr. Blythefield was nowhere in sight. A touch at her elbow made her freeze in her tracks. Mr. Lloyd?

"Miss Clavering, how unlike you to be standing alone. How did you shake off your bevy of suitors?"

Philippa turned in relief to Robert Whitmore, one of her brother George's best friends, whose welcome presence coaxed a small laugh out of her. That was cut short when she saw beyond Mr. Whitmore's shoulder the resolute stride of Mr. Lloyd. "Do not leave me, I beg of you," she said. "I believed to have shaken off Mr. Lloyd earlier, but he is on his way to talk to me now."

"That tedious bore?" Whitmore beckoned to two other friends, who came immediately to his side. "Duck, you had wished to dance with Miss Clavering, I believe," he said in a ringing voice, sending Mr. Lloyd in a different direction.

Mr. Oswald Duckworth, known as Duck, was a more recent addition to George's circle of friends. He was the biggest flirt of them all—and the least serious. "Of course I must dance with Miss Clavering, though she be ever famous for leaving a circle of slain hearts." He took Philippa's hand in his, lifted it to his cheek, then planted a kiss directly on her glove as he bowed over it, quoting, "'The robbed that smiles steals something from the thief.'"

Philippa shook her head and sent him an indulgent smile. As shocking as Duck's flirting was, no one was foolish enough to take him seriously. Society matrons tended to view him with an indulgent eye, as he was considered harmless. And even if Duck's outrageous behavior were not known, Philippa would not have been fooled. George's friends had always treated her like she was their sister as well—except for the flirting.

Nicholas Amos, a large man in height and breadth, possessed a quieter sense of humor at odds with his physique. He bowed as well, and when he lifted his head, teased, "Such an enchanting face might tempt the most stouthearted man to give up his freedom, were it not for a most protective brother. I, for one, am not foolhardy enough to attempt it."

"I dare not even request that you dance with me," Duck said, not to be outdone. "But I will tell you, I am in a positive *decline* until you promise me my suit is not hopeless."

Philippa chuckled. "As if each of you would not do precisely what you wished to. It is not fear of my brother that hinders you, though—admit it. If you're anything like George, it will be many long years before you are ready to settle down."

"I merely said you tempted us to the altar. I did not say we would actually consider taking such a drastic step," Amos said with a wink.

"Gentlemen, I only called you here to protect our Philippa from the unwelcome advances of Perceval Lloyd," Whitmore said, a teasing glint in his eyes. "I didn't expect I'd have to protect her from you!" He took a glass of champagne from a servant, then pulled a passing gentleman aside for a few words.

Philippa focused her gaze on the couples dancing, not regretting having sat this dance out. George's friends were more fun. "Do any of you know Mr. Merrick there dancing with my friend?"

Duck pulled out his quizzing glass and surveyed the couples dancing the quadrille, then dropped the glass. "As I am unable to discern who your friend is in this swirling crowd of people, I cannot tell you whether or not I know Mr. Merrick."

Amos laid a hand on Duck's arm. "How could you have forgotten? The fellow there with the nicely cut green coat, dancing with that redhead? Merrick was the one they bet on at White's after he'd boasted about being able to secure an heiress."

Philippa's mouth opened slightly, and she stared at him. "But my friend is not an heiress."

"Let us just say that those of us who bet on his success were not plump in the pocket afterwards." Amos looked conscious all of a sudden. "But we should not be speaking about this in front of you."

"Never mind that." Philippa dismissed the objection with a wave of her hand. "But when did this happen?"

"It was at the end of last Season, was it not?" Duck said.

"Indeed it was. Near end of June. He's a loose fish." Duck lifted his quizzing glass and ogled a pretty girl as she walked by with her mother. The young lady blushed and dropped her gaze.

"Duck, do stop flirting, would you?" Philippa said. "This is a serious matter. Susan cannot lose her heart to someone who will not care for her." Whitmore rejoined their circle, and Philippa attempted an air of nonchalance as she surveyed the crowds. "Where is Mr. Evans? You must tell him to make haste to London, for I have need of him."

Duck lifted a shoulder, already losing interest. "I have no idea where Evans is, so it would be a fruitless endeavor for me to try to reach him."

"It's true," Whitmore said. "George is more likely than we are to know where he is. Why do you look for him?"

"My friend, Miss Blythefield, is dancing with Mr. Merrick, who I've just learned is not quite *the thing*."

Whitmore cleared his throat, and Philippa turned her eyes to him. "So you think so, too? I am most attached to Susan and cannot help but feel she needs a guiding hand. I will need Mr. Evans in London to accomplish what I have in mind."

"Heaven help the girl," Duck murmured. "Philippa has decided to take on a project."

Amos directed his gaze to Philippa. "And now, why do you need Evans here? If it were not that you were playing matchmaker, I might think you had some interest there yourself."

Philippa laughed. "With Matthew Evans? Goodness, no. He might as well be my brother, since he stayed with us the first fortnight of every summer term. I've known him since I was in leading strings. It is only that I do not believe Mr. Merrick to be a worthy suitor for Miss Blythefield."

Philippa reflected that she could express her urgency for Matthew to return without *precisely* breaking his confidence. "Perhaps Mr. Evans would wish to fix his interest with Miss Blythefield. That is why he needs to return. To do just that."

All three gentleman turned to stare at her, and it was Whitmore who protested. "We can hardly get involved, my dear."

His reply did not surprise her since, as a whole, she found that the male race tended to abandon any challenge at the first setback. The discussion fell off quickly, which was just as well, for Philippa had caught sight of Mr. Blythefield. He stood some ways apart, and who knew how long that would last? She saw his gaze roam over the crowds as though in search of someone.

This, Philippa decided, would be the ideal time to find out exactly what Mr. Blythefield thought of Mr. Merrick. Perhaps it needed only a little nudge to help him firm up his resolve against the match.

"Gentlemen," she said, "you must excuse me."

CHAPTER FOUR

*J*ack had not been at the ball for an hour before he regretted having missed the Sommerses' engagement. There was nothing to interest him here, now that he had seen his sister move on from her first questionable dance partner, Mr. Merrick, to more suitable partners. He'd have to have a word with Christopher to find out why his brother thought the man an acceptable suitor for their sister's hand. Although Jack had nothing specific against Mr. Merrick, he'd always appeared to Jack as a man of shallow convictions whose vote was for sale to the highest bidder. There was no promise he would behave any differently in matters of matrimony, and Susan deserved better.

Jack had made it a point to greet all the men who would be likely to support his candidature as Leader of the Opposition but was smart enough to let them enjoy their evening free of politics. He also agreed to partner a young lady after Mrs. Yardmouth approached him to make the introduction, but her level of shyness went beyond the docility he searched for in a wife and bordered on stupidity. Miss Clavering had obviously not noticed what great condescension he had shown her by asking her to dance. He would not make that mistake again.

He glanced across the room at that petite angelic creature with cherubic blonde curls and noticed her holding court with three dashing blades surrounding her. *Holding court, indeed.* Jack curled his lips. That was precisely it. Miss Clavering would only be trouble. She likely flirted and cajoled and demanded, all the while keeping her suitors at arm's length. Far be it from him to join her court. He watched as she lifted a slender arm encased in a white glove and touched the cheek of one of the men. The man caught her hand and pressed a kiss on it. Jack turned away in disgust.

Had he gone to the Sommerses' house as planned, Miss Sommers would have taken great pains to see to Jack's comfort from the moment he entered the door. She had done so ever since they'd first been presented two years ago, but her manner of courting his attention was so subtle it had not raised any consideration for a more intimate connection. He had merely focused on how skilled she was at presiding over her mother's political dinner parties. It was only when he'd left for his estate at the close of Parliament that Miss Sommers's intrusion upon his thoughts had him questioning whether she was not showing him particular interest. That led him to ask himself whether or not he was equally interested.

After all, when a man decides it is time to find a wife, he will naturally look to the most suitable option. And suitable Miss Sommers was. If there was any defect to her appearance, it would be hard to find. Perhaps it was that her thin lips did not produce a spontaneous smile, and her complexion was rather too colorless to throw out a blush. But her dark hair contrasted prettily with her pale-blue eyes, and she never disordered one's senses by assaulting a man with unnecessary chatter. It was time he began pursuing her in earnest.

Jack folded his arms, suppressing a sigh as he looked around. He would have to remain at the ball for some time until his sister was ready to return home. He'd better prepare himself for a most insipid evening. And, he reminded himself, he'd better make haste tomorrow to go beg Miss Sommers's pardon for not having shown tonight.

"Mr. Blythefield."

Jack turned at the sound of his name spoken in a melodious voice and was struck anew when his gaze lit on Miss Clavering. She was not tall like Miss Sommers nor did she have such contrasting features as dark hair against a creamy complexion. Miss Clavering graced him with a natural smile, punctuated on either side by deep dimples in her fair cheeks. Her bright eyes captivated him with their intelligence. He had only time to recover from his initial jolt before she opened her full lips to speak. "I wished to find out what you thought of Mr. Merrick. Do you think him a worthy man?"

"I could not say." Surprised at her forthright question, Jack adopted a disinterested voice. "I hardly know the man. I will have to look into his affairs more closely before I decide. However, I should not wish you to trouble yourself with another family's personal matters."

He'd meant that for a heavy set-down, and a woman of greater sensibility would have taken the words to heart and have begged his pardon. Miss Clavering did not appear to be such a woman.

"It is no trouble, I assure you. After having encouraged Susan through her heartbreak last year, I can only rejoice that another man has deemed her worthy of his affection." She stopped and gave Jack a look he could not quite decipher before adding, "And, of course, he is a Tory, which speaks to his favor."

"Miss Clavering." Jack frowned down at her. She really was petite, but when she turned her face up to gaze at him, he thought she'd not be too small to… *Enough*, he scolded himself. "*I* am a Whig. That is hardly a recommendation."

She sniffed. "I am sorry to hear it."

Jack opened his mouth to speak, but before he could utter the hasty retort that had sprung to his lips, she gestured to where Mr. Merrick stood at the entrance to the card room. "Before you chase him away posthaste, you might give a thought for your sister's future. Especially her *immediate* future and yours. I am sure you will not wish to sit with Susan for hours on end, passing her your handkerchiefs when hers are too soiled with tears as she tries to make sense of why Mr. Merrick is no longer coming to call. Men are not generally equipped for such things, and you have no other sisters to bear the burden."

Jack did not know whether to laugh at her insight or shudder at the image she presented. "Susan does have a mother," he managed to say, although it lacked conviction.

Apparently Miss Clavering was more familiar with his family's situation than he'd realized, because she cocked her head and raised an eyebrow. "She does, indeed. However, if I am not very much mistaken, Mrs. Blythefield is passionate for social causes, and some of the more practical matters of the household must naturally fall into other hands, including dispensing sage counsel."

Jack studied her face with misgiving. Miss Clavering's expression was perfectly pleasant, and there was not an ounce of judgment to be read there, but Jack would have to speak with his sister. He most emphatically did *not* need his family's secrets being blabbed about. It was hard enough to keep some semblance of normalcy to his odd family, enabling him to continue his career in politics—which was looking to be a brilliant one—without his own sister inadvertently sabotaging his efforts.

He furrowed his brows. "If my mother is taken up by social causes—"

"Then she is a worthy woman with greater demands on her time than listening to a daughter's heartache," Miss Clavering finished for him. "If you are duty bound as Susan's brother to chase away poor Mr. Merrick, I advise you not to do so too quickly. It will only set up your sister's back and perhaps cause her to become more firm in her attachment. Approach the affair in a more subtle manner, so that she does not feel you are against her. If and when the time comes for tears, I will be happy to fill the role of confidant."

Jack's head spun with the idea that Miss Clavering did not appear to secretly despise his mother as most people did who became aware of her projects. Then there was the way she dared to instruct him—not to mention her advice about Mr. Merrick as a suitor, which had a grain of sense. It was all too much to take in, and Jack searched for a way to respond.

"The truth is, Mr. Blythefield, should you find Mr. Merrick's suit too objectionable to countenance, I have someone else in mind for your sister, to whom I think you cannot take exception. If you choose not to entertain the match, he is gentleman enough to withdraw from the lists. But I imagine his suit will prosper, for he comes with a handsome fortune."

Jack turned to examine Miss Clavering fully. She really was a puzzling creature. "Why should you care so much about who pursues my sister? First Mr. Merrick, now another gentleman? If I may speak bluntly, I have never met you before and have only learned of your existence on the carriage ride to the ball. I find your interest to be misplaced, as someone who is neither family nor on long-term acquaintance."

Miss Clavering tipped her chin up and met his gaze. A smile touched her lips before she spoke. "I understand you. It must seem odd, and I assure you, I am not in the habit of interfering in what does not concern me." She paused, then bit back a smile. "Well, perhaps that is not entirely true. But I only interfere in what I *know* to be for good cause. I may not have known your sister for years, but I have known Mr. Evans—"

"And this Mr. Evans is the unobjectionable suitor you spoke of, who comes with a handsome fortune," Jack clarified.

"The very one." Miss Clavering punctuated her statement with a nod. "He was present when Susan received her final rebuff from Mr. Browne, and he sent me into the retiring room after her to see to her comfort. So you see, he *cares* for her. Not only does his fortune make him respectable, his concern makes him ideal. I am determined that he shall at least have his fair chance with your sister before she is swept away by pretty words from a man of lesser morals."

"And by that, I can only assume you mean Mr. Merrick," Jack concluded. He narrowed his eyes in confusion. "I thought you would encourage the match."

"And so I do—but only enough to avoid giving the appearance of being opposed to the match, which might lead Susan to do something desperate. I am sorry to say this, Mr. Blythefield, but do try to keep up. I've already explained all this. Besides"—Miss Clavering assessed him with a mischievous smile—"I quite thought my approval of Mr. Merrick would bring about your renunciation, leaving the way clear for Mr. Evans. I know how much Whigs like to oppose."

Jack inhaled deeply. Not even the men who congregated before the debates were as conniving as she. "There is no need to put up a show of either support or opposition for me to question the suitability of Mr. Merrick. But as for this other man, I am far from convinced. Where *is* this Mr. Evans you speak of—and why has he not presented himself to me if he is so bent on pressing his suit?"

Miss Clavering settled a knowing gaze on Jack. "You mean, of course, why has Mr. Evans not presented himself to your *father*?"

Jack stopped, pierced with the embarrassing realization that he had allowed a glimpse of his strange family dynamic to leak out. His father could not be relied upon to filter anything, whether it be a business proposition or the suitability of a gentleman for their sister's hand. Jack was generally not betrayed into uttering anything so transparent about his home life—he, who was a politician at heart. At the same time, he was far from accustomed to discussing any aspect of his family's affairs with a total stranger—and this in the midst of a very public ball. He remained frozen for a beat, and Miss Clavering's dark-blue eyes, so very different to Miss Sommers's, held his gaze in such a steady way they only served to increase his discomfort. At last, he gathered his wits.

"As you say, madam. Any suitor with serious intentions must, of course, present himself to my father. As this Mr. Evans has not yet done so, I can only assume that his interest is not quite as strong as you have imagined it to be. Now, if you will excuse me, I see a gentleman I must have words with."

Jack turned without waiting for her reply, and—in what he could only accuse himself of being a most craven response—turned and fled Miss Clavering's presence. If she were a man, he would know exactly how to shut her down. But opponents generally did not have skin as fair as a lily and rosebud lips, and *that* was not something he knew how to manage.

***

The next day, Jack appeared at Miss Sommers's residence with a large bouquet of flowers and requested of the butler to seek an audience with her. His dignity still smarted from the uncomfortable conversation with Miss Clavering the night before. She had seemed to know much about his family—things he preferred to keep quiet—and although she did not appear to despise him or his sister for it, she did have an uncanny grasp of the tone of their household, something he had never permitted from any of his friends.

If his colleagues had remained in happy ignorance of Jack's odd family life, it was only because his mother did not mix with the same Society he did and was content with her crusade to reform the world. His brother did run with the same crowd, but he was considered at best, a Pink of the Ton—and at worst, a fop—and was generally viewed as harmless. And Jack had until now managed to hide his father's unfortunate predilection for bad business investments by covering the debts, diverting the intriguing new ventures that fell under his father's nose, and fabricating a better version of ventures his father tried to pass on to other gentlemen of means. In all areas, Jack moved the pieces to present a winning game to the world and mask the sense of shame that pricked at him.

Well, he had until last night.

Today, he would soothe his agitated spirit with Miss Sommers's calm good sense, and he had the perfect opportunity for paying a visit. He was here to apologize.

"Mr. Blythefield." Miss Sommers glided into the room, her statuesque appearance accentuated by a slimming, cinnamon-colored gown. "How happy I am to receive your visit. My mother will be in momentarily. She is still recovering from last night's soirée."

Jack bowed. "Forgive me. Perhaps I should have come later in the day. Of course you are both understandably tired."

Miss Sommers smiled and held out her hands for the flowers. "Are these for me? How kind of you."

"They are—with a thousand pardons for having missed your party last night." Jack handed Miss Sommers the large bouquet of white calla lilies. They had reminded him of Miss Sommers when he saw them in the florist shop. Tall, elegant blooms.

She examined the flowers before setting the bouquet on a nearby table. "You did not need to do such a thing, although we did miss your presence…" Miss Sommers ended her words abruptly and her gaze flitted away. She gestured to the chair. "Won't you please sit?"

The door opened, and Mrs. Sommers entered, a tall woman with an upper body of a drill sergeant, whose dress clung to her slimmer legs like an upside-down tulip. Despite her formidable appearance, she was not a forceful woman and preferred to host parties by slipping into the background and allowing her daughter to orchestrate its players. Mrs. Sommers had been a notable politician's wife until her husband retired due to ill health and eventually succumbed to the illness the year before Jack had made their acquaintance.

"What a pleasure to see you, Mr. Blythefield."

Jack bowed again and waited until both ladies had sat down before taking his own seat. "As I was explaining to Miss Sommers, I came to beg your pardon for having missed your party last night. My mother was suddenly unwell and asked me to take my sister to the Yardmouth ball. I could hardly refuse since my sister was dressed and looking forward to it."

"I thought there must be a simple explanation," Mrs. Sommers answered in a placid tone. "Some of the guests who arrived very late had come from the Yardmouth's ball and mentioned seeing you there. We could only assume the attractions of the ball had outweighed our humble party."

Jack placed his hands on his knees and sat straight. "I assure you, no. I was looking forward to the intelligent conversation your party would have afforded me and was not entirely pleased to find myself forced into a crowded ball instead." He smiled, hoping to put the discussion behind them. Although he had come planning to apologize, he did not want to give undue weight to his attention to Miss Sommers until he could be fully sure of his own interest. He hoped the flowers were not too extravagant.

A silence fell as Jack thought of what to say that was less open to interpretation. Both the Sommers women looked in different directions rather than attempting to further the conversation. At last, there was a soft tap as the footman brought the tea service and Mrs. Sommers gestured for him to put it on the table in front of her. She stood and retrieved the tea leaves, then prepared the teapot, allowing it to steep.

All this was done in a stately silence that Jack felt he should appreciate, as it was exactly the tone he was looking to install in his own home. Instead, it began to weigh on him as it appeared he was to carry the entirety of the conversation. He had never before made a morning call to Miss Sommers and only knew her from her skill at facilitating discussion—even skirting differing viewpoints with delicacy—at her dinner parties. Apparently, her skill remained at the evening parties she hosted and did not trail her to breakfast.

"Despite having deplored my absence, were you satisfied with your turnout last night?" he asked, offering a pleasant smile as he accepted the tea Mrs. Sommers handed him.

Miss Sommers nodded and opened her mouth to speak, but her mother answered in her place. "It was not what we could have wished for, as company was thin." She sighed as she took her seat. "And to think that we sent our invitations out before Mrs. Yardmouth. We had hoped that the lure of having Lord Sherwood at our gathering would attract more people, but he was unable to stay long."

Lord Sherwood. That was someone Jack thought he might win over on repealing the bill. Shame he had missed his chance to speak to him in an informal setting.

"Ah. I am terribly sorry to hear that." Jack sipped at his tea. "It is to be hoped that the next time I will not be called away again at the last minute." He had committed himself more than he would have wished for, but there seemed no other way to answer.

"No indeed." Miss Sommers's smile brightened as she rested her gaze on him. "Perhaps the next time your schedule will permit you to attend."

Silence settled again as the footman reentered to bring a second plate of cakes to accompany the tea. Jack helped himself to two and attempted more conversation as they ate and drank. *If Miss Clavering had been here, she would have dominated the conversation*, he thought with some irony. When the butler opened the door to the drawing room to announce more visitors, Jack stood.

"I shall not overstay my welcome, as I see there are others vying for your company, but will bid you both farewell."

The small party of newcomers looked him over as he took leave of his hostesses, and he noted that Mrs. Rainfair, a notorious gossip, was counted among their number. Surely a visit paid to a woman and her mother during calling hours would offer nothing for Mrs. Rainfair to gossip about. He certainly hoped not. Jack exited into the fresh spring air and took deep breaths. The visit had not lessened his interest in Miss Sommers, per se, but neither had it done anything to further it. He was just as unsure about his own mind where Miss Sommers was concerned as he was before he'd come.

However, there was one woman he had quite decided against. Miss Clavering would not be receiving any further signs of his favor.

CHAPTER FIVE

*P*hilippa picked at her breakfast and at last set down her fork before pouring herself more tea. Memories of Mr. Merrick dancing with Susan filled her with disquiet, particularly since Susan had spoken of nothing else the rest of the night. Philippa's first impression of him had not been favorable. Surely his smiles were too practiced to be trusted. Meanwhile, Matthew would have to admit defeat if he did not hasten to make an appearance.

Her thoughts drifted to Mr. Blythefield, who had surprised her in how different he was to Susan. For a second son, he certainly possessed firm ideas about how things should be done. The temptation to overturn those ideas had been too great to resist, and Philippa had to bite her lip over the sudden urge to laugh at his expression when she'd told him to keep up. *That was too bad of you,* she scolded herself. But it did not lessen her amusement.

In appearance, he was dark to Susan's fair—his hair brown with hints of gold that matched his eyes so well. Or perhaps it was just his particular color brown that was unusual. While Susan wore an expression of serious sweetness, her brother appeared to frown with enough regularity to form long creases on either side of his mouth. Philippa pushed the bit of egg on her plate, her chin in her hand. Mr. Blythefield, though she was loath to own it, was uncommonly handsome.

Her sister Maria entered the room. "Philippa, sit up straight. You must know better than to lean with your chin in your hand as though you were an urchin." Philippa obeyed as Maria went to the sideboard and chose two rolls before sitting at the table. "You were certainly distracted at the Yardmouths' last night. You barely spoke in the carriage ride home.

I will declare the ball a success, despite it being rather early to launch the Season."

"Quite a success." Philippa wiped her fingers on the napkin. "Of course, when one receives an invitation from Mrs. Yardmouth, one does not dare refuse it."

"No indeed. I am only sorry that we had to leave so soon in the evening, but what could be done? With the speeches ending so late every night, Charles was done in." Maria sighed as she reached for the teapot. "And with none of his particular friends there, no interesting discussions were to be had. Charles cannot be expected to devote his time to such flighty pursuits as late-night balls when there are more weighty matters to attend to."

"Certainly not. I am convinced that your husband's contribution in Parliament is indispensable. He must preserve his energy for more worthy pursuits." Philippa gave her sister a benign smile. Even if Charles were as important as he, himself—and Maria—thought him to be, Philippa was unimpressed by her brother-in-law's conservative approach. Lucius and George had no patience for Tory views, and after gleaning the crux of the debates from them, Philippa had to agree.

"Where is the apricot jam?" Maria gestured for the footman to bring some before turning back to Philippa. "It most certainly is. Charles is highly regarded in the Commons. Now, my dear. It is time we thought of your own future. Mother left you in my care—"

"Mother," Philippa interjected with contained ire, "did not precisely commit me to your care. She simply did not find it convenient to come to London, considering she is newly remarried herself."

"Philippa," Maria reprimanded in a sharp voice. "You must not interrupt. It is bad *ton*."

Philippa perfected a mask of indifference as Maria remained silent, testing Philippa's repentance, surely, by refusing to complete her thought until she was sure Philippa had truly been subdued. The apricot jam was brought, and Maria spread it on her bread, then continued.

"True though it may be that our mother would have done well to come to London herself, despite being newly married, she has reposed full trust in me to care for you—just as I have done since you were in the schoolroom. Now, it is only left for us to find you a husband and secure your future." Maria took a large bite of bread and swallowed it before adding, "I can only hope you will find such felicity in marriage as Charles and I have found."

The kind of marriage Maria and Charles had did not inspire Philippa in the least. She smiled innocently and added in a spirit of mischief, "And as Lucius and Selena have found."

She loved to remind Maria that Lucius also had married. The scandal attaching to Selena's family name had not endeared her to Maria as a sister-in-law. But that was through no fault of Selena's, whose noble character had shone through in her trials. Philippa held Selena in even greater affection than her own sister, who was flesh and blood.

Maria puckered her lips. "As you say. There is a standard to achieve where marital affairs are concerned, and we must waste no time in securing your future. After all, you are now nineteen years of age, and if you wait much longer you will be on the shelf. When I found out that you had turned down *two* perfectly eligible offers, I told Charles he was much too easy on you. I would have ordered you to accept them."

"Surely not both," Philippa said, blinking her eyes at her sister.

"Oh, no, no. Of course you could not have accepted both. But at least one. Mr. Gerson, I suppose I can understand, although if there had been no one else ... But it was the height of folly to have turned down Mr. Thackery, who is the *Parliament-driver*, Philippa." She laid heavy influence on those words, adding, "Although he appears to be willing to renew his suit, which I must say is most generous of him. If you refuse him, there is no guarantee you will receive another offer."

Maria buttered the rest of her bread with energetic stabs. "Not to say you are not a well-looking girl. You come from a perfectly good family with a respectable fortune. Those things would be foolish indeed to whistle away. But if you have the reputation of being a flirt..." She lifted her butter knife and pointed it in Philippa's direction. "There are other pretty young women making their debut, so you cannot be too choosy. The situation leaves you with some highly undesirable competition. There is nothing for it. You must work to make sure you catch the eye of a suitable man, and if that man is Mr. Thackery, why, you could not do better."

Philippa listened to this speech with only half an ear. Considering Mr. Gerson had in no way inspired any romantic fantasies in her young breast and that Maria had coupled the promise of Mr. Thackery's proposal with a warning that Philippa must not trouble him with her opinions, she knew it would be impossible to find common ground with Maria where marriage was concerned. It did not do to argue her case, however. If anything, Maria was relentless. As soon as she could, she would escape to Susan's house, where there was no one breathing down her neck at all, an idea which suited to perfection.

Charles entered the room. "Awake already, are you?" He leaned down to kiss his wife on the cheek. "Morning, Philippa."

She murmured a reply as Charles filled his plate and sat down to attend to his breakfast. Maria's husband inspired no romantic fantasies in her either, despite the *felicitous* state of marriage Maria had boasted about. With whiskers that grew in an unruly fashion almost to his nose and a tendency to corpulence and pomposity, Philippa was perfectly content to wait before entering the state of matrimony—at least if it promised to be to a man cut of the same cloth.

"You were thick with your young friend Miss Blythefield last night. How does she go on?" Maria asked Philippa before turning to her husband. "This is a family connection I think you need not be ashamed of. I understand Mr. Blythefield is a member of Parliament as well."

Charles looked up, answering with his mouth full of food. "Blythefield is a Whig. He and I cannot have anything in common."

Philippa could not bear to hear any more opinions spoken through mouthfuls of food. "If you say so, he must be a Whig, then. We have not exchanged enough words for me to know." She stood, the oppressive atmosphere of her house driving her from the room more quickly than usual. "As a matter of fact, I have promised Susan that I would come today, and I must not delay."

"I cannot approve of your tendency to run about with no one in attendance."

Philippa froze in place. If Maria forbade her to go to the Blythefields, she would go mad. Despite the fact that Susan was a new friend, she was the only female friend Philippa had. She had never been to school or had neighbors with daughters her age or lived in a household where people actually encouraged social calls.

Just as Philippa began to fear Maria would not let her go, her sister relented. "Although, I suppose it is permissible that you should visit another young lady, accompanied by your maid. Very well. Take Fernsby with you. In London, young women must not be seen unaccompanied."

"Of course not, Maria. I would not dream of going anywhere in London without at least a maid as chaperone." Philippa made her escape from the breakfast room, and after waiting a seasonable amount of time in her bedroom, for she knew Susan was not an early riser, she went downstairs and called for the carriage.

Philippa did not talk to Fernsby as they drove to the Blythefield residence—not because she was above allowing her maid to enter at least partly into her confidences, but rather because the prospect of the Season suddenly stretched bleakly before her. Last year, the lure of London and the excitement of the balls and parties had made up for the stilted atmosphere in the Holbecks' house. But this morning's meal was a stark reminder of what she would have to endure for the next few months in Maria's house, and she suddenly wondered if she could bear it.

Susan's townhouse appeared somber when Philippa arrived, with the grayish façade and the light film of grime on the windows. She stopped and looked around, her eyes lighting on yellow crocuses that had poked through the earth around the trees planted near the pavement. It suddenly dawned on her that much of her mood could probably be attributed to the dreary weather outdoors, rather than the true state of things, and she should not let such a thing as weather influence the quality of her reflections. It was as though winter was reluctant to let go, and although there was no precipitation, neither was there any sun. Apart from those determined crocuses—it seemed even the blossoms were timid at venturing forth.

Philippa took a deep breath and climbed the steps with Fernsby trailing behind. A low mood could be remedied. She needed only the fortitude of mind and some more cheerful company. She and Susan were not at all similar in temperament, but Susan was a comfortable person to be around and had a sweet disposition. Philippa tended to leave their time together with her mood greatly improved, and this was made even more agreeable when she'd also improved her friend's tone of mind.

The Blythefields' aged butler opened the door some time after the maid had let the knocker fall. Philippa waited for him to catch his breath before he announced, "Miss Blythefield is expecting you and will be down shortly. She asked me to have you wait in the drawing room."

Philippa, on familiar terms with the servants in this unusual house, did not wait for the butler to escort her into it, as it seemed unfair to make him move more than necessary. She entered the drawing room and was struck anew by the way the decor sucked out all the light that managed to pierce the dim interior, especially on days when there was so little sun. It was a shame, really, since the rooms in the Blythefield townhouse had tall ceilings and more space than was to be found in many London drawing rooms. This one had the potential to be charming. She walked to the center and let her bonnet fall on the worn settee.

The door opened, and Philippa turned. Mr. Blythefield entered. They stared at one another for a moment without speaking. Her visits to the Blythefield residence had not been numerous, and she had never crossed paths with him.

"Miss Clavering." Mr. Blythefield took a few steps into the room. "Why are you…" He stopped short, then glanced back toward the open door behind him. "I assume you are waiting for Susan?"

He hadn't bowed, so Philippa did not curtsy but simply inclined her head. "I am. Your butler said she would be down shortly."

"Which might mean a half hour," Mr. Blythefield said. He gestured to the settee where her bonnet lay. "Please—sit."

It felt more like an order than an invitation, but Philippa resumed her seat. When he sat as well, she looked around the room searching for inspiration. "You are not going to Parliament today?"

Mr. Blythefield sat upright and rested his arm on the chair. Then he spread his knees and leaned forward, looking like a lion about to spring. "No. Not at present. The debates today are not ones that interest me."

The man needed to unbend. Philippa would help him along. "I would have thought that all debates must concern you—that they cannot move forward without your opinion."

Her provocation fell flat. "Very likely true," he replied and rubbed his chin. "I may be a younger Member, but I believe men have come to rely on my good sense. It is only that this debate is a minor one, and therefore beneath my notice."

"Ah." There seemed to be nothing to say to that. What glorious self-importance. How could sweet Susan be related to such a pompous man? "I am sure you must be right," she answered at last. "No sense in wasting your time on less important pieces of legislation." A heavy silence fell over them, and Mr. Blythefield turned his face to the window and began to tap his fingers on the chair.

Philippa directed her stare to his hands. "Please do not feel obligated to stay—"

The door opened. "Oh, Philippa, how very glad I am to see you." Susan walked into the room, and Mr. Blythefield leapt to his feet.

"I will leave the two of you to your visit," he said, bowing when Philippa stood. She crinkled her brows and dropped a curtsy. It appeared he had remembered his manners at last.

Her mind was still attempting to decipher the perplexity that was Mr. Blythefield when Susan sighed loudly and dropped on the settee. Susan's mood appeared more morose than Philippa's, even taking into account her few minutes with the boring, self-important Mr. Blythefield.

Philippa laughed, trying to dispel the gloom that had fallen over them both. "Why, whatever is the matter? Did you not have a charming time at the ball last night? At last, you were able to see Mr. Merrick as you wished."

"Yes," Susan wailed, "but he did not dance more than one set with me. And he spent an equal amount of time dancing with Miss Fox."

"I believe he was attempting to stick to protocol," Philippa said, wondering why she was defending Mr. Merrick. "You know men cannot generally dance more than one set with a woman without setting tongues wagging. Or, at most, perhaps two."

"Yes, but he only danced *one* with me, and then he left. I begin to fear he is not as interested in me as Christopher said; otherwise he would not care about setting tongues wagging." Susan sighed again loudly and sprawled back along the chair. "I'm so tired of being a spinster. I'm so tired of looking at these same chairs and this same drawing room. I wish I was married and had my own drawing room to decorate."

Philippa let the spinster comment slide, allowing for Susan's disappointment. But Philippa did look at the drawing room with fresh eyes. It was clear there had not been a feminine touch here in some time. An idea began to form in her mind. "Has your family any particular reason for not making alterations to this drawing room?"

"I've never asked," Susan said, sitting up. She drew her brows together and followed Philippa's gaze to the window and the furniture lining the walls. "It has never occurred to me that we might do something to improve it. All I know is that we never have morning callers—or at least, only Mother's friends."

Philippa bit her lip as she contemplated the room. A big change would be welcome, and since she had absolutely no say in her own home, perhaps this was the very thing to occupy their minds—with the added advantage of keeping Susan's thoughts away from Mr. Merrick until Matthew might return. If only her brother George would arrive in London, as he had promised to do without delay, so she could get him to send word to Matthew.

She turned to Susan. "Is your mother at home? Might you ask her if she will give you the liberty to refurbish the drawing room? Or perhaps whether she would like to take on the project with your assistance?"

Susan scrunched up her lips in doubt. "My mother is quite taken up with other things. Her projects mean so much to her."

It occurred to Philippa that Susan might fear she would receive a snub concerning her mother's somewhat unusual behavior, and Philippa hastened to assure her. "And her projects of reform are *most* important. However, it does not leave much time for the affairs of the household, and those take some considering too."

With Susan looking at her expectantly, Philippa thought for a minute and gave the room a sweeping glance. "What fun it would be to decorate this room, if only you could gain your parents' consent. Susan—might you ask your mother? Perhaps she would be glad to have you propose it, for you could tell her it will be good practice for when you are married." She grabbed Susan's hands. "I should not wish to interfere in your family's affairs, but this could truly be a project we put our hearts into. Think of the fun!"

Philippa pointed to the draperies, which were an olive-green color, yellowed at the top and with a thick coat of dust near the ceiling. The wall hangings next to it were also of a deep olive color and patterned with gold. Together, they lent a dark tone to the room that absorbed all sunlight coming in. She walked over and fingered the drapes, then looked back at Susan, who still sat on the settee, which—along with the chairs—was positively Georgian.

Susan's eyes had begun to shine. "My mother is home. My father is too." She chewed her lip as a look of resolve settled over her. "I suppose I could ask them—although I don't know that Jack would approve."

Philippa looked at Susan curiously. Mr. Blythefield seemed to run this household. "What has your brother Jack to say to it? Gentlemen, as a whole, are not interested in household affairs such as decorating. It is up to your father, I believe, to make decisions pertaining to budget—and your mother as to questions of taste. If you wish to ask them, and they are in agreement, then there is no reason why we should put it off. I have nothing at all to do this afternoon. We might visit some of the drapers and have a look at catalogs to see what sort of furniture Sheraton has brought out."

"I think that is a most wonderful idea." Susan stood suddenly, and her voice trembled with excitement. "I shall ask them right now. Would you wait for me?"

Philippa nodded and silently urged her to go quickly, crossing her fingers that Mr. Blythefield would not choose to come back into the room in his sister's absence. Susan left, returning not ten minutes later.

"I was most fortunate, Philippa," she said as she breezed into the room. "I found my mother, and she said it was a wonderful idea. She has never found the time to refurbish the drawing room since she got married, although she said my father had urged her toward it early in their marriage. She came with me to see my father, and he agreed. He saw no reason to withhold the expense from such a scheme, as there is a most promising investment that he is about to commit to—" Susan stopped suddenly. "Although I don't suppose I should've told you that."

Philippa waved her hand. "Think no more on it. I will not share it with anybody. The point is, your parents said we might make changes. But does your mother wish to come with us?"

Susan shook her head vigorously. "She could not spare the time but said I might do so with you, and she is entirely sure you must have good taste."

"Splendid!" Philippa clasped her hands together. "Let us not delay. Shall we bring both our maids so they can help us carry packages?"

"An excellent idea. I will send word to the kitchen." Susan looked at Philippa, then hurried to her and took hold of both her hands. "Perhaps Mr. Merrick will hear of the changes, and it will induce him to come visit me so he may see the drawing room for himself. He will see what an admirable housekeeper I am."

"Oh … yes. I am sure he will." Philippa leaned down and swooped her bonnet up from the settee. The sooner they left the better. She had no wish for another taste of the overbearing Mr. Blythefield in one day. She had enough of *that* sort of thing at home. "The rain is holding off. Fortune has favored us!"

CHAPTER SIX

The large oak-paneled corridor leading to the Parliament chambers resonated with speech as men gathered together in small groups outside of it. It would be a lively debate if the number of men filing into it were any indication. Jack breathed in the invigorating scent of decisions and change—of power. His boots clipped on the stone floor, and the paintings of men who had gone before him lined the walls on either side. There were men of both parties gathered outside the room, but he was searching for Mr. Whitmore the elder. He hoped to learn before the business was introduced whether Mr. Whitmore had managed to persuade Earl Grey as to Jack's suitability for the position of Leader of the Opposition, as Mr. Whitmore had thought he might be able to do. Lord Palmer was already on board with the idea, which was most gratifying.

Before Jack could catch a glimpse of the gentleman he sought in the throng of people, Mr. Thackery, the Parliament-driver for the Tories, strode his way.

"Mr. Blythefield, spare me a few minutes of your time, will you?" There was nothing slipshod about Mr. Thackery. The neatness of his appearance would satisfy even Christopher's standards, and Jack felt almost shabby standing next to him. He had attempted to like the man but, for reasons he could not identify, found he could not.

"Of course, Mr. Thackery. How may I be of assistance?"

"I understand that it's your intention to support the motion to repeal the Corn Laws." Mr. Thackery glanced at the door to the chambers as more of the men headed inside. "I merely wanted to drop a word of warning in your ear that it's not likely to pass. You might better spend your time on a bill that will advance your cause in Parliament."

That surprised a laugh out of Jack. "I hope you're not banking on your ability to change my mind on Ricardo's bill five minutes before the House is called to order. I was with Ricardo when he drafted it, and I know there *is* support for it, and in both parties—more than you would have me credit."

Mr. Thackery indicated the door to the chambers ahead. "If you will have the goodness to walk with me, you will see that I have only your interests at heart. Rumors are circulating that your name is coming up for Leader of the Opposition, as you must be aware." He glanced at Jack, who nodded. "That would indeed be an honor if it comes about. In such a position, you could accomplish much—enough to leave quite a legacy. However, if you're leading the charge to abolish the Corn Laws, you may never have a chance to try. The motion to repeal runs so entirely against the interests of the landowners, and they are the ones who hold the power in the Commons."

Mr. Thackery stopped short of the entrance to the chambers and stuck his hand in his waistcoat. He was not much older than Jack, but he was a great deal more arrogant.

Jack was not learning anything he did not already know. But hearing it from Mr. Thackery, whom some had identified as a potential candidate for Prime Minister, lent a menace to his words. He ignored the people pouring past him as he answered.

"I need not tell you, Mr. Thackery, that there is growing unrest among the poor. If Parliament continues to fix the price of grain and forbid free trade the way we've been doing under the Corn Laws, laborers will not be able to eat." Jack raised an eyebrow. "And laborers who don't eat are more likely to cause mischief than turn their effort toward securing the prosperous future of England. Even men of power cannot subdue the force of the majority."

A few men glanced at them with a curious look as Mr. Thackery put his hand on Jack's arm. "You underestimate the will and creativity of men in power, Blythefield."

Jack suppressed the desire to throw off Thackery's hand—or wipe the smug look off the man's face. No wonder they were not better acquainted. He pasted on a smile. "Well, I invite you to listen with an open mind.

Perhaps I might change yours. After you," he said, gesturing into the room.

Mr. Thackery entered the room, climbing to one of the higher benches where he took a seat on the right side with the other Tories. Jack raised his eyes to see who Thackery's influencers—or lackeys—were. Mr. Merrick sat on the bench behind him, and he leaned forward to whisper something in Thackery's ear.

More and more undesirable for Susan, Jack thought.

Mr. Whitmore the elder caught sight of Jack and moved his way through the crowds in the chamber. A white-haired man known for patience and good sense, Mr. Whitmore had taken Jack under his wing since Jack had first entered politics. Mr. Whitmore had even advanced Jack's rise in politics over his own son, Robert, who had professed no interest in any position other than MP.

"Ah, there you are." He shook Jack's hand with a kindly smile. "I'm sure you are eager to know of my meeting with Lord Grey. I shall not keep you in suspense. He is of the same mind as myself, Lord Palmer, and the others."

Jack could not keep the smile from his face. What a coup! Ever since he'd begun studying at Oxford and found his sympathies were with the Whigs, he'd coveted the position of Leader of the Opposition—and to achieve such a thing before the age of thirty!

"However, nothing is set in stone as of yet. I would advise you to organize some sort of informal dinner party to see what you can do about repealing the Corn Laws. Earl Grey won't come, but Lord Palmer might very well attend." Mr. Whitmore cocked his head. "Shame you are not yet married, as I think the dinner will be more to our purpose with the women present. Men will be more likely to bend their views in the presence of the fairer sex, especially when it comes to ideas of reform."

Mr. Whitmore turned as the Speaker of the House took his place in the center of the room. "Ah, I believe we are about to start."

Jack nodded and went to sit, his initial euphoria now replaced with a sense of dread. How could he host any sort of dinner party at his own house? His family would only hinder the cause. Mr. Whitmore's words about finding a wife rang in Jack's mind. If anything could fuel his resolution to marry and settle into his own establishment, not much more was needed than the thought of attempting this dinner alone.

Robert Whitmore entered the room and came to sit at Jack's side. Younger by a few years, he had never resented his father's interest in Jack's career. Instead, they had quickly found a commonality of ideas, particularly concerning repealing the Corn Laws.

Robert glanced across the room at the conference conducted in the higher benches. "I saw that Mr. Thackery honored you by singling you out. As a more radical Tory, I assume it was to offer his support for repealing the Corn Laws?" His words dripped with irony.

"Hardly," Jack said, his eyes still on Thackery and Merrick as they spoke. "I do not know what he hoped to accomplish by 'dropping a word in my ear' as he put it. It was a feeble word that carried no real argument, except perhaps to deliver a threat, as he surely must have known."

The room was being called to order, and Jack waited until his bill came on the table before requesting acknowledgement from the Speaker of the House. Having been given permission, Jack stood and addressed the room. "Gentlemen. My lords. This is the second time since this year's Session opened that the subject of repealing the Corn Laws has come up before the Commons, and I claim your indulgence as I debate the matter before you today."

With barely a need to glance at his notes, Jack reminded the Members of Parliament of Mr. Ricardo's study of free trade and the economic boon it would be to England. He proved with examples that the day wages of common laborers could no longer cover the growing cost of bread, especially since they had again raised the tariff on foreign grains. He reminded his fellow MPs that most of these men were family men, and if they did not make enough to feed their families, the temptation to take to poaching, rioting, and further Luddite activities would become too strong to resist.

This was met by hissing that took the Speaker some time to calm down. The violent reaction caused Jack to reconsider his approach. *That was a novice's mistake.* Jack wanted to bury his head in his hands. He needed to appeal to his opponents' interests, not the interests of the poor.

His pause allowed the debate to turn, and Thackery gained a nod from the Speaker. He stood and began elaborating the proven benefit— or so he said—of relying on English-grown grains. He cited personal examples of such benefits among certain Members present, who nodded their heads in agreement. He went on to insist that English grain production would bolster the economy, for it would also provide more agricultural jobs.

Robert gave Jack a sympathetic smile as he resumed the seat next to him. Jack was unsurprised by Thackery's argument, which he knew very well, and he began to tune out. How would he arrange a successful dinner party to talk those wavering over to his side? Who would act as hostess? The memory of Miss Clavering at the Yardmouth ball sprang into his mind, a suggestion as surprising as it was wholly unwelcome. She would make an ideal hostess for a political dinner—if the men were desirous of abandoning all semblance of decision-making and meekly handing it over to the women. He shuddered at the thought, though he had to own she was as pretty as she was opinionated.

When the motion to repeal the Corn Laws had been put to rest—to be argued in a committee before being brought back before the Commons—the Speaker looked up from the papers in front of him.

"We have just one more issue on the table for today. We are bringing to vote whether or not to abolish the right for trial by combat after last year's debacle."

There was a general murmur on the floor and someone called out, "If the esteemed Mr. Laine still fears that abolishing the bill removes his right of appeal, I invite him to test out his rights to trial by combat—"

"I believe that threat has passed, now that Mr. Laine has managed to convince Mrs. Laine to the altar," Melton called out. "Her father is appeased."

Laughter rippled through the crowds on both sides of the bench, and the victim of the sally glowered. Mr. Laine was exacting on matters of the law but spoke in prolonged periods and was not generally well-liked. Jack knew Mr. Laine would not attempt a retaliation and thought it poor sport of Melton to have poked fun.

"Order!" the Speaker called out twice before he was obeyed and they were able to move to the final debates.

At the close of Parliament, Jack exited into the corridor where a stranger, who was older than Jack by a few years, caught Jack's gaze and approached him. He wore the casual attire of the gentry, and if Jack had to guess, he would say the man was a squire.

The gentleman gave a short bow. "I am Sir Lucius Clavering." *Perhaps not a squire.* "Since our paths have crossed, allow me to tell you that I appreciated your arguments today and am interested in the committee you're forming. This is not an easy crowd to convince, and I am not in the position to do so, but I wish you luck." He glanced at the men milling around them, some talking earnestly and others jesting with loud laughter. "I am a landowner, and although I want to see my grain sold at a good price, I work closely enough with laborers from all trades to know that they need to be able to eat in order to work cheerfully for me."

It was small encouragement, but Jack would take it. "Are you a Member of Parliament?"

Sir Lucius closed his eyes and shook his head. "No—and no desire to be. My only interest in attending was to hear the debates on the Corn Laws."

"I see." Jack was about to move on until he remembered. *Clavering.* Was this man any relation to the Miss Clavering he had met at the ball? In features there might have been some similarities, but in coloring there was none. "Clavering is a name that is now familiar to me. Do you have any siblings?"

"My younger brother, George. You might know him from the clubs or through his friendship with Robert Whitmore, whom I saw at your side. Although he is not any more involved in Parliament than I am." He gestured ahead to a portly man with reddish curls, who was in the process of exiting. "My brother-in-law there, Charles Holbeck, owns the seat in which Robert Downing sits. I don't know why he doesn't sit in the seat himself since he cannot bear to miss any of the speeches. I suppose he prefers to let someone else debate for him."

Mr. Holbeck was a Tory. So that was where Miss Clavering got her Tory tendencies. More was the pity, since Sir Lucius appeared to be a man of sense. Jack realized he was still clutching his hat, and he now placed it on his head, saying with studied nonchalance, "I met a Miss Clavering at the Yardmouth ball a week ago. Are you by any chance related to her?"

"Yes." Sir Lucius studied him with a bland look. "My sister. So you've met Philippa, have you?"

Sir Lucius folded his arms, and Jack wanted to blurt out that he had no designs on the young woman, but it would be foolish to grow defensive over someone he'd had absolutely no intentions of pursuing, anyway.

"A very lovely young woman," Jack murmured.

Sir Lucius wore an enigmatic smile. "As sweet as they come," he said, before taking his leave. Jack could think of other adjectives than sweet to describe Miss Clavering. *Forceful* was more like it—and scheming.

As Jack made his way home, an image flooded his vision of the supposedly sweet Miss Clavering, and he shook his head resolutely. She had the face of an angel, but he refused to devote any more of his energy to thinking of her, for a lovely face did not a woman make. All Jack knew was that Susan had been spending a great deal of time with Miss Clavering, and they were involved in some project that his sister was evasive about. But Susan had been more happy these past days than he had seen her in awhile, and that was something.

As Jack entered the house, he heard laughter coming from the drawing room, and it did not sound like Susan's. He paused in the entryway, listening. He stood there long enough that he eventually saw Shanks creeping up the stairwell from the kitchens. "Do not trouble yourself to hurry," he called out to the butler. "I will set my affairs on the bench."

He opened the door to the drawing room, but rather than finding Miss Clavering—for he'd grown certain that it must be she—sitting demurely with his sister as one would expect, he found the young lady standing on a chair next to the window, pulling down the heavy, green curtains that had been a mainstay of their house for Jack's entire life.

He stood on the threshold, thunderstruck. "What in heaven's name are you doing?"

"Wha ... what does it look like?" Susan turned with a handful of curtains, a pearl hairpiece sagging to the side of her head in a comical way.

Jack took in the two women removing curtains—*for heaven's sake, where did all that dust come from?*—without a servant in sight, standing on chairs, no less. "It looks as though you're embarking on a project well beyond your domain," he answered repressively.

Miss Clavering, rather than appearing upset at being in the midst of a family squabble, dropped her end of the fabric to a heap on the floor. "Susan has your mother and father's permission to make these changes. Your father assured her that he had fully intended for Mrs. Blythefield to refurbish after they were married, but it never had been done. And your mother was delighted at the idea of having a daughter who is such a hand at these things. I am here by invitation," she finished with a twinkling smile.

What in the devil! Who was this woman? Sweet, indeed. With difficulty, Jack pulled his eyes off Miss Clavering to glare at his sister. "And who is to pay for these changes?" He stopped short, suddenly realizing he should not be having this discussion in front of Miss Clavering. Jack could've spared himself the reproach, for she was the one who answered.

"Why, your father, of course. He has agreed to everything." Miss Clavering smiled, then pointed past Susan, directing her to the neatly folded pale cloth sitting on the table. "Now. If you will stretch out the new cloth, we may pull it over the curtain rod and judge how it falls. We shall see how it brightens the room, just as you said it would."

"Oh, no," Susan countered, eyes wide. "You were the one who said it—"

"And once we are sure in the choice of curtains, we may choose the color of paint and get your servants set to work. I believe it will only take a week to have this painted, and by that time the rugs and furniture will have arrived."

His sister clasped her hands together. "How exciting." With uncharacteristic energy, Susan pulled the settee over to the other side of the window and began to step on top of it.

Jack finally snapped to attention. "Moving furniture? You should have the servants in here doing this." He strode forward as Miss Clavering balanced on one foot and attempted to throw the cloth over the curtain rod. He reached up to take the cloth from her hands, and instead caught her in an armful as she tumbled from the chair. She was light and soft, and he pulled her close as he tried to catch his breath at the near fall.

"Oh." The exclamation escaped her like a sigh, and Jack found he could not set her down. Blood pulsed through his veins at the imminent disaster, and he seemed unable to loosen his tight hold on her in the weighted seconds that followed. His racing heart shifted from the near danger to something else as his eyes focused on her lips, and the impropriety of their position flooded his awareness.

"Jack, thank heavens you were here to catch her." Susan rushed forward to embrace Miss Clavering, whom he'd set carefully on her feet. Jack darted a glance at Miss Clavering, but she met Susan's gaze instead and laughed.

"How clumsy I am. I will be more careful." Miss Clavering paused for a moment, eyes vaguely fixed on the window and heightened color in her cheeks. Then, to Jack's astonishment, she made a move to climb back on the chair.

"You must allow me." Jack's voice was rough, and he was in no way pleased, although he imagined the strangled words that came out of his throat were from a different cause than irritation. The last thing he expected was to be met with an almost irresistible urge to keep holding Miss Clavering in his arms, frustrating woman that she was.

Still, how dare Miss Clavering take on such a project and in *his* drawing room? She might as well come and take up residence! Jack took a large portion of the cloth and examined the height of the curtain rod. The chair was the less steady of the two, so Jack made his way over to the settee, hesitating over whether to remove his boots. In the end, he decided that the settee was too old to warrant appearing in a state of undress before Miss Clavering and climbed up. He tossed the edge of the fabric over the curtain rod, catching it on the other side as a big cloud of dust from the rod fell on top of him. He coughed and climbed back down. Almost as if without thought, Miss Clavering reached up and brushed the dust off his shoulder then turned away before he could register the intimate gesture.

She then leapt forward to the window and, with nimble steps, pulled the fabric down on the other side of the rod. "It is simply lovely. This new cloth suits to perfection."

"It doesn't though," Jack argued. It came out like a grumble. "It clashes with the wall hangings."

"Never fear, Mr. Blythefield. We have plans to change that, too." Miss Clavering gave him a sunny smile that made Jack want to rip the cloth out of her hands.

Susan stepped forward with cards painted in various tones. "We have settled upon yellow, but are not sure which shade. Oh, Jack! You cannot know how happy I am. I have been too ashamed to have anyone come and visit me in the drawing room, for it is so old-fashioned. Imagine what it will look like when it's finished."

Jack moved back to examine the cloth in front of the window, using the time to regain his equilibrium. He brushed his hands together and looked around the drawing room. Why did this room need any changes?

He was accustomed to it the way it was. Then he glanced at Susan, who was generally shy and whose spirits were often oppressed. She was smiling and animated, entering into all Miss Clavering's plans with enthusiasm. For Susan, Jack could bear almost any change.

"Very nice. You will let me see the bills, will you not?"

Susan glanced at Philippa, who smiled back. "Oh, to be sure, Jack."

"Well then." Jack hesitated in front of the pile of old curtains before deciding to leave them near the wall rather than carry the dust with him. "If you have anything else to hang, please call a servant to do so. I would rather not have to send a note around to Miss Clavering's house to explain a broken leg."

He left, thinking that he'd rather not have to nurse Miss Clavering, either, while she healed from some injury occurring in *his* house. Miss Clavering's sweet temper, indeed. Surely her brother had been jesting. More like the bullheaded temperament of a Tory!

But at least Susan was happy.

CHAPTER SEVEN

*T*he air had grown colder when Philippa left the Blythefield residence, still satisfied with the way things were progressing with the renovations. It had taken her and Susan several days to choose and purchase the cloth that could be turned into curtains, to decide upon more modern furniture, and to choose the right color of paint to set off the tall windows and high ceilings of the room. Philippa was proud of herself for having steered Susan toward the more economical option when it came to choosing furniture.

Outside, however, the chill in the early spring air, and the softening light as it turned from late afternoon sun to evening sent Philippa's spirits plummeting. What awaited her at home? Only another dreadful party filled with dull political figures and their wives that Maria insisted Philippa attend. Not one of them bothered to speak to her as if she had anything to contribute, and the older men were more likely to pinch her cheeks in an odiously familiar way instead. Why, she must be the only young lady in all of London whose Season consisted of dancing attendance on men and women over forty.

In the faded light of the carriage interior, Philippa listened to Fernsby chatter about how she'd been allowed to eat cakes in the kitchen, thanks to the generosity of Miss Blythefield's cook. Fernsby's evident pleasure in spending the afternoons at Susan's house matched Philippa's own. How she'd lived through nearly the entire Season last year without this refuge, she could not say.

Philippa turned her thoughts back to the drawing room and their beginning attempts to put order—seeing their plans turned into action. What a relief to pull down the sets of dusty, drab curtains that were such an eyesore and let the light flood the drawing room. It would be even better when the walls were painted, and the new furniture and rugs had arrived. One would be hard-pressed to recognize it as the same room. And it was all her idea—her inspiration. Content, Philippa glanced down and brushed a bit of dirt off the front of her gown that lay uncovered underneath her pelisse.

True, she would not have gotten quite so filthy had they called the servants in for this part of the work. Philippa made a face. *And I would not have fallen into Mr. Blythefield's arms.* The sensation of being held tightly, his face inches from hers, had suspended her breath. His grip was like iron. She had no idea a man could have arms as strong as that. Despite having two older brothers, she had never been the recipient of more than a pat on her shoulder or a loose hug. She wondered if her brothers' arms held such strength as Mr. Blythefield's or if his was out of the ordinary.

You should have the servants in here doing this. Mr. Blythefield had clearly shown his displeasure. But that would not have been nearly as much fun as doing it themselves. The servants would have their role to fulfill when it came time to strip the walls and paint. Susan had already spoken to them, and they had promised to find more hands for the task ahead. The painting would begin that same week. All in all, it had been a most satisfactory afternoon—more fun than she'd had in a long time.

Philippa entered the front door of their townhouse, and Maria stepped forward, dressed in an evening gown and wringing her hands in agitation. "Philippa, child—you are late. I was beginning to worry. We are to have supper very soon."

"You need not have worried, Maria. I had Fernsby with me—and James as well. I was in perfectly good hands, and you knew I was with Susan Blythefield at her house." Philippa looked down to unbutton her pelisse, hiding her frown. "I will have a plate sent up as I dress. No need to hold supper on my account."

Maria hurried to assist Philippa with her pelisse, and a look of perplexity crossed her features. She reached forward and touched Philippa's hair that curled out from the front of her bonnet. "You have … it appears there is some sort of dirt on your hair. And on your gown, too. What have you been doing?"

Philippa lifted a hand to her head and tried to feel for the dirt Maria had spoken of. Now that she touched her hair, she could only imagine how it must look. Her curls were coated with some sort of film. "I assure you, it is nothing. Susan and I were only examining the possibilities for refurbishing the Blythefield drawing room. That explains why I am less than presentable at the moment, and why I was running late."

Maria's brows snapped together. "I am not at all sure the Blythefields are proper people for you to know if their drawing room is so dirty you must come home with your head covered in dust. Did you not remember that we had the Munster party tonight? You will never be ready on time if we have to wash your hair as well. Fernsby, you are going to have to take matters into your hands, and quickly. Unless I should come up with you. Perhaps I should—"

"Maria, it's fine. Fernsby and I can manage, and Charles will not appreciate having supper held back. Trust me to be ready on time." Philippa untied the strings to her bonnet. Maria's greeting did not further warm her to the evening that stretched ahead of her. *Ugh!* What a bore. She could have stomped her foot in frustration. An evening of Holbeck's political cronies who were—most of them—piggish and old, and all of them dull.

Fernsby stepped forward with a quick curtsy. "I'll do my best to have her ready, ma'am. Miss, I'll just fetch some hot water and send a plate of supper up straight away." The maid hurried toward the kitchen, and Philippa, intent on escaping further recrimination, went to her room to dress. There were times when it was best to obey her sister without a fuss.

After bringing up the basin of water, Fernsby helped Philippa to clean her face, then combed the more obvious dirt out of Philippa's curls. "No one will notice for tonight, miss. I will tie it up with the brown ribbon. But we shall have to wash your hair tomorrow."

In weary resignation, Philippa allowed her shoulders to relax under Fernsby's ministrations. "Tomorrow I have no great plans."

That was the sorry truth. She never seemed to have any plans at all, despite receiving a great number of invitations. Maria only accepted the ones *she* wished to attend, and only the larger of these gatherings attracted crowds that included people likely to interest Philippa. If only she could spend more of her time helping Susan to brighten her home. A frown pulled at her eyebrows. If only Matthew Evans would come to London and begin to woo the object of his adoration. She would be happy to see Susan so well settled.

Philippa sighed at the night that stretched before her—at the Season that stretched before her. If there was any good that came out of going to tonight's party, it was that she was not likely to meet Mr. Blythefield there. A Whig did not generally attend Tory parties.

At the Munster residence, Philippa trailed Maria and her husband into the glittering drawing room. She smiled and greeted the host and hostess, concealing her displeasure at being there, then looked around the crowds for someone she might speak to who would be slightly less unbearable than she was expecting. Chances were slim for success, but one never knew.

Why Charles insisted *she* accompany them to this stifling event Philippa could not say. He likely hoped that she would fall for one of his colleagues, thereby strengthening his position in politics. If what Maria said was true, he still held out hope for a match with Mr. Thackery. *That* was not going to happen.

"Miss Clavering, you are looking as ravishing as ever."

Philippa turned, and the very man himself—the devil, as she saw it—was standing before her. "Mr. Thackery. No need to be polite and come and greet me. On the contrary, I will not mind if you give me the cut direct the entire evening."

Mr. Thackery sipped at the champagne he held in his hand. His brown hair had grown longer at the bottom, and an additional year had only added to his distinguished appearance. "I see that entering your second Season without having achieved a match in the first has done no harm to your tongue." He smirked. "However, I believe time will do that."

Philippa skimmed him with her gaze, then looked away. His lack of feeling underneath the handsome exterior made him entirely unappealing. "I doubt that, Mr. Thackery. Considering I have no ambition to be married and lose the little say I have in my future—as you reminded me I most certainly would—I don't think any number of years will alter my tongue in any significant way."

"We shall see, my dear. I must own that you have taken me quite by surprise. No other woman has managed to catch my interest since last year." Mr. Thackery gave an enigmatic smile. "I am beginning to think I have settled on my choice and shall continue my pursuit of you."

Philippa widened her eyes. "After so thorough a rejection? I am all astonishment that you would attempt it. I cannot tell if it is your humility that is lacking—or your sense."

"Let us just say it is not my sense. I am a man who knows what he wants, but I am also a man who won't bargain unfairly. I told you what I expected out of the arrangement, which is more of a pound dealing than you'll get with most men." He indicated Philippa's brother-in-law, who was filling a plate on the other side of the room. "And if I know Holbeck, I don't imagine any resistance you attempt will last long."

"As Charles is not able to take possession of my body and move my lips to form the word *yes*, I am not in any way daunted by your threat. The answer is still no."

Mr. Thackery laughed and flicked her chin, then left.

The refreshment tables were full of dishes set out to tempt the guests, and although Philippa had eaten, she went to look it over. She took one of the plates from a liveried servant and chose a marzipan shaped like an apricot with green leaves and a ratafia cake. When she looked up, she startled under the gaze of Mr. Blythefield, who was standing across the table staring at her. *Him, too?* The night was turning out to be worse than she had imagined.

Mr. Blythefield circled the table. "We meet twice in one day." He glanced down at her plate. "Only sweets?"

"I am not any more enchanted than you are, Mr. Blythefield. And, yes, only sweets. We ate before coming."

She felt the weight of Mr. Blythefield's regard as she turned to watch the party, ignoring the delicacies she had just selected, until she could bear it no longer. "What?"

He was facing her, a small crinkle marring his brow. "Has something happened to bother you?"

Philippa shot him a look of surprise. "What makes you say that?"

Mr. Blythefield's eyes seemed to miss nothing as he studied her. "I cannot say. It is only that you appear more irritated than usual."

"More irritated?" Philippa mustered a smile with difficulty. "Am I really such an irritable creature overall, do you think?"

"Actually, no. It appears, on the contrary, that nothing ruffles you. But just now you seemed different. Unhappy, and most definitely ruffled." Mr. Blythefield glanced across the room. "I saw you talking to Thackery."

Philippa did not wish to go into her history with Mr. Thackery. "What are you doing here? I didn't expect to see a single Whig among us."

Mr. Blythefield pulled his gaze from Mr. Thackery to her and gave a soft chuckle that softened his features. "This was supposed to be a joint-party affair. At least that is what I was told. But considering the fact that I've been the dissenting voice in every conversation here, I'm beginning to think that was an exaggeration. I believe they are trying to poach me from the other side—and my influence with it."

Philippa raised an eyebrow. "Such efforts on your behalf," she observed. "Are you really so brilliant a statesman?"

Mr. Blythefield locked his gaze with hers. "I have great ambition. I have the talent to take me there. I lack only one thing."

"Modesty?"

Mr. Blythefield laughed. "Fair enough. Let us say I lack two things. Besides modesty, I lack a broader support to my bill. I carry weight in my own party and have been able to cross political lines and gain support from the other. Some of my sponsors expressed hopes in getting that for me here."

"Among the Tories?" Philippa asked. She looked around the room, and although she did not know many people, there was not one she could imagine who might entertain ideas from a Whig.

"There are sympathizers. The fact that the Prince Regent is drawn to Whig ideals does not go unnoticed. And I think…" Mr. Blythefield paused and searched her face—as if for understanding, she thought. "I think there are some, even among the Conservatives, who are beginning to see the need for reform. Those are the people I need to talk to tonight."

Philippa looked down at her plate, picked up the marzipan candy, and took a bite. She needed to distract herself from the earnest look in his expression that tugged at something inside of her—and that inexplicably brought up the memory of being in his arms. "Then I can only thank you for your condescension in having spent so much time talking to me."

"It was nothing," Mr. Blythefield said. He sipped his drink, eyes on her. "Everyone else was otherwise occupied."

Philippa lifted her head, her mouth twisted in outrage until she saw his laughing eyes. It was an unexpected sight, for Mr. Blythefield's lips barely crept up toward a smile. But in his eyes there was a light and humor that suddenly stole Philippa's breath. Perhaps there was something more to this overbearing gentleman than she had originally thought—some warmth and humanity. If anything, he wasn't entirely boring.

CHAPTER EIGHT

*N*oises of conversation, chairs scraping, and tools clattering emanated from the drawing room, bringing Jack to its door. He had entered this room more in the past couple of weeks than he had in the entire year. Generally, his feet trod the path from his bedroom to the breakfast room and out the door, where he spent the remainder of the day in Parliament and usually dined at his club. But the changes that were being made here roused his curiosity, and he found himself frequently coming to inspect them. Last he'd checked, they had been sanding down the walls that had been stripped of their wall hangings.

He opened the door and ducked as an unknown man turned with a ladder, nearly hitting Jack in the chest. With four other workers present, one of whom was his footman, Andrew, here was a flurry of activity unlike anything he was accustomed to seeing in his home. Much of the furniture had been removed and—he could only imagine—discarded. The rest had Holland covers draped over it, and more cloths covered the floors. His footman was covered in paint, including his hair, and the other men were similarly adorned. Together, the men had managed to complete two-thirds of the wall.

"You have begun the painting, I see. Who was it that gave you orders to start?" Jack's voice echoed in the tall-ceilinged room that was almost empty.

The hired men continued painting, but Andrew paused in the act of dipping his brush into a pot of paint. "It was Mr. Blythefield, sir."

Jack had nothing to say to that and simply nodded, gesturing for Andrew to continue. He supposed it was good his father was taking an interest in the renovations. He took a moment to appreciate how airy the room was without the curtains and noticed for the first time that there were pretty moldings near the top of the ceiling detailing leaves and berries, from what he could see. The walls were done in the palest of yellows, but the moldings had been repainted in white. The choice in colors was pleasing overall, but something about the whole process irked him. Miss Clavering had only been in town a mere three weeks, and his entire townhouse was in an uproar.

He left the drawing room and went downstairs to his father's study and tapped on the door. When his father bid him enter, Jack came in and found his father slumped over his accounts on the desk, his head in his hands. There was a half-drunk cup of tea at his side, and his father was unshaven. Jack recognized the signs of despair.

"I was coming in to congratulate you on having approved the changes in the drawing room, which were badly overdue." Jack hesitated on the threshold, unsure if he had the inner fortitude to take on his father's dashed hopes just now, as they were likely to increase Jack's own burden. He put his hand on the knob. "However, it appears I have come upon you at an inopportune time."

His father lifted his head and looked across the room, the hint of agony evident in his eyes. "No, you may as well come in," he replied, dashing Jack's hopes of being able to remain in blissful ignorance of the latest catastrophe. "I confess, son, that I did indeed invest in the frame-knitter venture, despite your having advised me against it. But I thought you were wrong. Why, these inventions are the future of England. One day it will not be by manpower but by machine power that we will become an even greater nation than we already are." The burst of energy that had accompanied this speech appeared to be spent when Jack's father got to the end of it, and he dropped his gaze to his hands.

"But the laborers were not happy to compete with a machine," Jack said softly, "and knew a machine could not fight back."

His father nodded. "Some of the troublemakers burned the entire factory down."

Jack absorbed this news in silence. He'd wondered about his father's cheerful mood these past weeks but had honestly been afraid to ask if his father had committed to a scheme Jack had advised against. He held affection for his father, despite his father's weaknesses, and he could not look at such brokenness and add to his burden by delivering a heavy reproach. Nevertheless, this could not happen again. The Blythefield estate was barely solvent.

"I knew that scheme could not prevail, Father. Not in that city and at this time, in any case. Where there are masters looking only to profit, who are not concerned with the workers under their care, we cannot be surprised when those same workers, who are hungry and have families to feed, rise up in anger at the threat of job cuts. We need to seek out the investments of men who are taking into account the needs of their workers."

Jack's father sighed. "You were right, of course. It was a difficult proposition to turn down, however. If only those union men had not turned violent—if they had only waited another three months before carrying out such a wasteful protest—until I could have earned my share in the profits ... Now, as it stands, I have lost everything."

Jack came over to the desk and lay a hand on his father's shoulder. "How much?"

"Two thousand pounds."

A few minutes of silence ticked by, and Jack swallowed. Their household could ill afford it. "Who else went in with you on this venture?"

Mr. Blythefield shook his head. "No one else, by my invitation. I was told of the scheme in the strictest confidence. They said there were not enough shares as it stood, and that I should keep the investment to myself."

There was that, at least. Jack would not have to worry about other men who had been led astray by his father's gullibility. "Who were the men who pulled you into this?" When his father wouldn't answer, Jack reminded him with the greatest degree of gentle respect at his command, "It is rarely the case that investors will not make room for more shareholders. Anyone who tells you that the investment must be done in secret is not likely considering your best interests. Who knows if such a factory even existed?"

"It did exist, I am sure of it," his father insisted.

Jack shrugged. What difference did it make anyway? He had said it before, but it bore repeating. "I wish you would come to me with the investments you're considering before you hand over any sum of money. If I don't know whether there is value in the venture myself, I can more easily find it out than you—and without tipping my hand if the investment proves to be sound."

His father nodded but with such a look of misery Jack could not bear to rub it in any further. "Susan has not sent me any bills for the drawing room as she promised. You may send them all my way."

His father's eyes snapped open at the mention of bills for the work in the drawing room. He had clearly not thought through the consequences of having given approval for the changes when his own investment had just failed. And the bills were likely to be sizable. Susan had mentioned having ordered furniture over breakfast yesterday. He had to lay the whole initiative at Miss Clavering's feet. His sister would never have had the idea of refurbishing the drawing room on her own.

Perhaps he would need to have a conversation with Miss Clavering about not meddling in affairs that did not concern her.

Jack left his father's study and, before he could make up his mind to go to the club, he crossed paths with Susan in the corridor.

"Have you seen the changes in the drawing room, Jack? Are they not all that is marvelous?" Susan's excitement would have been contagious were it not for Jack's sour mood. But she didn't seem to notice and squeezed his arm. "I know we live in what is considered a desirable location, but we so rarely have visitors. Perhaps now that we are remaking the drawing room into something of this century, we will begin to have more."

Something of this century. Was that Miss Clavering's judgement? She would soon learn that the Blythefields did not need to be edified by her opinions on family affairs. What a pity. Last night he had found her company diverting.

"Don't you think more people will begin to come now?" Susan's eyes had grown anxious when he didn't answer.

Jack made a noise of assent, but he was thinking it was more likely that visitors were afraid of getting swept up in another one of his mother's projects than they were of being accosted by a set of ugly drapes. "I don't see why not," he said.

Susan sighed. "It's a beautiful day today, and I am stuck inside. I so wish to go out. Will you come with me to the circulating library? Philippa has recommended a book she said will lift my spirits, and she was astonished I had not read it yet."

Miss Clavering again. At least she recognized the need to keep up his sister's spirits—which had always been easily depressed—and actually applied herself to the task.

Jack paused before answering. After his conversation with his father, Jack was hardly in the right humor to accompany Susan. He would have preferred to spend time alone. However, he knew how few companions his sister had, without anyone to escort her to *ton* parties. She had little opportunity to leave the house without his occasionally taking pity on her. That had been one of the benefits of Miss Clavering's frequent visits, despite her thinking their drawing room gothic. "What is Mother doing?"

"Mother has gone to reform the gin houses. She asked me to go, but I was not ready and she could not wait." Susan uttered these words as she tied on her bonnet—as if he had already agreed—adding, "But I'm ready now."

What an odd family he had. Jack had never known his mother to be interested in anything other than reform, although she was generally affectionate with her offspring. As much as he was glad that Susan did not seem embarrassed by their mother's activities, he would prefer his sister not join in. It was one thing for a married woman, who might be called eccentric, to tackle such ventures, but his sister would likely be labeled a bluestocking. And Susan did not have the presence to carry such a title.

"Very well. I will not attend Parliament for another few hours, and I suppose I can spare the time. Have Andrew bring around the carriage, and I will take you up. Would you like to go to Gunter's afterwards?"

Susan's eyes lit up. "Oh, yes. I have not had a strawberry ice in nearly a year."

Susan did not require much time at Hookham's. She came out with a small book, wrapped in paper. They then drove to Gunter's tea shop, and Jack left Andrew in the courtyard with the horses as he escorted his sister inside. The tea shop was bustling with clientele with few available tables, but they did manage to get one near the far wall and placed their orders.

Before they had much time to look around the room at who was in attendance, Jack heard a man's voice on his left. "Excuse me."

He looked up to see Mr. Merrick, who bowed before Susan. "Mr. Blythefield, Miss Blythefield, I apologize for my forwardness, but I saw both of you from across the room and had hoped I might join you. Is this seat taken?"

Jack had no favorable opinion of Mr. Merrick, but he could not refuse him. Miss Clavering's warning about not chasing him away too quickly niggled at him. Besides, it would give him a chance to get to know the man better. Susan was smiling shyly up at him.

"It is not," Jack said. "Please have a seat."

Mr. Merrick sat in the empty chair on the other side of Jack's sister. "Miss Blythefield. It is an unexpected pleasure to see you here."

"I believe we have not met since Mrs. Yardmouth's ball." Susan leaned back as a servant placed a dish of strawberry ice in front of her. Jack received his dish of chocolate ice and lifted his spoon.

"Will you take anything?" he asked Mr. Merrick.

"No, thank you. I've already had tea and some of their cakes. I am not a fan of the ices. And Miss Blythefield, you are correct. I have not been able to go to as many events in recent days as I would have liked. The Sessions have run late, and I've had prior engagements."

Though it was true that Parliament often finished late, Jack could not help but think if Mr. Merrick were truly interested in his sister, he would have found a way to come during calling hours. However, it was not his place to push a suitor on his sister—especially one he was not sure he approved of.

Susan dipped her spoon in her ice and took a small bite. "I suppose it is a good thing you have not come calling, for we would not have been able to receive you. Our drawing room is being refurbished."

There was a slight pause, and Mr. Merrick raised his eyebrows just slightly. "How interesting. You must let me know when you will again be available to receive callers."

It seemed to Jack as though Mr. Merrick had had no intention of calling at all. Miss Clavering's warnings returned in full force, and he wondered if he should ignore them. As much as he was tempted to give her a rebuff for being too interfering, it might be prudent to tread cautiously where Miss Clavering was concerned. He would need her to comfort Susan when Mr. Merrick's attentions wandered, as they surely would.

Jack looked up as the bell over the door rang with the newcomers who had just entered the salon. He recognized Sir Lucius from their brief meeting at Parliament, and he had his arm around a woman who must have been his wife. Lady Clavering was holding a small baby in her arms, and the two of them, side-by-side, nearly hid the figure of another who entered behind them before the door was shut. When Sir Lucius's wife turned back to speak to her, Miss Clavering lifted her head to answer before glancing across the room.

Her eyes met his, and he saw a smile light her face, which he could not help but return, despite wishing to give her a set-down. There was more friendliness there—or at least less antagonism than their previous meetings had held. Then her eyes drifted over to Mr. Merrick, and her smile fell. She turned back to her sister-in-law, following Sir Lucius to a table some distance from the door, where she sat with her back to the rest of the room.

"There is Philippa." Susan stood, and it was a testimony to her affection for Miss Clavering that she excused herself from the man she professed feelings for in order to go and greet her friend.

While she was gone, Mr. Merrick laid a hand on the table. "I hear you were at Munster's on Thursday. Who convinced you to go?"

"I was invited by Mr. Munster himself, as he said there were people he wished me to meet." Jack took another bite of his chocolate ice before looking up at Mr. Merrick. "I don't know if you realize, but your party is more divided on repealing the Corn Laws than might be apparent in the debates."

Mr. Merrick gave a short nod and cleared his throat. "I am counting the votes, and I know that as much as some speak of simply reforming the bill, there is also support for abolishing free trade all together. However, I am afraid the Tories will be able to carry the reform through, which means any hope we had of repealing a bill that encourages unrest in our country will be shot down."

Jack paused with his spoon on the way to his mouth. "We? So you do not count yourself among those who wish to simply implement a reform?"

Mr. Merrick leaned back in his chair. "Let us just say that I have enough sense of the good repealing the law would bring about to be persuaded. I have interests of my own, of a more personal nature, that could influence my decision."

Jack studied him, registering the clink of spoons and murmur of conversation around them. "And what is it you want?" His gaze flicked to his sister and back to Mr. Merrick again. *Surely not Susan?*

Mr. Merrick followed Jack's gaze to the table across the room, where Susan was still talking to Miss Clavering. "I profess to have an interest in your sister and think we might make a fine match. But I must warn you. Although I would see that your sister is well taken care of, I am not motivated by feelings of passion. Indeed, I do not believe I possess them." He met Jack's gaze. "If I were to hazard a guess, I would say you are of the same mind."

Jack pressed his lips together and nodded. After all, he was pursuing the idea of a wife with the same logic. Still, the thought of aligning his sweet-tempered sister with a man who would not offer her any of the more tender feelings did not sit well.

"Good. Then we are in agreement. Miss Blythefield is an uncommonly pretty girl, and her quiet nature is just what a man in politics could wish for. Despite being of different political parties, you and I, we might create an alliance—not an official one, mind you, but a meeting of the minds that we can use for the good of the country. What do you think?"

"I think your objective for an alliance is not a bad one." Jack fingered the handle of his spoon. "But I do wish to see my sister happily settled."

"And so she shall be. It is only that more objectives will be met than a simple marital union, which I think we can both agree is a noble aspiration."

Mr. Merrick picked up the napkin that Susan had set down in her haste and glanced up at her, now bending over the Clavering's baby. "There is another matter at stake, however, which has me wondering if there might not be a wiser move to consider. I have been attempting to persuade Thackery on the restriction of coal duties and with little success. I have found him more distracted as of late since it appears he is suffering from an infatuation. Nothing will do for him but to take Miss Clavering to wife. Besides her having strong Whig tendencies, according to Thackery—"

Mr. Thackery and Miss Clavering? Jack could not see the two together. Mr. Thackery lacked the openness and finer feelings Miss Clavering appeared to possess, despite her somewhat meddlesome nature. Jack had difficulty imagining her settling for less than someone as open as she herself was. Then again, what woman did not come to London with the intention of elevating her status through marriage? She could not be any different.

The second thought came crowding in on the first. *Whig tendencies?* Jack had thought she sympathized with the Tories. His mind was reeling. How had he arrived at that conclusion? Oh, yes! When he'd announced he was a Whig, she had goaded him by saying she was sorry to hear it.

"—I am looking to introduce Mr. Thackery to a marital candidate with less strongly-held political notions. Since your sister possesses just such a docile nature, I thought perhaps she might be brought to make Mr. Thackery's acquaintance. Your sister is a most worthy young woman, and it would be my delight to align our households. But, as I said, marriage is a matter of political gain for me. And my heart is not so engaged that were Mr. Thackery to take an interest in Miss Blythefield, I would gladly step aside for the good of the party."

Mr. Merrick cleared his throat. "Knowing what I do of your family, I imagine I will be doing you a great service by marrying your sister off to someone so eligible, whether it be Mr. Thackery or myself."

Susan appeared to be taking leave of her friend, which was just as well, as she had let her ice melt considerably. Jack's gaze met Miss Clavering's across the room, and she held his for a brief moment before turning back to her brother. He would like to greet her but could not conjure up any excuse for doing so that would seem natural. Then he remembered what he'd just learned. Miss Clavering was more likely to appreciate a greeting from Mr. Thackery than from him, and he shouldn't waste his breath.

Mr. Merrick had no more to say, it appeared, but it had been more than enough. In one earful, Jack learned that Miss Clavering had a powerful suitor, and that the same Miss Clavering had been goading him when she professed to be a Tory. He'd also learned that his family's eccentricity was more widely known than he had realized and was generally considered an impediment to his sister being married. Jack set his spoon down, knowing he would not be able to swallow anything after that.

He glanced up to see Susan moving their way and leaned over to Mr. Merrick. "How do you know Miss Clavering won't accept Mr. Thackery's offer?"

"I don't." Mr. Merrick narrowed his eyes as if in irritation, then transformed his features into one of delight when he met Susan's gaze.

Jack followed Mr. Merrick's conversation with his sister for another five minutes without adding any of his own until Mr. Merrick took his leave. It was clear to Jack that the man's objective had been more to have words with him than with his sister. Mr. Merrick planned for a marriage based purely on what could advance his own gains, but he did not realize he would be hurting Jack's sister in the process. The fact that Jack was also planning a marriage in just such a logical way did not escape him, but he could not think that Miss Sommers possessed the same gentle, sensitive nature as Susan.

"What's wrong, Jack? You appear entirely glum, but is it not wonderful that Mr. Merrick should have chanced to be here at the same time as us?"

"Indeed." Jack looked at the puddles of ices in their bowls. "Shall we go?"

After Jack had paid, they turned to leave, and he darted one last glance at Miss Clavering. She was not looking his way, but Sir Lucius caught his eye and waved him over. Jack swallowed down a sudden lump of nerves. As he approached the table, Miss Clavering looked up and smiled.

Sir Lucius stood and shook his hand. "I merely wished to introduce you to my wife, Lady Clavering, and my son." He smiled fondly at the baby who lay in his mother's arms, watching her every movement. Lady Clavering dipped her head in greeting, her expression warm.

"How do you do, my lady?" Jack bowed and turned his attention to Miss Clavering. When she lifted her face to his, his heart began beating in his ears. His body was betraying him, and it annoyed him. He bowed again. "Miss Clavering."

"How do you do, Mr. Blythefield?"

Miss Clavering's eyes shone, and the corners of her lips curled as though something secretly amused her. Jack wanted to sit next to her until she confessed what it was. He shook away the distracting thought and remembered that her interests likely lay elsewhere.

"I also wished to find out when your committee will meet next to discuss the plans to repeal." Sir Lucius glanced at his wife, then back at Jack. "I still have no interest in politics, but on this particular issue, I might be able to lend my counsel based on my own experience. This is a worthy cause."

"That would be excellent. We have not set the date, but if you have a card, I will send word around, letting you know the particulars." Jack glanced at Miss Clavering. "After all, we Whigs must support one another."

Miss Clavering bit her lip and looked away, but not before he caught the look of guilty amusement on her face. Her playfulness stirred something in him—he did not have enough of that in his life—but he remembered what Mr. Merrick said and could not see why she would turn down the eligible Mr. Thackery for him.

Steel your heart, he admonished himself. He had no time to waste pursuing a woman whose interests lay elsewhere—a woman he did not desire anyway!

CHAPTER NINE

*L*ate afternoon, Philippa returned to the Holbecks' from her outing with Lucius and Selena, which consisted of a ride in Hyde Park after their stop at Gunter's. It had been a stroke of luck to meet Susan there, who did not often have the opportunity to go out, and Philippa had been surprised to learn that it was her brother who'd escorted her. Nothing in what Susan had shared about Mr. Blythefield had led Philippa to believe he had time or inclination to take his sister anywhere. In fact, she had the impression that Susan led a very lonely life, which was one of the reasons Philippa held her in affection. Her own life was not much different.

Mr. Blythefield had scarcely looked at Philippa after that first glance in the tea shop, and she wondered whether it was studied avoidance rather than disinterest. Mr. Merrick was at their table, and the two men were taken up in conversation. She could not imagine what topic it was they had found so interesting, but she made sure to keep Susan with her as long as she possibly could so Mr. Merrick had less time to work his charm. She was beginning to despair of—and for—Matthew Evans.

She opened the door to the drawing room to find her brother sitting on a chair, one leg crossed over the other. He looked up at her and waved, and a rush of affection came over her. "George! At last you are here. What has taken you so long to get to London?"

"Why should I hasten to London? What have I to do here?" He ran his hand through tousled curls and sent her a lopsided grin. "Well, I suppose I should attend the speeches at Parliament, as it appears that is to be my brilliant future."

"You don't sound half-pleased," she said. "Don't you like the idea of making a difference in the world? If I were a man, I would be sure to get involved in politics. And no one would better me in a debate."

George laughed. "To be sure. I certainly would not attempt to take you on as an opponent. And, well, yes, I suppose to some degree the debates can be interesting, especially when someone clever speaks—short, to the point, and droll. But when you get one of those fellows full of hot air, it is beyond what anyone can bear."

Philippa came and sat next to him. "Where is Mr. Evans?"

"Evans?" George's brows snapped together. "Why are you interested in him? I hope you're not contemplating …"

"George, don't be ridiculous. Mr. Evans is like a brother to me, just as much as you are." Philippa bit her lip as she studied him. "It is only that I know of something, but I cannot say what. He left me with a particular charge, you see—"

When she saw that George was about to protest, she added, "No, do not worry. It is nothing you could not like. But I believe I shouldn't gab it about—even to you."

"As if you could resist." George pierced her with a hard look. "My friend communicating with my sister and swearing her to secrecy? No, I don't like it."

"You must trust me, for it is absolutely innocent, I assure you. And it has nothing to do with me." Philippa laid her hand on his arm and gave it a gentle shake. "Now where is he, and when is he to arrive in London? He's already missed the first month. Just *tell* me and put aside any ideas you might be entertaining of a secret courtship."

George was not one to be overly suspicious, and he relented. "Very well. I do trust Evans. And you're not one of those chits with more hair than wit, so I suppose you won't go and do something addle-brained." George frowned and pulled out his snuff box. "Come to think of it, Evans did ask me to write to you to tell you of his plans. He said you would want to know."

"Which of course you did not do," exclaimed his sister. "Yes, do tell me. I have been waiting this age for his news, for I am trying to bring about a … a project on his behalf."

George examined her, then snapped his snuffbox shut. "This is about a lady, isn't it?"

Philippa closed her lips and shook her head. "What did Matthew wish for you to tell me?"

"Oh, so now it is Matthew? You are sure this *lady* is not you?" George leaned back and stretched his legs out, crossing his Hessians on the rug.

"Go on—tell me," Philippa urged, half-exasperated.

"*Matthew* wished for me to tell you that he regretted not being able to come to London earlier. As a matter of fact, he was concerned for his father's health. The old man went into a deep decline and was quite ill, and the local sawbones told Evans to prepare for the worst."

Philippa put her hand over her lips, for she knew Matthew was attached to his family, and most particularly to his father.

"However, the old man has rallied. He is much stronger than many gave him credit for. Evans comes from good stock. So he'll be in the Cotswolds for a few more days, and then he will make his way to London"—George shot Philippa a look—"for whatever nefarious purpose you have in mind. Philippa, you know you are entirely too busy on other people's behalf. Perhaps you should think about your own future."

"My own?" An irrational surge of anger toward her brother rose up in her. "Would you have me married to Mr. Thackery?"

"On no account." George stood and wandered across the room, placing his back to the fire. "I should rather hope Maria is not urging you to *that* alliance. If I know Lucius, he would have something to say about it. I know I would."

"I am very glad to hear it," Philippa said. "How I could have used his support last year—or yours. Lucius was busy with his new bride and not in London at all. *You*, however, had no such excuse. You were in London the entire Season, and still, I am not sure I saw you above five times."

She paused for breath and pressed her lips together as if to repress her ire. "Maria exerted her influence in the most heavy-handed way, as you can imagine, but it was Charles who was the worst. He all but threatened me—of course he had no power to actually carry it out, and he knew it—to make a match of it with Mr. Thackery." She sent George a wry look. "They are in perfect agreement on political matters."

George narrowed his eyes. "What a gapeseed Holbeck is. I should never have allowed it. I know Thackery—not well, mind you—but he would never do for you. He is much too likely to order you about and would expect you to have no opinion on any matter. Anyone who has spent five minutes with you knows such a thing is impossible."

"How wonderful to be understood." Philippa said dryly. She remained silent for a moment, then turned her gaze to her brother. "But you do not send me word, George—not that I expect my older brother to keep me apprised of his doings. How can you say you will not allow it when you are not here to take up my cause? Even this Season you've left me here for weeks now without telling me when you were planning to arrive. What kept you so long?"

George shifted his gaze to the window. "Lucius gave up his hunting box for me to entertain some friends, and that is precisely what I did."

"But I saw Duckworth, Amos, and Whitmore here. Who were you with?"

"Nothing that needs concern a little sister," he answered repressively.

Philippa chuckled. "You were indulging in all manners of jollification. Well, I am glad you are here now." She raised her hand dramatically to her brow. "So you may support me in my time of trial."

"Maria coming down hard on you, is she?" George asked with sympathy. "I will come here more often than last Season. To own the truth, my conscience did begin to trouble me at the thought of leaving you alone with Maria so often, but I thought you likely could handle her. You always do. This time, I'll make sure Thackery doesn't haunt your doorstep."

Philippa smiled up at him. "I must say, I never thought to see the day."

George returned to the chair and sat, taking a pinch of snuff from the box he had been holding. "By the bye, you will never guess who I ran into when I was at Lucius's."

Philippa peered at him from the corner of her eye. "Let me guess. The amiable Lord and Lady Harrowden."

"The very ones." George laughed. "If appearances did not deceive, they were in the midst of a row when I chanced upon them. I do not believe their wedded bliss lasted very long after their hasty marriage."

"How could it when their marriage began with deception and a flight to the border? I have no sympathy for them. They were both awful to Selena, and I am glad Lucius rescued her out of that situation. Did you see the Widow Harrowden?"

"Yes, Old Lady Harrowden has put up at the dower house. She seems to have found a pleasant companion. A Mrs. ... oh, I don't remember her name. When I stopped in to see her—"

"Your spree cannot have been so very wild if you had time to visit old ladies," Philippa teased.

George brushed the snuff that had fallen on his pantaloons, hiding a smile in the process. "No, not so wild as that. We played games of chance and went hunting—had a few parties, but you need not know more about that. I did indeed have time for at least one visit to Lady Harrowden. She was kind to us when we were little, and she's not likely to get any affection at all from her nephew and his wife in her old age. In any event, I believe she's happier than she has been, now that she found company to keep her occupied."

Philippa stood and went to the door, saying, "Well, I cannot tell you how good it is to have you in town. Life has been rather glum. I had best go up and change for dinner, and so should you. Charles does not like to have his dinner kept waiting."

George stood and trailed her to the door. "As I find myself of the same mind, for once, I will not complain."

***

Several nights later, they were scheduled to attend the opera, which promised to be more amusing now that George would be joining them. He seemed to be making good on his promise to come around more and had twice stopped by the Holbecks since his arrival. As they piled out of the carriage, Philippa whispered a warning for him to come and save her should Mr. Thackery make an appearance.

The opera opened with a comedy, and from the Holbecks' box seat, Philippa pulled out her lorgnette and examined the theatre. The chandeliers were burning brightly, and more people in the crowd were staring at the other theatre-goers than the performance, just as she was. She could not find Susan or anyone else of interest, but Mr. Lloyd had his quizzing glass pointed in her direction. *How fortunate*. It looked as though she had more than one gentleman to hide from at intermission.

When the curtain came down on the first act, Philippa stood. "I am in need of refreshment."

George leapt to his feet. "I will come with you."

"I might wish for some champagne," Maria began when—to Philippa's relief—a friend of her sister's entered the box "for a comfortable coze," as she put it, and Maria put all thoughts of leaving aside.

"Timely escape," Philippa murmured to George, as they left the box.

"As long as Holbeck doesn't decide to join us," George replied.

The corridor was thronged with people, and they wove their way through the crowd. At one of the refreshment tables, Philippa saw the back of Susan's head and wished to go to her but was prevented by the number of people blocking the space between the tables.

"I'll be just a minute," George said. Before Philippa could protest, he called out to a friend and crossed the corridor to see him—with much more ease than Philippa was able to do. She turned to find that Mr. Merrick had made his way to Susan's side. Not even her affection for her friend was enough to compel Philippa to join a group that included Mr. Merrick. She did not know why, but she couldn't like him.

The crowds pressed upon her, and Philippa turned to look for George—who had disappeared from view—and instead ran flush up against Mr. Blythefield.

"Miss Clavering." The din of the crowd seemed to grow muted as Philippa stood in front of him, her eyes at the level of his chin. At least the crowds had stepped back, giving Mr. Blythefield room—and her with it. He glanced above her head, hesitated, then simply bowed without saying anything else. His expression was closed.

Philippa squeezed the lorgnette case through the fabric of her reticule, waiting for the easier conversation they had shared at the Munster's party, and wondered what had made it disappear. *Not that they had ever been the best of friends.* Civility forced her to speak.

"How often we seem to meet of late. Did you enjoy your ice at Gunter's?"

Mr. Blythefield lifted one dark eyebrow, and his gaze focused on Philippa. "Immensely. Thank you." *What has come over him? He has never been this unfriendly before.*

Philippa found it difficult to breathe, as much from the oppressive mood under which he seemed to suffer as from the press of people. She darted a glance in the milling crowd but recognized no one nearby. "You were sitting with Mr. Merrick, I believe. Have you approved his suit for your sister?" She hoped he had not wavered in his disapproval.

Mr. Blythefield shifted on his feet and looked at her questioningly. "I thought you were not in favor of Mr. Merrick. Why do you ask if I now approve?"

"Only idle conversation." Philippa pursed her lips and broke the stare that was becoming too searching for her comfort. Cheeks hot, she pulled her ivory-stick fan out of her reticule and began to stir the air.

"Perhaps you are merely trying to distract yourself." Mr. Blythefield gave Philippa a measured glance that held her captive. "Where is your court of admirers who always seem to flock to your side? Has one of them caught your interest?"

Philippa dropped her fan to her side with a huff of annoyance. "You need not try to stare me out of countenance. I assure you I have not met with any particular interest—at least none I welcomed." She hesitated, then shifted tactics. "The truth is, I hope you have not approved Mr. Merrick's suit, for I have received news of Mr. Evans. He had been detained at home because of his father's health, but his father is now on the mend. I expect him in London any day now."

A modish woman whose dress labeled her a courtesan rather than a lady strolled toward them, escorted by a young gentleman who glowered at any man who looked her way. The woman's gems gleamed in the light of candles, as did the diamond pin in the man's cravat. Mr. Blythefield stepped aside to let them pass, moving closer to Philippa. "It appears the opera will start again soon. May I escort you to your box?"

Philippa was irritated with his behavior tonight. He seemed bent on setting up her bristles. She tried to think of an excuse, parted her lips to say something, but found herself trapped by his unwavering gaze and relented. She laid her hand in his arm. As Mr. Blythefield accompanied her toward their box seat, he leaned in and pitched his voice low so only she would hear. "As much as you try to champion your friend's cause, Mr. Evans does not hold the sway and power of a man such as Mr. Merrick— or someone like Mr. Thackery—who will elevate to the highest social circles the lady he chooses for a wife. Is that not a strong consideration for a woman such as yourself?"

Philippa darted him a glance of surprise and felt her cheeks grow warm. *Why had he mentioned Mr. Thackery?* "If I may speak frankly, I doubt your sister would be happy in such exalted circles. She has a gentle nature and can be easily persuaded—and easily crushed. She would be a lamb among wolves."

"And what of you? I cannot see you as a lamb. Do you aspire to such circles as those which Mr. Thackery inhabits?"

Philippa gave a sharp laugh and stopped, releasing Mr. Blythefield's arm. "Mr. Thackery's circles do not interest me. I do not think of him at all."

Mr. Blythefield's jaw hardened, and he fixed his stare on her. His eyes seemed to search her face for something, but she had no idea what. He gave a brief nod. "I must not detain you. I believe the next act is about to start."

CHAPTER TEN

*J*ack received an invitation to the Sommerses' next dinner party, and this time he was determined not to miss out. There was no time like the present to begin spending time with Miss Sommers if he was to fix his interests with her—and that was what he would do. Miss Sommers had everything he needed. She was a handsome woman who knew the art of conversation. Her family was esteemed in London, and in the political circles in particular. And she never put herself forward in a disagreeable way by attempting to tell him what to do.

When Jack arrived, the drawing room was full. Mrs. Sommers was deep in conversation with one of the MP's wives, but Miss Sommers moved toward him immediately, her hands extended to greet him. Jack was struck anew by her grace and elegance. *I believe she is the right choice.*

"Mr. Blythefield, our party is now complete with you here." Miss Sommers indicated for the footman to take his coat. "I think you will find many interesting people to talk to tonight."

Jack bowed over her hand. "Wherever you are, Miss Sommers, there is sure to be entertaining conversation."

"I did not take you for a flirt," she said with a laugh, linking her arm through his. He could tell she was pleased. "I believe you know Mr. Merrick already? He has been asking about you."

Jack wondered what Mr. Merrick wanted that they hadn't already discussed. He was no further along in deeming Mr. Merrick an acceptable suitor for his sister. The evening suddenly seemed less palatable with him here. "Why, yes. Mr. Merrick, how do you do?"

Miss Sommers gave them both a shallow curtsy before turning to go. "I will leave you gentlemen to discuss politics. After all, that is why you are here."

Mr. Merrick signaled for a servant to bring a glass for Jack. "I came during calling hours to visit your sister last week, but I was turned away. I hope I have not fallen out of grace."

Jack took a sip of the wine he had been given. The Sommerses did not skimp on the quality of their refreshments. "Not at all. It is only that my sister was still refurbishing the drawing room." He could not help but grimace as he added, "With the help of Miss Clavering."

"Indeed." Mr. Merrick's eyes widened. "Then Miss Clavering is a great favorite at your house."

"Not with me." Jack was still out of kilter after having met her at the opera, and that irritated him. He did not appreciate how troubled he felt in her presence, especially knowing she was likely to form an alliance with Mr. Thackery, whom he could only look at as a political opponent. Despite Miss Clavering's assurances to the contrary, Jack did not believe her. Women never revealed their matrimonial targets, and she would not turn down such a good catch as Thackery. Mr. Merrick had presented it as an almost sure thing. "I find her much too meddling for her own good."

"From the little I know of Miss Clavering, that is an accurate assessment." Mr. Merrick laughed. "I should hope for Thackery's sake that his suit does not prosper. A wife like that will cut up his peace and distract him from his political endeavors."

"But if you consider him in danger," Jack said, "you are ready to sacrifice your hopes for an alliance with my sister."

Mr. Merrick paused, his hand lifted midair to bring his drink to his mouth. "Have you been having second thoughts about my intentions? Perhaps I brought up the matter prematurely."

"A crowded table at Gunter's is perhaps not the most ideal location to discuss such personal matters," Jack affirmed.

Mr. Merrick drank and kept his gaze fixed steadily on Jack's. "I am a man who prefers to put all his cards on the table. Giving the appearance of seeking a love match when I know my motivations are more practical-minded is abhorrent to me. I do not like to make false promises. You cannot fault me for that."

Jack shook his head and glanced across the room, where he saw Lord Palmer. That was someone he'd hoped to speak with. He turned back to Merrick. "I cannot fault you for such a thing. But I am not sure your intentions toward my sister are as clear to *her* as they are to you. I can still wish for a better situation for Susan than that of a pawn."

"Fair enough. Then let us agree to this," Mr. Merrick said. "Give me leave to pursue your sister without any promises on my side or yours. I give my word that I will not trifle with her, and if we find we do not suit, we shall part amicably."

The likelihood of his tenderhearted sister being capable of declaring they did not suit was slim. However, Miss Clavering's words came back to him. If he forbade the match outright, it might drive Susan to do something drastic. Better he let his sister see for herself that Mr. Merrick's intentions were not serious. Still, he doubted what was the best course. How much easier were politics than matrimony.

"Do not raise any false hopes in my sister, and I shall be satisfied."

Mr. Merrick nodded. "You have my word."

There was a silence, and Jack glanced around the room. "Mr. Thackery is not here."

"No, he went to the country for the weekend on some personal business." Mr. Merrick set his empty glass on the tray of a passing servant.

Jack wondered how much he was in Thackery's confidence. "You said you thought Mr. Thackery had some chance of his suit prospering. Is he still pursuing Miss Clavering?"

Mr. Merrick's eyebrows shot up. "Do I sense a rivalry? Have you some interest there, too, Mr. Blythefield?"

Jack was irritated with himself for being so transparent. "It is only that she is my sister's friend. Forget I said anything. In any case, it is none of my affair."

"Nor should it be mine, though I've made it so," Mr. Merrick said. "Let us turn our attention to our common affair. I saw you speaking to Lord Sherwood after Wednesday's debates. How many sure votes do you have for repealing the Corn Laws?"

Jack was not about to give away any of the voting preferences he had so assiduously gathered. "I think the vote is too close to call—there are too many still undecided. Miss Sommers orchestrated this dinner party well. She has invited some of the more liberal Tories, so perhaps I will discover more in favor."

"No doubt. I am never disappointed when Miss Sommers puts together an evening's entertainment. I wonder that she is unmarried." Mr. Merrick gestured near the fireplace. "Look—Mr. Matheson is free. Let us go and talk to him, for he is one of the more uncertain votes."

Jack could think of better uses of his time than accompanying Mr. Merrick around the room as though he were the man's subordinate. "Ah. Not quite free. He's talking to Mr. Balding, and I must say, I am surprised Mr. Balding is here. I had thought him entirely too entrenched in Tory ideals to be budged on anything."

"Nobody is a lost cause, if you ask me. Balding is looking for alliances more than he's looking to uphold certain ideals. He also has an eligible daughter, if you should be interested." He glanced over at Miss Sommers. "Unless you have someone else in mind."

Jack's desire to move on to different company was growing by the minute. "Let us just say that right now my interests are focused solely on politics and not on home life."

"Are the two not intrinsically tied? I had thought them to be. At least, in my case they are." Mr. Merrick's smile did not reach his eyes.

Jack had begun to move forward, aiming to join another discussion and lose his current partner, but at this he paused. "Then I must say, I am surprised at your showing any interest in my sister. She is not likely to advance your political cause in any way."

"Except for being the sister of a political figure I admire." Mr. Merrick stepped forward, and Jack walked beside him. "Kingdoms are united through marriage. Why should not political agreements be conducted the same way?"

A dry laugh escaped Jack. "Me—change policy based on sentiment? You must not think that I am so easily persuaded."

"Not on matters of deep conviction, of course," Mr. Merrick hastened to reassure him before they joined Mr. Balding and Mr. Matheson.

Jack did not find Mr. Balding so malleable as Mr. Merrick had seemed to think, but he was able to gracefully exit that conversation and join ones that were much more fruitful. He spent such a pleasant evening, and it was only at the end of it that he realized he hadn't once spoken to Miss Sommers, although some of his discussions had included some of the women present. Shouldn't he have been drawn to her as one with whom he was thinking of building a life?

It was with a look of chagrin that he sought her out at the close of the evening. "I bid you good night, Miss Sommers, and ask you to excuse me for not having spent more time talking to you."

"You are forgiven, Mr. Blythefield." Miss Sommers gave him an enigmatic smile.

"Well, I do thank you for the evening, which has been most entertaining, just as you promised."

She inclined her head. "We shall hope to see you here again soon. Don't neglect your social calls amidst your political ones." She arched a brow. "Of course, when the two can be combined, there is nothing better."

"I highly agree," Jack said, thinking that she sounded like Mr. Merrick. He hesitated, then finally bowed and took his leave.

***

The next day, Jack walked by the drawing room and heard nothing but silence. He had looked in the previous day and saw that the servants were in the process of replacing the vases, statues, and bibelots on the gleaming furniture and hanging the artwork on freshly painted walls. The absence of sound today told him the room was finished.

Jack turned the handle to the drawing room and stepped in. At once, his eyes were drawn upward to where the cheerful yellow walls met the white molding on the tall ceiling. The pale curtains allowed light to flood the room, and the white and gold silk threads on the new rug gleamed in the sunlight. The beige-cushioned chair near the writing table made him long to sit and draft all his correspondence here rather than at the dark tables of his club. He could breathe in this room, and he wondered whether any of the changes were his sister's or whether they all belonged to Miss Clavering.

He stepped fully into the room and looked at the new sofa on the right, which had been hidden by the door. There Miss Clavering sat, drinking tea alone.

"Miss Clavering!" Jack hesitated, then advanced to greet her, annoyed that his heart sped up. *Her heart is likely engaged*, he scolded himself once again. But this involuntary reaction seemed to happen whenever he ran into her unexpectedly as of late. He thought back to the Munster party, and his heartbeat was steady enough there when he saw her. Although, when Jack thought about it, his stomach *had* done a small flip when she looked up at him across the table. Very irksome, since he had no intention of pursuing the woman.

Miss Clavering stood, and if her heightened color could be believed, she was also experiencing a touch of embarrassment at meeting him unexpectedly. "Mr. Blythefield, I do not live at your house, though you must sometimes think it. Susan has only gone upstairs to change because she believes Mr. Merrick will call today."

Jack bowed, willing his nerves to be steady. *Just pretend you are about to address the Commons.* "Do you believe Mr. Merrick will call today? You cannot wish it—you're not one of his devotees."

Miss Clavering had removed her gloves, and she ran a slender hand over her muslin sleeve. "To own the truth, I do not care whether Mr. Merrick comes or not. I am of the mind that Mr. Evans will be here today, for he paid my brother a visit yesterday and declared his intention of doing so. I wished to lend my support and also to see him, since I was out when he called."

Jack looked at her with amusement and was relieved that his equilibrium seemed to be returning after the initial jolt. Perhaps his common sense would return with it. "You really are bent on this scheme of yours to fix my sister with your friend. I own to some curiosity to meet the man myself."

"Then, by all means—stay." Miss Clavering sent him an impish smile. "And have a seat."

Jack had to laugh at being offered a seat in his own house. The woman had no shame. If nothing else, she was amusing.

He sat, and Miss Clavering poured him a cup of tea as if it were the most natural thing in the world that she should play hostess in his drawing room. His heart rate threatened to speed up again, but he tried to focus his attention elsewhere. Miss Clavering leaned forward to lift the cup, then paused. "I should have asked if you take milk."

"I do," he said in a mock-stern voice. "And now you've ruined a perfectly good cup of tea."

"No. I shall merely add a cloud of milk into tea that has"—she gasped—"*already been poured into the cup* and shock the entire English world. Do you take sugar as well?"

"Three spoons," he said.

"So many?" She handed him his tea. "Is it in hopes of balancing out your bitter nature?"

Jack's lips twitched, although he tried valiantly not to smile. From the corridor, he heard a rap on the front door and set his cup down on the table next to him before getting to his feet. Miss Clavering gave him a questioning look, and Jack realized how odd it must appear to her. If only she knew how slowly Shanks moved.

Fortunately, Jack heard the shuffled feet of their butler going to open the door, and he resumed his seat. Miss Clavering held his gaze, and although her look was one of perfect innocence, her eyes danced at the sound of the butler inching his way across the hallway to the drawing room. At last the door creaked open and Shanks announced, "A Mr. Matthew Evans, sir."

Miss Clavering smiled with satisfaction as Jack said, "Send him in."

Mr. Evans entered the room, and Jack was unimpressed. He couldn't imagine that his sister would feel differently. Evans was of no very great stature, had a head of thin hair that threatened to part ways with him before he reached the age of forty, and returned Jack's gaze with large, pale eyes set under blond eyebrows. Despite his insipid appearance, however, he showed no hesitation in his manner.

"Good afternoon," he said with a bow. "I am Matthew Evans. Thank you for receiving me."

Jack stood as well. "I am Jack Blythefield. Please allow me to welcome you to my father's house. If Miss Clavering is to be believed, you are here because you have some interest in my sister, Susan."

If Jack had hoped to disconcert the man by calling out his intentions, he was to be disappointed. Mr. Evans merely smiled at Miss Clavering. "How are you, Philippa?"

They were on such intimate terms as to use each other's Christian names?

Miss Clavering returned the smile and lifted her hand for Mr. Evans to bow over it. "I am very well. You have come at last."

Mr. Evans nodded, then returned his attention to Jack. "Yes. And to tell the truth, I am glad for an opportunity to speak with you while Miss Blythefield is not here. I have not had time to press my suit, for it came rather late in the Season last year, and we were not on such terms that I could write to her over the summer. I cannot speak for her interest in me, but I assume she has very little at present—if she remembers my existence at all. However, I have sustained what can only be described as a violent love from the very first time I set my eyes on her."

Jack was astonished that 'violent love' could in any way be attributed to such an unprepossessing man, and he attempted to assess how to answer. "Please sit."

Miss Clavering began to prepare another cup of tea, and he could only assume it was exactly in the way Mr. Evans preferred it. "If I may speak bluntly, so that we do not waste one another's time, are you in possession of a fortune that could support my sister?"

"I am." Mr. Evans took the cup from Miss Clavering's hand and nodded his thanks. With the room redone in a new style, Jack was beginning to feel as though he were a guest in someone else's house.

"I am to inherit a substantial amount of land," Mr. Evans said, "although I am not in any hurry to receive it, for that would mean losing my father. If I may be permitted to boast of my own abilities, I am skilled at investments, and I have increased my father's fortune in the years since he put me in charge of it. I am in possession of fifteen thousand a year. I can assure you, your sister would be well taken care of."

Fifteen thousand. So much. She would be one less family member to worry about, and the thought was tempting. But Jack could not sell his sister off simply for a comfortable fortune where her heart was not engaged. *And that is exactly what you are contemplating with Mr. Merrick,* he accused himself.

"I thank you for your honesty, but I must leave it up to my sister to see whether she might be persuaded." As soon as Jack had spoken, Susan entered the room.

CHAPTER ELEVEN

When Susan walked in, Philippa turned her gaze to Matthew and was witness to the sudden tremor of his hands as he shot to his feet.

"Miss Blythefield."

Susan stopped short at his greeting, and her mouth dropped in surprise. "Mr. Evans, I did not expect to find you here."

Matthew glanced quickly at Philippa before turning back to Susan, and she could not help but feel sorry for him. All the ease and assurance in his possession disappeared at the sight of the woman he loved. His face grew red as he stammered out, "I … I hope it is not a disappointment."

Susan had a tender heart, and the proof of it was in her reaction to his obvious nervousness. She moved forward quickly, as though anxious to reassure him. "Oh, no. I hope I could not make you think such a thing. Your visit is always a pleasure. Please, won't you sit?"

Matthew resumed his seat, and Susan sat in one of the newly-purchased chairs to form a cozy circle of four. Philippa wondered what Mr. Blythefield thought of the prétendant for Susan's hand, but the man's expression was impossible to read. Matthew had been at ease before Susan came in, and Mr. Blythefield seemed impressed when he'd spoken of his fortune. However, Mr. Blythefield had stated that he was in no way ready to give his sister away where her heart was not touched, and Philippa could only respect him for it. What a rare thing.

Matthew fell silent. Philippa tried to catch his eye to urge him toward that animated conversation she knew him capable of, but his gaze was glued to his hands. She could not fathom why he could not seem to string two words together when he was around Susan, who was such a gentle creature. What had he to fear?

Susan took a deep breath and smiled. "You were not here at the start of the season, I believe. Were you visiting family?"

Matthew sat upright, and if his nod was a tad eager, her question had at least loosened his lips. "I did wish to visit you sooner, but I was detained. My father was in poor health—"

"Oh!" Susan's mouth puckered in her concern. "I hope to hear that he has made a swift recovery."

"Swift—no." Matthew sat back again and relaxed the grip of his hands as if forcing himself to be more natural. "But he is recovering, and that brings me a great deal of relief."

Susan poured herself a cup of tea and set it on the table at her side, then directed her attention back to Matthew. "I am so very glad to hear it. Where is your father's property?"

"It is in the Cotswolds. Near Chedworth."

Philippa was enjoying their exchange too much to contribute anything. Matthew was doing a fine job now that Susan had put him at ease.

Susan lifted the cup to her lips, and some of the tea that had spilled on to the saucer now dripped on her white dress. "Oh dear, I..."

Susan brushed at her dress as both her brother and Matthew reached for a napkin at once. Matthew was first, and he handed it to her. She smiled in thanks and, as she wiped her dress, said, "I do not know that area, but I hear it is quite beautiful."

"It is, indeed. I hope that you might be persuaded to visit it one day."

Another knock on the front door was heard in the drawing room, and Susan's expression brightened in anticipation, but she was too kind to waver in her attention to Matthew. "I hope so. There are many places in England that I would like to visit."

The butler appeared to have remained stationed in the corridor, for it was not long before he ushered in Mr. Merrick and Mr. Thackery. Philippa groaned internally at the sight of the latter gentleman. Susan's house had been a place of refuge, and now that man was invading it.

Mr. Thackery raised an eyebrow when he saw Philippa, and his lips jerked upward in a self-satisfied grin. *He needn't be so surprised to find me here*, she thought with irritation. Had he done any investigating in the matter, he would've discovered that she was frequently at Susan's house.

Mr. Merrick strode directly across the room and shook Jack's hand, then bowed before Philippa and Susan. There was a seat between Matthew and Susan, and Mr. Merrick took it, turning his back on Matthew and claiming Susan's attention. Her pleasure at seeing him was only too obvious, and Philippa glanced at Matthew to see how he took it. If his clenched jaw was any signal, he knew precisely who his competition was.

Mr. Thackery also greeted Mr. Blythefield, then came and bowed before Philippa. She offered up thanks that the only remaining seat for Mr. Thackery was on the other side of Mr. Blythefield, so she was not obliged to sit next to him and listen to any quiet innuendos he might wish to send her way. She would not put it past him, but Mr. Blythefield was too effective a barrier for that.

"I'm surprised to see you at home, Blythefield." Thackery leaned back in his chair, and Susan realized her duties as a hostess. She leapt up and asked the two gentlemen how they took their tea, which she prepared for them, then rang for more hot water.

"I do occasionally spend my afternoons here." Mr. Blythefield frowned when he at last answered Mr. Thackery, and the cold reserve he'd used with Philippa at the opera returned in full force. Did he not like Mr. Thackery, either? "I'm not always desirous of going to the club before I attend Parliament."

Mr. Merrick's gaze had followed Susan as she moved over to the cabinet to fetch more tea leaves, but at this he turned and addressed Mr. Blythefield. "That is not what I would have wagered. I see you more often at the club than I do anyone else, and it's always in some political discussion. A man cannot be about politics all day long, though it seems it's all you have a mind for." He grinned broadly. "In fact, I suspect you pepper all your social discourse with political matters."

Mr. Blythefield's lip lifted slightly. "If you'll notice, I was not the one who brought up Parliament today."

Philippa looked down to hide a smile. If Mr. Blythefield did not annoy her so much, she would actually like the man. He always seemed to have an answer for everything.

Mr. Merrick's jovial expression fell slightly. "Very true."

Mr. Thackery called to Philippa from across Mr. Blythefield. "Miss Clavering, what Society event is likely to be graced with your presence next? Perhaps our paths will cross."

Philippa was not to be pigeonholed that way. "I am not quite sure," she replied. "There are so many interesting engagements to choose from, and I can never say in advance where my fancy will take me."

Mr. Thackery would not be put off. "Except, if I am not mistaken, you don't have much of a voice in deciding where you go." Mr. Blythefield had leaned forward slightly, and Mr. Thackery was forced to lean as well so he could finish his statement to Philippa. "Holbeck tells me that you go wherever he decides, since you are staying with him and your sister for the Season."

Philippa glanced at Mr. Blythefield, but his gaze was fixed on some spot across the room as if he was not at all following the conversation. She wondered if he had cut off Mr. Thackery's line of sight on purpose. She did not appreciate Mr. Thackery presenting her situation in such bleak terms, especially in front of Mr. Blythefield—although why she should care at all what Mr. Blythefield thought of her situation, she could not answer. A long pause fell before Philippa answered.

"As I'm staying at my sister's house, it is only natural that I should accompany Maria and Charles to various events. But as you see, I do sometimes manage, with their blessing, to attend morning calls on my own. I am here without my sister, after all."

Mr. Merrick drew his brows together and glanced around the room as if noticing the absence of chaperonage for the first time. He turned to Susan. "Does your mother not sit with you during calling hours?"

He had asked a delicate question. One of the reasons Philippa appreciated going to Susan's house was because chaperonage there was light—or nonexistent. Philippa could not bear to be under anyone's thumb when that was all she faced at home. However, she had to own that in cases like this, where there were two unwelcome gentlemen, a chaperone would serve to keep off unwanted advances.

"I am here in the guise of chaperone today," Mr. Blythefield said. "My mother was otherwise engaged."

Philippa darted her gaze to his in surprise. If she had not heard the words directly from his lips, she would never have believed he'd use the word "chaperone" in reference to himself.

"Mr. Blythefield has been most effective in his role," Philippa added with a grin. "He is protective of his sister." Their eyes met, and there was a moment of complicity between them.

Mr. Thackery narrowed his eyes. "But who is to chaperone *you*, Miss Clavering?"

"I am here with my maid. My sister allows me to visit Susan, who is a particular friend of mine, as long as my maid accompanies me."

"But your maid is not here in the room," Mr. Thackery insisted, "and you are with several gentlemen."

Philippa used the same overly polite tone when she replied. "But one of the gentlemen's sisters *is* in the room." She darted a glance at Matthew, not worried she would have to beg him to remain discreet, for she had clearly been alone with Mr. Blythefield in the room before Matthew stepped in. Philippa wondered vaguely if she possessed no maidenly sensibility. As a young unmarried woman, she should have been shocked at being alone with a man she was unrelated to. Nevertheless, she had not felt the need for protection until Mr. Thackery walked in the room.

Mr. Merrick folded his hands and at last brought his gaze to Matthew. "I see you have other visitors, Miss Blythefield."

Susan's hand flew to her mouth. "Forgive me for being remiss, Mr. Evans. I did not perform the introductions."

Mr. Blythefield held up his hand. "No, the apology falls to me. Mr. Evans. I'd like to introduce you to Mr. Merrick and Mr. Thackery. We know each other from Parliament. And Mr. Evans, I believe, is a particular friend of Miss Clavering."

Mr. Thackery directed his gaze to Philippa. "Indeed! How is it that you two are acquainted?"

Matthew answered, "Her brother, George, is one of my closest friends, and I have known Miss Clavering since she was a girl. We have a relationship akin to brother and sister." Philippa did not appreciate the reminder of her youth, but it could only help her cause and her reputation that Matthew presented himself in the guise of a protector.

Mr. Thackery appeared to accept this, and for an insane moment, Philippa almost wished Mr. Evans had lied and announced his intention to marry her, just so she could get rid of Mr. Thackery. She was hard put to contain the laugh that threatened to break out at the thought. Matthew could never play such a farce, and word of course would eventually get around that they were not to wed. Philippa did not know how she could rid herself of Mr. Thackery without an obvious sign that she was unavailable. He seemed impervious to barbs.

Their conversation touched on other polite subjects, and even though Matthew had surpassed the customary amount of time for his visit, he was clearly loath to leave the field to the two other gentlemen. Mr. Blythefield did not contribute much to the conversation at all, so the volley of uninteresting questions and responses went back and forth between Mr. Thackery, Philippa, Mr. Merrick, and Susan—with the occasional attempt at conversation from Matthew Evans.

Poor Matthew was easily outmaneuvered. A man not comfortable with words could not hope to shine in the art of conversation against a glib politician such as Mr. Merrick. When at last the guests decided to leave, with Matthew reluctantly taking his leave at the same time as the other two, Jack saw them out.

Philippa was not ready to leave until she had a better idea of Susan's frame of mind. Although she could not think much good was gained for Matthew's cause, she'd hoped that Mr. Merrick had not advanced much in his. "What are your thoughts about this morning?"

Susan smiled and lifted a dreamy gaze to the ceiling. "He did not comment on the drawing room, but I do think he noticed it. Did you not think Mr. Merrick the most handsome, attentive gentleman?"

Philippa's heart sank. She could see for herself that Matthew did not have much of a chance, but it still stung. Matthew would be the better man for Susan if only she could be made to see it.

"Mr. Merrick is most handsome and attentive, as you say." Philippa took Susan's hands in hers. "I only ask, as your friend, that you not give your heart to Mr. Merrick until you have given Mr. Evans a chance. I promise you, he is a most worthy gentleman, and he deserves at least that. Bounds of matrimony are broken only by death. If one should end up unhappy…"

Susan drew her brows together. "Mr. Evans is kind; I will give him that. And I did have more of a chance to see his good nature today than I have in the times we've danced. Then he seemed too nervous to say anything at all. However…" She bit her lip and raised her eyes to Philippa's. "I must confess that my heart is not engaged where Mr. Evans is concerned. He does not inspire me with love the way Mr. Merrick does. Besides, the thought of being bound in matrimony is a *pleasurable* thought to me. My dear friend, you take such a pessimistic view of marriage. I can only hope that you find the one man who inspires you to think differently."

Philippa hoped the same. Finding a husband was growing to be quite the complicated affair, especially when she desired something more than a mere position of wife.

The door opened, and Mr. Blythefield walked in, his expression brooding. Susan's earnest look was still fixed on Philippa's face, and he stopped short. "What are you talking about?"

"Nothing." Philippa sat back, releasing Susan's hands.

"Marriage," Susan countered. "And my ardent wish for Philippa to be brought to that happy state."

Mr. Blythefield's brooding turned into a positive scowl. "I should not wish to hinder the intimacy of your conversation. I shall take leave of you." He bowed. "Miss Clavering, I bid you good day."

He left abruptly, and Susan stood to collect the tea cups and place them on the tray. "I cannot think why Jack was so put out."

Philippa shrugged. Mr. Blythefield was a most unaccountable man. She would not have thought upon first meeting him that his moods could be so easily changeable. Then again, she could not say he'd left her with a particularly favorable impression at all.

CHAPTER TWELVE

*I*t was the warmest day of the season so far, and Jack was inspired to send a note around to Miss Sommers to see if she would like to accompany him for a ride in Hyde Park. He feared this was likely to set the gossips' tongues wagging, but he supposed he had to start somewhere with his suit if he was ever going to make her his wife.

Marriage as a whole was too tedious a topic to think about, despite his sister's and Miss Clavering's interest in the subject. Jack was in favor of a simple courtship, not a convoluted one. The dinner party Miss Sommers had hosted left a favorable impression on Jack's mind, as much for the meeting of notables in the political arena as for the way Miss Sommers disappeared into the background and let the men talk through their ideas. He could imagine many more evenings like it, especially if it meant influencing his opponents to see his point of view.

Jack was for reform, so in whatever way he could guide other men toward similar ideals, it would bring good to the country. And if his home life could be congruous to his mission, why then all the better. Miss Sommers was a woman of distinction, and she suited his ideas of a wife exactly.

If the thought that flitted across his mind next was of Miss Clavering's impish smile, it was quite against his will, and he quickly dismissed it. Mr. Merrick had hinted that she was already taken—or if not publicly engaged, then at least on her way to being so. When they had met during calling hours, she had not shown herself to be under Thackery's spell, but women were not known for being transparent about their feelings. Besides—what woman would turn down an offer from such a man as Mr. Thackery, who was rich, influential, and hailed on the Marriage Mart as a catch? No, it would be better that Jack avoided her completely. He didn't want to sit back and watch Miss Clavering succumb to Mr. Thackery's fawning and flattery.

He received Miss Sommers's positive reply and had his horses hitched to the phaeton. Despite his decision to completely avoid Miss Clavering, his thoughts turned back to her union with Mr. Thackery as he drove and her absence of showing any visible interest in the man. Perhaps Mr. Merrick had it all wrong. It could very well be the professed interest was only on Thackery's side. Still! Jack guided the horses to the end of the street, where he turned the corner neatly. That woman would make a terrible politician's wife. She was too forthright and did not measure—or mince—her words. She was much too young and was not likely to lend a distinguished air to any event. She would certainly not lend consequence to such a man as he.

Nevertheless, Jack had to own that there was something about her that was appealing. His heart responded to her; and if they were in the same room, he became aware of her position by the way his pulse sped up when he turned in that direction. *Very much against my will,* he protested to that traitorous organ. And because Jack was on his way to court another woman, he, firmly this time, put all thought of Miss Clavering out of his mind.

Jack left his footman standing with the horses while he knocked and was bid enter. Miss Sommers did not keep him waiting long and soon descended the staircase in a jonquil day dress and white pelisse.

"How do you do, Mr. Blythefield? I have only to put on my bonnet, and I am ready." She did so quickly and tugged on her gloves, and before Jack could feel any of the impatience his sister and mother inspired in him, they were in his phaeton on their way to Hyde Park.

The calm street she lived on soon gave way to a busy thoroughfare, and Jack fell quiet as he navigated the traffic coming in two directions, as well as the crowds, which threatened to shove the people hawking their wares into the path of his horses. An old woman pushing a cart with a kettle of what was likely hot salop steered it into the road, heedless of any danger. He breathed in sharply and tugged on the reins—strong enough to avert the danger, but with a light touch that would not spook his horses.

"You are a fine whip." Miss Sommers had stayed quiet while he drove, which he'd appreciated. But she chose to praise him now, just when he most felt the difficulty of London driving.

Jack risked a glance at her, then pulled his gaze back to the road. "I assure you, I am no candidate for the Four Horse Club. In fact, to be perfectly frank, this road is stretching my limits. I've not come this way at a time when there were so many people or such traffic."

Miss Sommers held on to the side of the phaeton as he was forced to swerve around a dog. "So you admit to weakness. How unlike a man of influence to do so. The prevailing idea among men, I've found, is that one must put on a show of strength if one wishes to move ahead in the world." She did not lose her perfectly modulated tone, and he wondered if truly nothing rattled her or if she was simply well bred.

Jack did not return an answer until he had safely navigated them past the crowded road and on to the broader lane that led to Hyde Park. There, he finally allowed his shoulders to relax as his horses now went unheeded at a light trot. "Do you think so? For myself, I find people are more willing to follow the lead of a man who can admit to his weaknesses."

"Oh, perhaps the common man might be so easily won over." Miss Sommers paused as if for reflection before adding, "But not other men of influence. Influential men need to see a leader's strengths before they are willing to follow him."

At last, Jack drove through the gates of Hyde Park, where his pace was brought to a more sedate walk with the number of carriages already driving on Rotten Row. They took their place in the progression.

"I must disagree with you, if I might do so without giving offense." Jack turned to Miss Sommers and smiled, hoping she would hear him out. He did not know her well enough to be sure. "I think leaders who hide their weaknesses tend to be mistrusted by peers and common man alike. Much better a man who will ask for help. In that way, he may learn from the wisdom of others and overcome his difficulty more quickly. Of course, we are no longer talking about carriage driving, but it's a fair recommendation for any number of challenges."

Miss Sommers clasped her hands loosely on her lap, and he heard a noncommittal noise from her closed lips.

He laughed. "You may as well give it up. It is clear you do not agree or share my view."

"It matters not what I think. But you have me puzzled, Mr. Blythefield. Until you admitted to having trouble on the road, I had not seen any weakness in you. Does that mean you have none, apart from driving?" Miss Sommers asked in a light tone. "If you believe in being honest about your shortcomings, surely your frailty or humanity would be readily expressed and visible to all."

"I do have weaknesses…" Jack drew his brows together, unable to finish.

His thoughts flew immediately to his family. They were his weakness. To have a mother who could not be trusted to behave with the decorum expected of an older, distinguished woman. Or a father who could not be trusted with the family inheritance—who was forever thinking himself up to snuff on matters of finance. An older brother who was a ne'er-do-well, who lived only to dress and strut—to see and to be seen and to throw his life away in the pursuit of pleasure. At least with his sister he found less to accuse her of. Indeed, he could scarcely fault her at all. For who could develop a genteel character without having witnessed it from her parents?

"You have fallen silent, sir," Miss Sommers said. "Are you reflecting which weakness to bring to light for public consumption?" She laughed, but he could feel the weight of her regard as she studied him.

When he brought his gaze to hers, he could not read her thoughts. It was as though this disaccord had dropped a veil between them, so they could not understand one another. He needed to bring the conversation back to something lighter.

"I suppose if I am forced to talk about my weaknesses, I would have to confess that I am not a man who excels at hosting parties." Jack shook his head tragically. "And that is a weakness indeed for a man of politics. However, such a thing can be remedied." He looked off at the line of trees on the other side of the path, knowing he was perhaps taking an irrevocable step. "Were I to take a wife who was skilled at such things, the weakness would quickly be vanquished."

Miss Sommers laughed again, a light, tinkling laugh as if the idea appealed to her. "Then you shall have to try your hand at hosting so this weakness can become a strength. I should like to assist you in the endeavor, if you should wish it. I do not propose to host at your side in an official capacity—merely that I lend my hand in making up for this deficit which you claim to have."

Jack pulled the phaeton to a halt as the people in the carriage in front of them stopped and called out to their acquaintances. He took the occasion to glance around the park, but there were too many faces for him to discern anyone he knew. Did he wish to host a party with Miss Sommers, even in an unofficial capacity? He hardly knew. But he had broached the topic with her and needed to see it through. In any case, he still had not come up with a ready solution for the dinner party Mr. Whitmore. had advised him to organize.

"You have the right of it, Miss Sommers. After all, we've just refurbished our drawing room and have begun on the dining room, which is a much easier task as the paint is at least new enough. Perhaps it is time to have the silver polished and try my hand at hosting a dinner in my own home. A political dinner, of course."

"Wonderful." Miss Sommers opened her parasol and smiled at him broadly. "If you'll heed my advice, you will create a guest list of such distinction that no man of influence will want to miss it and their wives will wish to attend, too."

She waved at one of the Almack's patronesses before turning back to him. "I must say that if your way of overcoming a professed weakness is to host a party of that scale, I wonder at there being any weakness at all."

Jack gave a feeble smile. "I will not attempt to convince you. But it is decided then. I will host a dinner party with your help."

Jack turned his mind to what such a party would entail. The guest list would be easy to sort out as he knew who needed to attend. He would host a party that brought together the more moderate of both the Whigs and the Tories and bring about the vote he desired. It was the other details, such as food and invitations that were more difficult.

As if Miss Sommers had read his mind, she said, "I can recommend a shop to order invitations. You will want to have flowers sent as well."

They had come to a larger stretch in the road that was less crowded, and Jack turned his head to see who was on the other side of it. An open barouche was parked underneath the shade of a tree, and Jack recognized his sister and Mr. Merrick on the forward seats, so he waited until a carriage passed before turning his phaeton to go over to them.

"Those are helpful ideas. Would you mind if we greet my sister? I had not known she would be in the park today."

When Jack came abreast their carriage, he perceived who was sitting across from his sister—the bouncing, golden curls of Miss Clavering, and at her side, Mr. Thackery. Jack frowned. He had all the answers he needed seeing them together like this.

"Good afternoon." His greeting lacked some of the enthusiasm he had been feeling when he first realized it was Miss Clavering.

As Mr. Thackery's carriage was facing the opposite way, Jack's seat as driver was closest to Miss Clavering. He wanted to ignore her but something in her eyes tugged at him. He was beginning to see nuances in her expression, and he wondered if she and Mr. Thackery had quarreled. He then glanced at his sister, who did not look happy either, though she was seated next to Mr. Merrick. Had Mr. Merrick given Susan false hopes only to dash them, despite his assurances to the contrary? It was a curious party, as none of them looked particularly happy to be there.

"Miss Sommers." Mr. Thackery called out to her from across both Jack and Miss Clavering. "I see you are taking advantage of this beautiful weather. How clever of Mr. Blythefield to invite you to ride. I was just asking Mr. Merrick here if you'd planned to organize any more dinners. I was sorry to have missed your last one. One can be assured of the success of your parties."

Miss Sommers smiled bashfully at her hands for a moment before lifting her eyes. "Mr. Thackery, you are too kind. As a matter of fact, I was just discussing with Mr. Blythefield the idea of hosting a dinner in his home."

Miss Clavering's eyes rested on Jack, and he saw surprise in the lift of her brows. Susan's mouth fell open.

Miss Sommers quickly rectified what she said. "I do not mean to imply that I would be hosting the party *with* Mr. Blythefield. I meant only to say that the next political dinner will likely be at the Blythefield residence rather than my home."

"Splendid. We have just had the rooms redone." Susan's face lit with pleasure at the idea, and she gave a soft clap of her hands. "At last, *we* are hosting something."

Jack could not appreciate Miss Sommers having announced his dinner when he was still considering how to send his family away. He'd also had reservations about inviting Mr. Thackery, who was not likely to further Jack's objectives—although he probably could not avoid it now.

Mr. Merrick leaned across Susan to speak to Jack. "I believe your dinner will be the very thing." With a glance at Susan, he added, "and I hope the women will be invited as well."

Jack opened his mouth to answer, but Miss Sommers performed the office for him. "Why, of course. Any successful party must have women present."

Jack studied Miss Clavering, who had remained silent. This was unlike her from the little he knew. "Miss Clavering, when I host the event, I do hope you will join us as well."

Before she could respond, Mr. Thackery said, "Absolutely. I will bring you myself, Miss Clavering. I am sure your brother-in-law will give his blessing."

Miss Clavering returned a tight smile. "It is most kind of you, Mr. Blythefield. I cannot imagine I would have anything to add in a political discussion." A slight protest erupted from Mr. Thackery's and Mr. Merrick's lips, and a louder one came from his sister. Miss Clavering met Jack's gaze. "I do not see that an invitation will be necessary, but I thank you."

Jack didn't understand why she would not want to come, but he would not beg. If Miss Clavering was not inclined, after all the effort she had put into refurbishing the drawing room, he was not going to try to force her into it. "I shall not insist," he said. "Gentlemen, Miss Clavering—if you will excuse us, we must be on our way. I should not like to have Miss Sommers home too late. Susan, I will see you at home."

They drove off, and Miss Sommers said, "I assume you will have your mother host your party?"

Jack was not ready to begin thinking about that troublesome aspect. "I am not sure. I shall have to see."

"You have mentioned before that your mother is frequently unwell or busy. If that is so, there is always your sister to act as hostess for your dinner party. Although she is young, I will do all I can to help her."

"Thank you," Jack said. "I will have to speak to her about it."

He responded with a distracted air to the preparations that Miss Sommers had begun to make. However, as they approached her house, he began to listen more carefully and add his thoughts. After all, Miss Sommers was kind enough to assist him. And it would be the first dinner party he had ever known in his house.

He would simply have to make sure none of his family would make an appearance.

CHAPTER THIRTEEN

The sound of Maria's half-boots clicked across the wooden floor outside the library, and Philippa propped her book in front of her nose and sat upright. If someone asked her what the book was about, she would in no way be able to answer.

"Here you are. It is nearly seven o'clock, Philippa. You must dress for the Ridley's ball this evening, for we are to leave promptly at eight-thirty."

Philippa lowered her book, her gaze still fixed on the page before her. She allowed a couple of seconds to slip by before lifting her eyes to meet Maria's gaze. She spread a vague smile across her face. "Oh, Maria—you are home. Is it seven already? I suppose I must go and change."

"Do. And wear your blue gown. Mr. Thackery has said he likes the color blue, and the pale shade of that gown is just the sort of modest color a man like Mr. Thackery would appreciate." When Philippa allowed her gaze to focus on the window in front of her instead of responding, Maria could not contain herself. "Go. I have ordered Fernsby to lay out your dress and the aquamarine set of jewelry, which is not too showy."

"Very well." Philippa stood. "May I not wear the gold set with diamonds instead? They are not so large as to be vulgar."

Maria clucked her teeth and shook her head in a decisive manner. "No. The aquamarines will go very nicely with that dress. Hurry."

Philippa picked up her pace, though her heart was heavier than she had ever remembered it. Was this her future? To exchange Maria's house for Mr. Thackery's with only a few insipid balls and parties in between? Why weren't her brothers telling Maria to back off from her marriage schemes?

I suppose they might if you'd told them how disagreeable Maria's and Charles's hints have become. That's what Philippa got for trying to prove to everyone she could manage for herself. In theory, she could. But where was an unmarried woman supposed to flee to when she was dissatisfied with her home environment? Not everyone was fit to be a governess.

At the door, Philippa turned back. "I don't have any intention of marrying Mr. Thackery, no matter how many invitations you accept on my behalf and how often you throw him my way."

Maria had been reading the details of the invitation and she looked up at this, her expression showing surprise. "Young ladies do not have a say in whom they marry. I certainly did not."

"But you wanted to marry Charles," Philippa protested. "You told me so."

"I happen to possess common sense. I knew what consequence a marriage with Charles would bring me." Maria walked toward the door of the library and shooed Philippa into the hallway. "And if you had any sense, you would know the same of Mr. Thackery. Why, he's being talked about as the future Prime Minister. Only *imagine*!"

"Yes, but I would have to live with him every minute he's not reveling in his glorious career. Besides, there is no guarantee his rise to that position will ever happen," Philippa replied crossly. "He might get kicked in the head by a horse before then."

"Don't talk nonsense," Maria scolded. "Now, off with you."

Fernsby had laid out the blue dress on Philippa's bed, and she looked at Philippa doubtfully, as experience had taught her what kind of mood Philippa would likely be in when Maria had decided to apply pressure. Philippa eyed the blue dress—which she adored—with distaste. She did not want to wear anything that might further tempt Mr. Thackery.

"Fernsby, hand me the water pitcher and a glass. I am thirsty."

Philippa's maid did so, and Philippa stood over the dress and poured the water from the pitcher into her glass, spilling the excess contents all over the front of the dress. She allowed her hand holding the glass to shake as well, drenching the dress further. Fernsby gasped and covered her face with her hands.

"Oh, how careless of me. What a shame that I could not wear my blue dress tonight. You may take this to dry and set out my gold dress." She thought for a minute, and added, "And the aquamarine necklace."

"But, miss! That set don't go with the gold." Fernsby paused with the damp dress in her hand.

"Never mind that. You must hurry, for Maria will howl if she is kept waiting."

Fernsby kept her eyes downward as she performed these tasks, but her lips quivered with remonstrance and amusement.

When Philippa was dressed for the ball, she met Maria and Charles in the drawing room at the last possible minute. Charles was looking at his pocket watch when she entered the room, and Maria gave a gasp of dismay.

"Philippa—what on earth? Where is your blue dress?" Maria glanced at Charles, who'd slipped his pocket watch into his waistcoat and reached for his coat.

"Maria, it was so unfortunate." Philippa stepped forward, pulling on her gloves. "I am devastated because I know how becoming that dress is on me! But I was holding a glass of water, and I accidentally let it go—so very clumsy of me—and now the gown is drenched and won't dry in time. But I did wear the aquamarines as you told me to."

Maria *tsked* in irritation. "You cannot wear an aquamarine necklace with a dress of that color. Run up and have Fernsby attach your gold chain with the diamonds—I am sorry, Charles. I really am. But she cannot go like that. Make haste, Philippa."

Philippa hurried up the stairs and was able to accomplish the swap in a matter of minutes since Fernsby had already polished the necklace and was holding it out for Philippa to wear.

Her maid deserved an increase in pay.

***

It was the largest event since the Yardmouth's ball, and Philippa had made Matthew Evans promise to be there. She'd reminded him that he could not win a lady's heart if he were not present to attempt the deed. And apart from the one morning call he'd performed without Philippa's bolstering presence—in which Mr. Merrick also was in attendance—he had all but conceded defeat.

"You must not give up so easily," Philippa had urged him when he visited her. "Susan's heart may be engaged by Mr. Merrick, and I understand your hesitation on the matter. But I am far from convinced that Mr. Merrick is the best one for her. In fact, I fear he is interested in her for mere appearances, and that he has something to gain politically by attaching himself to her."

Matthew had frowned and put his hand on her arm to halt their progress toward the door. "You think Mr. Merrick is interested in an alliance with Mr. Blythefield and that he could bring it about by marrying Miss Blythefield?"

"I am far from being certain." Philippa had attempted to put words to why she thought so. "It's just an instinct I have. I don't see the sincerity in Mr. Merrick—and believe me, if I thought he were perfectly suited to her and would treat her well, I would advise you to give it up and look elsewhere. It is only that I cannot believe Mr. Merrick has such innocent intentions. I cannot even place my finger on why. It's just in the things he says. Or perhaps he is too smooth in his attentions."

"And that, I am not," Matthew had replied glumly. In the end, however, he'd agreed to come.

When they arrived at the Ridley's, Philippa quickly separated herself from Maria and Charles and searched the room until she found George standing next to Whitmore, Amos, and Matthew. She gave a firm tug on her brother's coat.

"Where have you been? May I remind you, dear brother, that you promised to save me from Maria's machinations, and I haven't seen you near the house since the night of the opera."

A look of chagrin crossed George's face. "I know. I've been taking care of Duck. He's had a nasty fall and has broken his leg."

"Oh, no, has he?" Philippa glanced at her brother's friends. "So are you all forced to keep Duck occupied as he convalesces?"

"Not him." Amos jerked a finger at Whitmore. "His father has been keeping him too busy in Parliament for him to be of much use."

"We hear of your knack for chess, Whitmore. But what's the use of being a formidable chess opponent if you're never around to apply yourself?" George quipped. "Duck has only Amos and I for partners."

Mr. Whitmore took a sip of his wine and looked across the room. "I am merely playing a different type of chess. And there goes my rook."

Philippa followed Whitmore's gaze. "Mr. Blythefield?" Matthew turned to look as well.

"The very one. My father and his cronies have him in mind for the next Leader of the Opposition. They don't think Tierney will last long. I am to assist him in bringing about the abolition of the Corn Laws, for m'father is not certain he will be chosen without that victory."

"I don't follow politics closely, and even I know Tierney is not a favorite in his party," George said. "So Blythefield? He's awfully young. He can't be much older than us."

"Twenty-nine." Whitmore shrugged. "But what has that to say to anything? Pitt was only twenty-four when he became Prime Minister."

"Mr. Blythefield has a brilliant future ahead of him, it seems…" Philippa began and let her voice trail away when the men turned to look at her. She had appeared overly interested. Apparently, Mr. Blythefield had not been boasting without merit.

"I don't mean to say it's a sure thing, for there are many vying for the position. Speaking of young men who are rising in esteem"—Whitmore's glance at Philippa was full of meaning—"Mr. Thackery's name is also being talked about as a possible Prime Minister. Although that day will not come quite as soon. Thackery might not give such an impassioned speech as Mr. Blythefield, but his ability to work behind the scenes to gather the necessary votes is impressive. He's naturally fallen into the role of Parliament-driver."

"That does not surprise me in the least," Philippa replied. "Mr. Thackery is certainly obstinate to the point of pigheaded when it comes to going after what he wants. The Commons would do better to follow the direction of a man like Mr. Blythefield."

Amos, not at all involved in politics, had given the impression of disinterest as he let his gaze wander around the ball, but he now faced Philippa. "Miss Clavering, we are not in ignorance of your feelings toward Mr. Thackery. Why do you spend so much time in his company?"

Philippa glanced at George, who'd had his attention drawn elsewhere but now brought it back to the conversation. He waited until Philippa answered.

"Well, George. Must I out you for your lack of chivalry?" She smiled at his friends. "Apparently, George was too busy last year to see to the affairs of his younger sister when Mr. Thackery declared an unwelcome interest in me. My brother-in-law did not see fit to send him packing, because he wants Mr. Thackery to whip the votes his way on the matters that concern him. And now, despite my very obvious snubs, Mr. Thackery does not take the hint. I don't seem to have the fortune of possessing older brothers who concern themselves enough with my pitiful bleats to chase the unwanted suitors away."

George raised his hands in defense. "Now, Philippa, you know I was not aware of the situation last year, for you never told me about it. You didn't even mention it when we saw each other over the summer—"

"And since I do not wish for a family squabble at a public ball," Philippa interjected, "let me simply conclude by saying that the subject *did* come up, but my brother was distracted and otherwise engaged."

George shook his head, but conceded the point with a small bow. "Please accept my apologies, Philippa." He paused, his attention diverted. "Gentlemen, Mrs. Ridley is slowly making her way over to this side of the ballroom. I would say it's an ideal time to head into the card room, wouldn't you agree? You don't mind, do you, Philippa?"

Philippa rolled her eyes. She couldn't expect a miraculous conversion of brotherly concern overnight.

"I will join you in a minute." Matthew's gaze had drifted from his friends and focused to Philippa's right where the Blythefields stood.

Throughout the conversation, Philippa had been aware of Mr. Blythefield's presence, though she was trying not to look in that direction. Therefore, her heart gave a strange leap when, from her side vision, she perceived Mr. Blythefield moving her way. A quick glance was enough to remind her what a handsome man he was, and his features were only set to advantage by his black coat and the starched white neckcloth. The absence of facial hair revealed a decisive chin and firm lips.

Susan was at her brother's side. "I convinced Jack to bring me over to see you. Isn't this an enchanting ball? What an idea to have only white flowers of all sizes as decorations. I predict this will be the next fashion."

Matthew had lit with pleasure when Susan joined them, and when she transferred a smile to him—even if it seemed to be a benevolent one—he looked to be done in. He bowed, and in the most natural way, pulled Susan aside for conversation by asking how her guests were finding the changes in the drawing room. *Well done, Matthew,* Philippa thought. They were still discussing it as he led Susan off, presumably to dance.

Meanwhile, Philippa was experiencing a curious emotion she could not quite account for—and one she'd never remembered having known before. A stab of disappointment shot through her that it had not been Mr. Blythefield's own desire that had brought him her way. Philippa swept away the regret and greeted him in a perfectly natural manner.

"You look very dashing, Mr. Blythefield." She gave a playful curtsy by way of belated greeting.

"I must say the same about you." Mr. Blythefield bowed deeply, and when he lifted his head, his eyes rested on her for a long, unsettling pause. "This is a very becoming dress on you. A perfect match for your golden curls."

Philippa thought she detected a flush of consciousness in his expression, as though he had not meant to say that. A blush of pleasure tingled on her cheeks, and she drew in a deep breath to clear her head. "I am told you delivered an impressive speech yesterday."

"You mean to say, of course, an impressive speech for a *Whig*." Mr. Blythefield gave her a raised-eyebrow look of skepticism.

"Even Whigs are capable of giving fine speeches," Philippa said, biting her cheeks to keep from smiling. "I will concede the fact."

Mr. Blythefield took one step closer so that their faces were inches apart, which removed her urge to smile—and her ability to breathe all together. "Come now, Miss Clavering. You and I both know you are sympathetic to the idea of reform. Let us leave off this pretense of supporting the Tories."

At his teasing, the smile returned to Philippa's face before she could prevent it. "And who has told you such outrageous lies about me?"

"Someone hinted at it, and your brother, Sir Lucius, confirmed it yesterday at our committee meeting. He informed me that not only does he share my Whig views—but that you do too."

A laugh was surprised out of Philippa. "Lucius has betrayed me. But you are correct. I am a Whig sympathizer. It is only my brother-in-law who is a Tory. But, of course, all that is neither here nor there since women have no say—or place—in politics."

"Do you really think so? Miss Sommers believes that women do have a place in politics, and it is the role of hostess. Her interests lie in organizing events that bring men and women together to discuss ideas more suited to an informal setting—and over a good bottle of wine."

Philippa had no urge to smile at the mention of Miss Sommers's name. She had seen her at the ball and had identified her as the woman

Mr. Blythefield had in his carriage in Hyde Park. Miss Sommers was dark while Philippa was fair, tall while Philippa was petite, and she had perhaps five years on Philippa, giving her a worldly air Philippa did not possess but eagerly wished for. She paused before replying.

"Miss Sommers is perfectly right. Nevertheless, we cannot watch the debates in Parliament, nor can we sit. We cannot give debates ourselves. We can scarcely educate ourselves and must rely upon the generosity of our menfolk—or their negligence, as in the case of my brother-in-law, who leaves his papers lying about so I can follow the latest news. It is no surprise that the views of women are so little considered if we do not have access to the same education as men to formulate our ideas."

"I agree that it is a hardship for women not to have access to the same education, but it is not insurmountable." Mr. Blythefield stared across the room. *Was he searching for Miss Sommers?* "Until the world is ready to catch up to your ideas, there are always brothers and husbands with books at their disposal to share."

"Brothers with books, I will agree with you—*if* they should be the reading sort. But husbands? I hardly think husbands will do the work of educating their wives." Philippa let her gaze skim the crowd. Across the room, Mr. Thackery lifted his glass and nodded in her direction with a wolfish smile. She clenched her teeth. "It seems more that husbands are in the mind of shutting them up in the guise of protecting them."

"I'm sorry to hear you think so." Mr. Blythefield paused long enough that she turned to look at him. "You must not have any role models that can prove you otherwise, but I assure you, not all men think the same."

It was perhaps crossing over into dangerously intimate terrain, but Philippa could not help but ask, "Do you think the same way, Mr. Blythefield?"

He was standing nearer to her than he ever had, and he held her gaze, pausing until her breath was suspended in anticipation of his response. "If I had a wife, she should have access to every paper and book in my house that might possibly interest her. And I would speak with her on any topic she should wish. My protection would be shown in a different, more gallant manner, and not in keeping any knowledge from her that she might wish to gain."

Philippa's head grew light. Could such a man exist? She could not break his gaze, and something shifted between them. A trust. A common bond. Attraction so suddenly strong it could be felt. Two women passing by glanced at them and leaned in to whisper behind their fans, and Mr. Blythefield took a step back.

One of the women stopped and slipped her arm out of the other's, holding a gloved hand to her lips. "Miss Clavering. We haven't met this Season, and I was wondering if you had perhaps left London." She glanced at Mr. Blythefield then back at Philippa. "Still unmarried, are you? I would have thought you might have persuaded some gentleman to commit last year. But ... who is your friend?"

CHAPTER FOURTEEN

*ack heard Miss Clavering draw in a quiet breath. "Mr. Blythefield, may I present Lady Harrowden?" Miss Clavering's face had closed up. It appeared this was a woman she did not like. And for some unnamed reason, he had a hunch he would not like Lady Harrowden either. "She is married to an earl whose property borders my brother's hunting box. Lady Harrowden, Mr. Blythefield." Miss Clavering offered Lady Harrowden's companion a polite smile.

"Mr. Blythefield! What a divine coincidence. I had not dreamed you were so young." The way Lady Harrowden appraised Jack with open admiration seemed to add an unspoken regret that she was married and unable to pursue him for herself. He thanked the heavens she was. "Lord Harrowden has been anxious to meet you, for he has gained a seat in Parliament and he has ideas regarding some bill or other. I've forgotten the details, but I must introduce you without delay." Her searching gaze around the room spoke her intent to do so at the instant.

Jack had rather liked the conversation he had been having with Miss Clavering before they were interrupted. It had revealed a side to him he had not been entirely aware of—that he wanted a knowledgeable wife he could converse with and not simply a quiet mouse of a woman who kept a good home. His second revelation unsettled him, however. Perhaps he craved the sort of conversation he could have with a woman like Miss Clavering, who challenged and excited him.

He pulled his thoughts back to his surroundings. "Lady Harrowden, I can see you are at present engaged with a companion, but I will be glad to meet your husband at some other point this evening. Or, if he wishes, I will be in Parliament on Monday, and he is welcome to seek me out there." Jack bowed, hoping it would be enough to make her leave, but he had overestimated the level of sensitivity of Lady Harrowden.

"Why, no. You don't mind going to the refreshment table without me, do you, Mary? I will go now to fetch Harrowden. He won't want to miss meeting you, Mr. Blythefield."

Lady Harrowden strode off on her mission, and Jack faced Miss Clavering again, who offered up a weak smile. "I am not overly fond of Lady Harrowden."

"I could tell," he said. "What has she done to you?"

"To me? Nothing. She could not have hurt me in any possible way. But Lucius's wife, Selena—my dear sister-in-law—was her governess, and she made her life vastly unpleasant in the short time Selena had to live with her." Miss Clavering exhaled and looked in the direction Lady Harrowden had gone. "I think I will not stay. As much as it astonishes me that Lord Harrowden should take an interest in politics, and I am curious as to why, I am not overly fond of him either."

She curtsied and gave Jack only time to bow before she was gone. Miss Clavering was the most independent woman he knew. She was unafraid to walk alone in a ball, whereas his sister could not take three steps without being on someone's arm. Miss Clavering apparently also had strong opinions and wished for further education on political matters. As much as Jack had spoken the absolute truth about wanting his wife to be educated in any area that interested her, he did not wish for a wife whose strong opinions might lead her to take an undue interest in a project outside the home. Despite the fact that he liked Miss Clavering a surprising amount, he feared she would do precisely that.

Jack had sworn to his brother that all he wished for was a quiet wife, who caused him no problems. Miss Sommers was intelligent and threw successful parties, but she had the ability to sink into the background once she had enacted her hostess duties. She would never put herself forward more than to see to a man's comfort. It would not do for him to forget that she possessed these desirable qualities in measure.

Mr. Evans brought Susan back to Jack's side and bowed over her hand. "Miss Blythefield, thank you for the honor of dancing with me."

The words had no sooner left his lips than Mr. Merrick appeared at Susan's side with an engaging smile that completely shut out Mr. Evans. "I believe this next dance was promised to me, Miss Blythefield."

"Yes, I believe so, Mr. Merrick." Susan's cheeks turned rosy under his attention, and she walked off on his arm. Mr. Evans stared after them, the longing evident on his face.

Mr. Evans breathed in then turned to Jack. "I've heard that Parliament is going to propose a bill to regulate the southern whale fisheries. Do you have any interest in it?"

Mr. Evans was an unassuming man, but he was direct—Jack would give him that. He commanded respect in his own quiet way. "I am aware of the bill but know nothing of its contents. I have not yet reviewed it. What is *your* interest, if I might ask?"

"Only that your sister has told me of your father's interest in various investments. It is being spread about that investing in the fleet is a sound bet, but it appears to me to be more of a speculation." Mr. Evans accepted a drink from one of the servants who passed by. "Mr. Blythefield, I should not wish to presume in any way, but if someone were to ask me, I would advise them against it. There has already been an increase in whaling ships since the peace treaty, and I don't believe it will be long before the market is saturated."

"Thank you. That is most interesting." Jack studied Mr. Evans, wondering how much to disclose. "My sister spoke to you of my father's investments?"

Mr. Evans gave a small shake of the head. "I want to assure you she revealed nothing indiscreet. It is only that I prompted her to talk about herself, and her affection for her family propelled her to speak on the topic, particularly since she knew investments were an interest of mine as well. But I am not a man to disclose another family's affairs."

Jack was beginning to like the fellow. "My father has spoken to me about whaling. With the oil lamps being put up in Bristol—I thought it could not hurt to invest in such a venture, although I've neither encouraged nor discouraged my father on the matter. I don't know enough. Nantucket has the smaller share of the market, I've heard. I thought perhaps England would be gaining hers."

Mr. Evans dismissed that with a decisive shake of his head. "Although Nantucket will never be what it once was, the whaling companies are expanding in Australia now. Even if we managed to light the entire streets of London with oil lamps, we should still have more than we need, I believe."

Mr. Evans followed Susan's movements across the room. "Even if your sister's heart should belong to another, I would be glad to be of service to your family. There are other investments that will prove more sure, and if you would trust me with the task, I will do some research and come back with recommendations."

"I would appreciate that." Jack was moved to hold his hand out to shake that of Susan's admirer before Mr. Evans excused himself to speak to a friend.

The ball had begun to grow packed and warm, and Jack was reminded why he did not love balls overmuch. Better to be in the chamber of Parliament—or the comfort of his own home, especially now that it had become so inviting. He looked across the room and easily sought out the gold silk dress of Miss Clavering, who had gone from the hands of one partner to another since the last time he'd looked. Her smile was bright, and she seemed to have no interest in anything other than what her current partner was saying. It was a rather irritating sight.

It occurred to Jack that he had not yet partnered with Miss Clavering—an error that should be remedied. Then again, the last time he had asked, she had directed him toward another woman, whose name he had promptly forgotten. The maneuver was not one he had been prepared for, and certainly not from a pretty chit like her.

Jack could not pull his gaze from Miss Clavering as she spun on her partner's arm. He wondered if she were still opposed to dancing with him. He quite thought they had made progress in understanding one another.

"Good evening, Mr. Blythefield."

Jack turned at the sound of the cultured voice. Miss Sommers was at his side, her black hair swept back and her dark-blue gown complimenting her ivory features and pale-blue eyes.

He bowed. "Good evening, Miss Sommers. Are you enjoying yourself?"

She held her fan closed between her gloved hands. "Very much. I have danced, partaken of the refreshments, and have had several delightful conversations. Everything a soirée should be." She turned from watching the dancing couples to face him.

"Everything yours usually are," he replied with a smile. Lady Harrowden had not returned with her husband, and Jack was under no obligation to wait for her. "Are you too fatigued to dance again?"

"With you? Not at all. We may talk about the dinner party you are to host." Miss Sommers lifted an eyebrow, as if challenging him with the reminder of his vow. He had not yet gone to her house as promised to discuss the details, such as what she might recommend his cook to serve.

"Very well." Jack held out his arm, and she placed her hand in his as they joined a set that was forming. Miss Sommers was the picture of elegance, and he should be more active in his pursuit of her. Was she not his ideal? Beautiful, without a hair out of place, an easy conversationalist whose ideas never shocked a person, skilled at hosting … There was only one small point that he was not certain should be a matter worth considering. He had never experienced the unnerving sensation of having the floor shift when Miss Sommers turned her gaze his way. It was otherwise with Miss Clavering.

"I received your note about the date for your dinner party," Miss Sommers said as they took their place in the set forming.

"What did you make of my guest list?" Jack asked, wondering if she would offer her own ideas on the people he had named.

"I am sure anyone you see fit to invite must be a perfectly acceptable choice." Miss Sommers closed her lips, and her artful look made Jack suspect she wished for him to beg for her opinion. She would be disappointed. It was too much trouble to coax opinions out of people. Much better they give them up voluntarily.

The music began, and another couple took their place at Jack's side to form a square. It was Robert Whitmore, who had partnered with Miss Clavering. She smiled at Jack, since they had not long since parted, and Robert had only time to bow to Miss Sommers before the dance began.

The music started, and Jack received his chance to take Miss Clavering's hand whenever the partners changed. He found himself calculating how long he would have to turn around Miss Sommers before Miss Clavering's hand would again be in his. It made it difficult—nigh impossible—to make any conversation at all. When the dance paused in between sets, Miss Clavering stood opposite of him, laughing with Robert Whitmore, and it was with difficulty that Jack turned his attention to Miss Sommers.

When he did, she was studying his face. "I was thinking, Mr. Blythefield. Why did you invite Sir Lucius Clavering to your dinner? This is not a name I know—unless he is related to Miss Clavering? He must be, since the name is not so common."

Clavering. The one name he could not get out of his head, and now it hung in the air between them. "Sir Lucius is her brother. I've invited him and Lady Clavering because he and I are joined together on a committee." Jack glanced at Miss Clavering and caught her gaze at the moment she looked away from her partner. Her eyes danced, and he wondered what Whitmore could possibly be saying to make her that pleased.

Whitmore could be a dull fellow.

"And Mr. Whitmore the elder is to come as well. A *coup*!" Miss Sommers seemed determined to discuss their common project, and Jack knew his wandering attention was not fair to the lady he had partnered for this dance.

He turned his face away from the sight of Miss Clavering and directed it to Miss Sommers. "Yes, indeed. In truth, it was Mr. Whitmore's idea to host a dinner in the first place. He is leading the group that wishes to appoint me and must be at anything I organize." Jack studied Miss Sommers, wondering for the first time just how much she advocated for reform. "And with his support, I will convince the others that opening up for free trade on grain is the best way to serve England's interests."

Miss Sommers opened her fan and raised her eyes to him over it. "I am sure you know best, Mr. Blythefield."

It was just as he preferred it. No contrary opinion to trouble him from a candidate for the role of wife.

A change in music announced the next set, and Jack took his place next to a different couple, partly relieved that Miss Clavering would not be next to him to befuddle his mind, and partly disappointed by the same. He forced himself to show Miss Sommers more attention than he had before, and her pleased expression was his reward. Perhaps that was why the floor didn't shift when he met her gaze. No woman was at her best when she was being overlooked.

As he led Miss Sommers off the dance floor, she put her hand in his arm. "It seems you have everything well in hand for your party. What might I do to further assist you?"

He directed his steps to where her mother was sitting with other widows and elderly ladies. "There is the food, which we may discuss this week. I will come and call when it is convenient for you. Besides that, perhaps with your experience, you might think of something I am overlooking?"

"*Hm.*" Miss Sommers did not speak until they were a few feet from where her mother sat. "With the number of guests you've invited, have you considered where the gentlemen will stable their carriages while they attend the soirée?"

He raised his eyebrows. "I see I was not wrong to seek your advice. I confess I had not thought about it. There is a private mews on the cross street from our house, and I have heard of his letting it out on occasion. I will send someone to speak to him about doing so that evening."

"That should answer." Miss Sommers dipped her chin. "If I think of anything else, we may discuss it when you call. Otherwise, if you do not object, I will arrive an hour early for the party?" She let the question dangle, and he answered with a sense of relief. She was not officially his hostess, but he couldn't imagine organizing the affair without her help.

"That would suit me very well. And I will send word if I must beg your assistance for anything else." Jack took her hand and bowed over it.

"It will be my pleasure." Miss Sommers curtsied and returned to her mother's side, and Jack turned back to the crowded floor, searching the countless figures for a golden dress when his gaze landed upon Susan, standing beside Christopher. It was unexpected, as he rarely saw his brother these days. He wasn't even sure if his brother had seen the renovations in their drawing room.

He walked up to them. "Christopher, what a surprise. What brings you here?"

"A man must show his face every once in a while or Society forgets about him." Christopher was wearing another of his outrageous creations with yellow breeches and a bold blue coat. His neckcloth was printed with large violets.

"I don't believe anyone would forget you." Jack could wish his brother were more discreet and that he were a man who could be relied upon. However, Jack had not been blessed with what one would call a normal family. He and Christopher had been close as boys, and he smiled whenever he remembered the larks they had got up to—left, as they often were, to their own devices. Mother and Father had been more amused than shocked at their doings, if they'd even noticed them at all.

It had bewildered Jack when he and his brother started to drift. Around the time Jack came of age, he had inherited a small fortune from his godmother. It had seemed about that time that Christopher became distant, and while the madcap adventures quickly became a thing of the past for Jack, his brother had plunged headlong into a shallow, dissipated life. Jack had become a responsible man of substance, and Christopher had become dependent on a father who was not able to keep his estate afloat. It was as if he had given up caring for the future of the estate—as though the battle against debt was not one worth fighting.

Jack was standing in the middle of a crowded ball—the cream of Society. He was courting the attention of a desirable female, who would assure him success in the political arena as well as his home life. He was up for the senior most position in his political party and was about to host a dinner for the most influential of them. And he was lonely.

Susan was looking at them both fondly, and Jack experienced a rush of affection for his little sister. She was the least eccentric, and he did want to see her happily married—she deserved it. "So, are you still of the same mind regarding Mr. Merrick?"

Susan linked her arms through her brothers' arms, forcing them all to stand close. "I am. I was afraid the last time we met that perhaps he was not as serious in his intentions as he had at first seemed. But tonight, he paid me particular attention." Susan beamed. "He is most gentlemanly. And so handsome, don't you think?"

Jack narrowed his gaze at her. "You cannot honestly expect me to answer that."

Susan giggled.

"Well, he has not spoken to Father"—Jack remembered Miss Clavering's implicit rebuke about him usurping his father's position of authority—"and he has not made any sort of official declaration. Even if he had, we have not looked into his financial matters. But, you know, I only want what is best for you."

Christopher extricated his arm from Susan's. "As much as this happy family party warms my heart through, I should not like to make anyone ill by the sight of it." He bowed, preparing to leave, and for once his expression showed none of its usual irony. "Although let it be known that I, too, dear sister, want what's best for you."

Jack could only wish that the concern Christopher professed to have might encourage him to take a more active leadership role in the family.

CHAPTER FIFTEEN

*P*hilippa was putting on her bonnet by the front door when Maria caught sight of her and strode down the corridor. "Philippa, wait."

She had been about to visit Susan, for they had not had a chance to speak at the ball and Philippa had not been to the Blythefield's house in some days. She finally had to admit to herself that she was hiding from Mr. Blythefield because he'd stirred emotions in her that she would rather not experience: a desire to know in just what gallant way he would protect his wife—all while sharing his books, his learning, and his conversation. But today, she was anxious to be gone because Mr. Thackery had hinted at another dismal soirée last night that he would be paying a morning call today and that he should hope to find her at home.

Maria shook her head at Fernsby, who had been about to hand Philippa her cloak, then turned her attention to Philippa. "You are up and about early, but I've been listening for you as I didn't wish to miss you. Remove your bonnet, for you may not leave just yet. Mr. Thackery has expressed a desire to speak with you in private, and I have granted him his wish. He is to arrive early this afternoon."

Philippa turned on her heel to face her sister. "Maria, you know very well I have no intention of accepting Mr. Thackery's offer. Why you should hope to bring this about *still* is a mystery to me. My answer is no. Can you not spare me the pain of having to say that to him directly?"

Maria glanced at the footman, whose attention was ostensibly directed elsewhere, and ushered Philippa into the drawing room. "I do not think you have thought this through. Mr. Thackery is known by everyone to be quite a catch. He is handsome—which I'm sure you yourself cannot deny—he is wealthy, and he has an important role in Parliament. He is a man of influence. And, despite all the lures cast his way, he has fixed his regard on *you*. That is a crowning success, Philippa. I cannot let you throw that away."

"But you would not have to live with him—" Philippa began.

"If Mr. Thackery's character runs true, neither will you." Maria raised an eyebrow, and Philippa's heart chilled at the words. "You will have your own bedroom, and he will be spending his time at the clubs and elsewhere. Once you present him with an heir, you may do as you please. Furthermore, you will be mistress of your own house and will run in the first circle of Society. I cannot imagine what of this image has no appeal for you."

"Because you have no heart—" Philippa cut her hasty words short and instead pleaded with her sister. "I am sorry for those words, Maria. But you must understand, my feelings do not run deep for Mr. Thackery. On the contrary, his manner of living raises every sort of abhorrence in me. He assumes much and gives little. I cannot love him."

"What has love to say in the matter? Besides, you never know whether feelings of practicality will turn to love—much as has been the case for Charles and me. My marriage is a happy one, as much as you say I have no heart." Maria walked over to the sofa and gestured for Philippa to sit. "You are under my charge, and I forbid you to leave this house. As an unmarried girl, you must do as I say. I will remind you that I am your guardian this Season. And if I say you will marry Mr. Thackery, believe me, I have ways of bringing it about. Now sit."

Mere threats, Philippa thought, but she followed her sister to the sofa and removed her bonnet, placing it beside her as she sat. If Maria chose to remain prey to delusion, a firm refusal given to Mr. Thackery directly should settle the matter. Although anger turned the blood in Philippa's veins to ice, she donned a bored expression. Maria did not need to know just how distressed she was and add that weakness to her arsenal.

Without another word, Philippa picked up the embroidery that was always lying on the table in front of the sofa and began setting stitches. Let her sister think she was going to be docile about the matter.

"Well, isn't this nice?" Maria bustled over to get the tea leaves and brought them to the small table next to a chair, before sitting. "I suppose I should find something to keep me occupied while we wait."

There was a loud knock on the front door, signaling that a wait would not be necessary. Better to get this over with sooner rather than later. Philippa heard the voice of Mr. Thackery in the hall, and just the sound of it turned her stomach. Maria, on the contrary, sat up straight and brightened. *Maria, I almost suspect you wish Mr. Thackery were coming here for yourself.*

The butler opened the door and announced Mr. Thackery, who came into the room and bowed. "Good day, Mrs. Holbeck. Good day, Miss Clavering. I am delighted to find you home, just as I requested."

He sent a significant glance to Maria, which she interpreted, for she stood. "I will go see that the tea platter is prepared." It almost appeared to Philippa as though her sister danced out of the room. She continued setting stitches with a steady hand, but it was growing increasingly difficult to hide her anger and revulsion as the charade continued.

Contrary to Philippa's expectation that Mr. Thackery would immediately begin his assault, he sat facing her in silence. Crossing one leg over the other, he leaned on the armrest, his chin in hand as he observed Philippa. "You are very pretty today."

Philippa was wearing a morning dress in that color blue Mr. Thackery apparently liked. She had hoped Mr. Blythefield might have been at home to appreciate it.

"Thank you, sir." Philippa kept her eyes cast downward on her work. It was not from any sense of modesty but rather a perverse desire to infuriate her suitor by appearing uninterested in anything he had to say. She *was*, after all, uninterested.

After a small silence in which he seemed to be examining her, Mr. Thackery announced, "I am considering changing my tactics and throwing my weight behind a political bill of Mr. Blythefield's. That is, I mean to say he has taken it up this Session, though the idea has been bandied about for years."

That was all he would say, and Philippa rose to the bait. "And what bill is this?" She punctured her needle through the embroidered cloth.

Mr. Thackery seemed to be enjoying her irritation. "It is to repeal the Corn Laws and allow free trade on grains. As I'm sure you must be uninformed on the subject—"

"English landowners have fixed the price of grains so as not to permit any imports from foreign lands. In that way, they assure the success of the

English economy—and their own, of course." Philippa pulled the green embroidery thread to its length.

He raised both brows. "Learned as well as beautiful. I admit, you still surprise me, although I am beginning to be unsurprised by the surprise."

"You flatter me," she answered in a bored voice.

"How did you learn about the contents of this bill?" Mr. Thackery lifted his chin from his hand and clasped both hands on his lap. "You have a natural interest in politics?"

"Oh, no," she demurred. "Women should not have any strong opinions on politics. Much better they put their focus on running a household to their husbands' satisfaction and making the place welcome for when he comes home." Philippa began making reckless stitches that she would just have to undo. She silently dared him to prove her wrong when she added, "Any sort of political ideas are out of place in a woman's mind when such a thing is better left to the men."

Mr. Thackery opened his hands, as if her comment had surprised him—despite his determination to be unsurprised about the surprise. "It gratifies me to hear you say that. And I suppose this leads me naturally to my next topic."

Philippa fought with all her might to keep her expression perfectly closed, but her heart began to beat quickly. It was one thing to despise a man and be determined to refuse him. It was another thing to be forced to face such unpleasantness. *But let him speak,* she thought, *for then he may be done with it.*

Mr. Thackery was not content to speak. To Philippa's horror, he got up from his chair and walked the few steps to her sofa where he lowered himself on his knees in front of her. He took her hands in his, and revulsion almost caused her to snatch them back, but she resisted the urge when she felt the force of his grasp. She wasn't sure he would release her, but to know it for a fact would be frightening.

"Never did I think to find myself on my knees declaring my love for a woman. But you have brought me to this, Philippa—"

"Miss Clavering, if you please—"

"*Shh!* What began as an idle flirtation, followed by a determination that no one would satisfy me but you, has quickly become an obsession. I cannot see you in a room without forgetting every other woman present. I cannot look upon my home without imagining you there. And even if my political career will always be my true wife, and you my mistress, I believe I shall have no need to look for any other mistress while you are at my side. With that welcome home you are so determined to create for your husband"—he pulled her hand to his lips and kissed it fervently—"a most noble aspiration, my love, I can only imagine that you will satisfy my every need. So I ask you —"

At that moment, the door opened, and Maria stepped through with the footman hard on her heels, carrying a platter with teapot, saucers, cups, and cakes. Maria stopped short at the sight of Mr. Thackery on his knees with Philippa's hand in his, and the footman bumped into her from behind.

"You clumsy oaf," Maria cried, turning to leave the room. She pushed him backwards, closing the door quickly, and Philippa heard a loud clatter from the corridor, followed by a series of muttered oaths. She was at last encouraged to lift her eyes and look at Mr. Thackery, the humor of the situation giving relief to some of her indignation. The proposal could not get any better than this.

Mr. Thackery did not share her humor. Irritation for having been interrupted in his passionate declaration was written all over his face. Philippa could only assume he was not interrupted very often in Parliament.

He got up from his humiliating posture and sat at her side. "I am asking you to marry me." His irritation removed all traces of the warm, passionate feelings he had been referring to before. "Please make me the happiest man alive and accept my proposal."

As this was said in a voice tight with annoyance, Philippa was hard put not to laugh, despite her ardent wish to be anywhere but here.

"I thank you for your proposal, Mr. Thackery," she replied, "but I am afraid I must refuse it."

Mr. Thackery sat back on the sofa and folded his arms. "You cannot refuse it. I feared you might try resistance, although perhaps I deluded myself into thinking you were beginning to come around with your rational words just now." He regarded her with a smug expression. "I have already spoken to Holbeck, who has accepted on your behalf."

Philippa paused, horrified. Surely such a thing was not still done in this modern age. Only a small quake in her voice could be heard when she replied. "Charles cannot accept on my behalf. He is not my guardian. My mother is."

"I am sorry to contradict a lady," Mr. Thackery said. "However, your sister has assured me she has your mother's written approval to the match. I am afraid you will have to resign yourself to the inevitable, my dear, and take my offer. There are worse proposals than mine, you know."

"Such high praise for yourself," she replied in an icy voice.

"And yet, true."

Philippa stared ahead of her, refusing to turn to him. That her sister—and even her mother—would approve the match, despite her insistence that she did not wish for it, hurt more than she thought possible. Her expectations about receiving any maternal support and affection were low, but this went beyond anything. Their blatant disregard for her feelings …

She would not give Mr. Thackery the satisfaction of knowing how much his gloating victory hurt. "I will fetch Maria. The two of you will have many things to discuss." Philippa clutched her bonnet, then stood and walked toward the door.

"Ah!" Mr. Thackery cried out in a voice of delight. "I am glad to see you are so easily brought to reason. We shall rub along very well together."

Philippa paused at the door and faced him. "We may not have time to rub along together, as we will not be spending any time together at all. I would like to make one thing perfectly clear, Mr. Thackery." She opened the door where sounds of the footman cleaning the broken porcelain echoed through the corridor. She paused at the threshold and looked back. "I will not marry you."

Philippa shut the door to the drawing room and stepped over the spill. She hastily tied her bonnet under her chin as she strode to the front entrance. Her pelisse was no longer in sight, and she decided it was possible to do without it. The footman stood at the door ready to open it.

"Philippa!" Maria's voice rang down the corridor as she came up from the kitchen. "Where do you think you're going?"

"Out!" Philippa stepped over the threshold and—without waiting for the footman—yanked the door shut from the outside with a loud *clack*.

CHAPTER SIXTEEN

*J*ack paused at the door to his father's study, about to knock, when a quick rap at the front door informed him of his brother's arrival. No one else but Christopher had quite the same imperative knock. There was some shuffling movement coming from the dining room, which was likely Shanks. Their butler never seemed to be near the door when there was a rare visitor. It would be more expedient for Jack to open the door himself.

"Jack. I had not thought to see you here." Christopher strode into the corridor, wearing a lime-green coat paired with pale-yellow trousers. Jack supposed it was slightly better than some of his other outfits, although if his brother was going to wear such garish colors, Jack wished he would stick to the more form-fitting pantaloons rather than the wide-legged slops he had on.

"Are you trying to avoid meeting me?" Jack stepped aside as Christopher removed his hat and cane and set it on the bench. "If so, you have accomplished your purpose. I don't believe you have been here since Susan has made all the changes in the drawing room."

"You mean all the changes Miss Clavering made," Christopher said. "Susan told me about it, and it appears most of the ideas were her friend's."

Jack walked over to the drawing room and threw the door open. "Well, see for yourself. Whether or not it was Susan or Miss Clavering, the effect is pleasing. You may almost wish to move home."

Christopher looked around the room and up at the ceiling, then gave a slow shake of his head. "Very nice. But, no—I do not wish to move home. Why? Are you worried about me racking up too great a bill at the Hart?"

"Peace, brother. It was not my intention to start a fight." Jack stepped away. "I was just going to see Father."

Christopher shut the door to the drawing room behind him. "I will join you, then. That is why I have come, as it is time for my quarterly allowance, although it pains me to have to remind Father to give his approval to the solicitor. Better he let me deal directly with the man." Christopher stopped short. "What is this I hear in the dining room? Surely it is not Shanks making such a noise! Has he learned to dance?"

Jack laughed at the thought of their aged butler doing anything so unlikely. "No, this was my doing. After such an impressive change in the drawing room, I thought we might improve the dining room as well. After all, we do have one of the more sizable houses in London despite the lack of a ballroom. Shame we never invite anyone to use it." He rapped on his father's door and heard the permission to enter.

Christopher followed behind him. "Are you thinking of entertaining? Things have changed around here then. At whose feet may we lay this extraordinary novelty?"

Jack did not answer. Despite Mr. Whitmore's advice to throw a dinner party, Jack did not think he would have had the courage to attempt it if Miss Clavering had not brought about such a magnificent transformation to their drawing room.

Jack's family came from centuries of affluence, and he sometimes wondered what his ancestors would have thought of the way the fortune had dwindled. The furnishings in their house had only reflected the demise. Miss Clavering had seen the potential and had wasted no time in bringing it about—and all this she accomplished with an economy he could only admire.

Inside the library, their father was sitting in contemplation before the fire. For once, he was not poring over ledgers trying to make ends meet or envisioning a great future from his latest acquisition. He seemed in a listening mood, and Jack thought there was no better time than the present to approach his father with his objective. "Father, I came to talk to you about this dinner party I mean to host."

"Good day, Father," Christopher added with a wry look at his brother before taking a seat in one of the armchairs.

"Yes, Christopher has come," Jack said. "We've settled on the date, and Miss Sommers reminds me that we should hire a temporary use of the mews on Carlisle Street. I am not sure if we need a permit."

"Only for crowds above fifty," Christopher said, surprising Jack with this bit of worldly knowledge.

Jack pressed his lips together in thought. "We are not quite that. But perhaps it would be good to speak to the local magistrate to make him aware of the party, just so everything runs seamlessly."

"Am I invited?" Christopher asked with a half-smile. "I find myself impatient to see how your first attempt at hosting a dinner will be. I assume you have engaged the help of Miss Sommers?"

"No, you're not invited. You won't like it anyway." Jack attempted a smile as though he were joking, but he knew his eccentric brother would not fit in with the other guests. "It's just going to be a dinner with political allies on both sides trying to hash out a reform bill—that *will* pass. You would have nothing to say to the matter."

Their father had been silent until now, and Christopher glanced at him. "Is Father invited?" This was asked in a quiet voice, and Jack heard the taunting in it. He knew it was because he was running the house again as if it were his own.

Jack looked at his father and revised his first thought of his being in a listening mood. Mr. Blythefield seemed more depressed. Jack did not want to ask what had happened to bring out the somber mood. "Our father needs no invitation to an event that is held in his own home. However, Father, I do fear this gathering will be more than you should wish for. I know you are not fond of entertaining. I just came to inquire if we should add a place setting for you."

At these words, his father turned his head and focused on what Jack was saying. "No, you are right. I do not enjoy entertaining, and I do not think I will have anything worth contributing to the discussion. I have no knowledge of this bill you are seeking to pass. I think I will stay in my study."

Jack wanted to sigh with relief. "As you wish. I will see that Cook has a plate sent to you, since the fare is likely to be excellent."

"Why? Because you are paying for it yourself?" Christopher interjected.

Jack was irritated at Christopher's insinuation that whatever the Blythefields had to offer was not enough for his friends. He knew his brother would have preferred that Jack's inheritance had gone to him as the future head of the family. However, Christopher had his own responsibilities, if only he would own them rather than waste his days on foolish pleasures.

All the same, there was some truth to the fact that the Blythefield estate could not cover the costs of an elaborate dinner without the addition of Jack's own fortune. "I want the best of everything. The future of England depends upon it."

Christopher snorted in derision.

Jack walked over to the chimney and turned a log so that it burned more brightly. The sun had hidden behind a cloud, and it made the room chilly. Mr. Blythefield seemed to grow frail as the years went by, and as much as his father often frustrated him, Jack did not wish for anything to happen to him.

Christopher let a small silence go by before speaking. "Father, if you don't mind, I should like to go over my quarterly allowance with you."

At Christopher's words, Jack put another log onto the fire and walked to the door. "I will leave you then. Christopher, don't be such a stranger next time."

Christopher raised his quizzing glass to examine Jack as he opened the door. "Really, brother. I could almost imagine you wished to see me."

"I have only one brother," Jack reminded him, and he left the room. Why was family such a weighted, painful thing? Why could they not be happy and cheerful?

"Jack!" His mother was descending the stairs, carrying two bags of what looked suspiciously like Methodist tracts if the even folds of paper sticking out of it were any indication. "I have just received these from the printer, and I need to carry them to Mrs. Arcot, who is directing this project. Can you accompany me? I am unable to take them by myself."

Jack did not have anything of particular importance to do, since there were no speeches today in Parliament. Despite the opening in his schedule, he was hardly in the mood to escort his mother around the city. "Cannot Andrew do it? I have not needed his service today, so I am sure he is free for other duties."

"Oh…" Mrs. Blythefield seemed to sag under the weight of her tracts. "I suppose I can ask him, but I had hoped you might accompany me. I am going to Covent Garden. He does not yet know the city the way you do, and I don't believe we can leave Shanks alone for that long. He will be tired, poor man."

Jack saw the justice in this. Andrew was their steward's nephew and newly arrived from the country. He could not be expected to find his way around London yet with ease, and Shanks would have difficulty without additional help if anyone came to the door.

"Very well, then. I will take you." He called for Andrew to have the phaeton sent around, and he took the bags from his mother and set them by the front door. When the carriage was brought, he carried the bags outside, and the groom handed the reins to Jack. "Shall I come, sir?"

Jack put the tracts into the carriage and climbed up. "No, it will not be necessary. Help my mother up." The groom did so, and when she was settled, Jack clicked his reins and they moved forward.

The streets were clear, and Jack was able to drive easily through them. They went much of the way in silence, listening to the clip-clop of hooves on the packed road. But when his mother sighed, Jack heard it and thought it sounded plaintive. "You are not often at home, Mother. If you are tired, perhaps you should spend more time resting rather than running about town."

His mother looked down and patted one of the bags that was sitting on her lap. "I could never do that. I am needed. Mrs. Arcot said I was the most important person to this movement, and I cannot abandon her now."

Jack wondered if his mother was needed, or rather if it was his mother's need to feel important that urged her on. "Yes, but you could take a few days to rest and recuperate your strength. What do you have in the coming weeks?"

"Mrs. Arcot's house is on Russell Street just ahead." His mother lifted her face to the sun and closed her eyes. "Just some visits of great importance," she said vaguely.

Jack was not sure he was going to receive any promises from her, so he let it drop. "Mother, do you know the party I told you about that I will host—the political party to be held in our house next week? It will be a somewhat dull conversation about political matters, and Father does not wish to attend. I assume you will not wish to either?"

He phrased the question in such a way that would make it seem beneath her interest and was relieved when her answer came. "No, that is not where I am most useful. My work is in carrying out the reform on the streets rather than talking about it in the dining room." She looked straight ahead and clasped her hands over her bag.

Jack experienced a pang of sadness. His mother had noble ambitions, surely. But she drove herself hard, and he could not imagine her life to be a happy one. Had she been more content when she was newly married?

"Shall I wait for you while you deliver these?" he asked.

"Oh, no. Mrs. Arcot and I will be spending a considerable amount of time discussing how we shall handle the willing converts once we've managed to convince them of a life away from gin. I will take a hackney home when it's time." She picked the other bag up from the floor of the carriage.

Jack had learned better than to ask his mother for more details about her projects. If she grew carried away, the horses would be kept waiting. "Very well. Here, let me hold these for you while you climb down. There. Can you manage?"

"Yes, I will be fine." Jack's mother waved at him, then picked up the two bags and lugged them to Mrs. Arcot's front door. He felt a twinge of remorse for not being more accommodating or helpful to her causes. But truly, a man could not be everywhere at once. And he had his own battles to fight. He clicked the reins, and his horses were off.

Jack turned down Bow Street and kept his horses at a steady trot until he reached the Strand. The sun had reappeared, and, although it was too chilly to feel anywhere close to summer, it was still nice weather. He wished he had some greater purpose than just going back to his house, and he had no desire to go to the club or even to embark on another debate. Despite his home being a vast improvement, there was not much for him there, and he could almost wonder at himself that the idea of marrying and setting up his own home had not occurred to him earlier.

Before turning at Charing Cross, a movement on the side of the street caught Jack's attention, and when he glanced over, he perceived the form of a young woman who looked familiar to him—one who set his heart pumping. He pulled in the reins.

"Miss Clavering," he called out. When she kept walking, he puzzled his brows. She surely must have heard him. "Miss Clavering," he called out again.

At this, she turned, and he was struck by the variety of emotions that could be read on her face. Pale cheeks, full lips pursed, eyes that had just a hint of red in them, but also an expression of defiance that showed she would not accept the defeat of dissolving into tears. She stopped and looked at him. "Mr. Blythefield."

Her voice was hard and sounded unlike her. She had no cloak on, and she was unaccompanied. He could not fathom what she was doing here, or why she was so lightly clad. She must have been freezing. "I regret that I cannot alight to assist you; I have no one to hold the horses. Please—allow me to escort you somewhere."

She hesitated, biting her lip, and it appeared she was trying to gain control over her emotions. After only a slight pause, she came to the carriage. "Very well. I was hasty in leaving my sister's house, and I've no money for a hack, no maid, as you can see"— Miss Clavering gave a brittle laugh—"and not even a cloak. So your arrival just now is providential."

She climbed into his phaeton and, due to the nature of his sporty carriage, was forced to sit close to him. He tried not to focus on her nearness, but on her distress instead. He unbuttoned his cloak with one hand then handed her the reins. "Here. Hold these."

He wrapped his cloak around her then took the reins from her. "Now. Will you tell me what has troubled you?" Jack urged the horses forward again. "And where shall I take you?"

Miss Clavering was silent for a moment. "I suppose my brother Lucius's house. He lives at 5 Whitehall Court."

"That is easy enough," Jack said. He gave her time to answer his first question, but she did not do so right away, and he was forced to prod. "If you are uncomfortable sharing with me what has happened to distress you, I will not press for details. But if I can be of assistance, please know that I am your servant."

Miss Clavering gave another laugh, as if she were one of those steam engines he had once seen, letting out bursts of steam when the pressure became too great. "I am too angry to return a lucid answer or speak rationally, I fear, on any subject. Suffice it to say there are some who think my life is for them to order about. And I do not intend for anyone to make decisions about my life other than me."

A marriage proposal was Jack's first thought. What else would cause an unmarried woman to wish to rebel? *She's being forced into a marriage.* He allowed the noise of other carriages and people on the street to fill the space between them.

"You are right that your life is only for you to decide," Jack said at last. He steered his horses around a corner adorned with a wrought-iron fence, regretting that this particular drive was not a long one. He would not be able to spend more time with Miss Clavering, as he would have liked. "If I may…"

He hesitated, afraid to finish the sentence. He glanced at Miss Clavering, and there was something in her vulnerable expression that pulled his words out of him. "I hope you will see me as your friend—and that you will come to me if you should need anything."

She looked down at her hands clasped on her lap, and when he glanced at her, she swallowed in a way that seemed fragile and unlike the Miss Clavering he had come to know.

"I could use a friend," she said.

Too soon, he had pulled up in front of Sir Lucius's door. "Once again, I offer my apologies that I cannot assist you to alight. But I'll wait and see that you are received at Sir Lucius's house. I will not leave until you've been admitted."

"You are too kind." Miss Clavering sat up and prepared to descend from the carriage.

In guise, he supposed, of a bow, Jack reached for her gloved hand and held it up to his lips. She turned her gaze to his in surprise, their faces inches apart, and he could feel her soft breath on his cheek. There was no confusion or shrinking back. It was as if they had been friends forever—as if he had done the most natural thing in the world and she had responded in kind. Then the spell was broken.

"Good day, Mr. Blythefield. Thank you for rescuing me." Miss Clavering unwound his cloak from around her shoulders and handed it back to him. It now smelled like orange blossoms. She turned and lifted the hem of her skirts as she climbed down, then walked up the stairs and knocked on the front door. In a few minutes, the door was opened and the house swallowed her up.

Jack stayed in place until his horses began to fidget and stamp impatiently. He let out his breath slowly. What kind of pressure was she under, and how could he help? He was practically a stranger, but what he wouldn't give to be able to rescue her. With a shake of his head, he set his horses in motion toward home.

CHAPTER SEVENTEEN

"*I*nform Sir Lucius and Lady Clavering that I am here," Philippa announced when the footman opened the door. The butler hurried out of the morning room at the sound of her voice and told the footman in a rather austere manner that he would take care of announcing young Miss Clavering's presence to her ladyship.

Philippa's emotions had gone from despair to quite the drastic detour when Mr. Blythefield had interrupted her walk. He was the last person she'd expected to see, especially between Maria's house and Lucius's. She associated him with Susan, with social affairs, with glittering balls and all the times when Philippa was at her best. She did not associate him with overwhelming distress.

It had been hard enough to keep her emotions out of the public eye without being offered such heartwarming declarations of friendship as Mr. Blythefield had given her. It was much easier not to think of him at all, particularly after she had seen him dancing with Miss Sommers and knew that the *ton* expected them to make a match of it. Miss Sommers was his equal in grace and elegance and had all the necessary connections to host brilliant parties. Philippa just had youth on her side, as well as an overbearing sister who expected her—quite unreasonably—to do as she was told.

The butler came back presently and said Lady Clavering would be happy to receive her in the nursery. Philippa climbed the stairs to the third floor and entered the room where her sister-in-law was reading. The walls had been painted to look like a sky and someone had done a rather poor imitation of cherubs floating in the clouds that Lucius said resembled 'swaddled potatoes'.

Selena drew her brows together when she saw Philippa. "My dear, something has happened. Briggs said you have not even come with your maid. I know Maria would never permit you to leave like that."

"Maria was not forewarned of my exodus. She was otherwise occupied with cleaning up broken porcelain and, if Mr. Thackery stayed around long enough, with soothing the wounded sensibilities of a rejected suitor."

"Oh my," was all Selena returned in response. For once, baby Hugh was not sitting in her lap but was sleeping peacefully in a cot near the wall. Selena closed the book she had been reading and patted the seat next to her on the sofa. "Make yourself comfortable. How can I help? Shall I have tea sent? It should be ready, for I generally take some at this time."

The invitation was a welcome one. Philippa sat and nodded. "I am cold." She slowly pulled at the silk ribbons from her bonnet.

"Let us take care of you, then." Selena stood and rang for the footman to come, then went over to a trunk and pulled out a blanket. This, she wrapped around Philippa's shoulders.

A lump formed in Philippa's throat, but she dampened the emotion. She had too much to do to put up with tears. "To answer your question, I believe I am more in need of Lucius's help than I am of yours. Except…" She glanced at Selena, assessing her face, which showed nothing but kindness. "Do you think it would be possible to stay here? I should not like to be a burden."

"I shall have to ask Lucius, of course." Selena put her hand on Philippa's arm. "But that is more of a formality. For I shall insist that you stay here. Is Maria causing you problems?"

"Maria is applying such tremendous pressure for me to marry Mr. Thackery, as if she could bring such a thing about when I am unwilling." Philippa spoke the words bitterly but fell silent when the footman entered. Selena gave him the request for the tea to be brought then turned to Philippa.

"No one likes to be forced into a marriage, but is he really so bad?" When Philippa glared at her, Selena put her hands up in defense. "I admit I have heard little of him, but what I *have* heard has been impressive. A handsome man with a fortune, a catch in the Marriage Mart, a rising star in politics. Is this not everything a woman would dream of?"

Philippa looked away, and it was a moment before she could muster the strength to answer. "He is not capable of love, and although he is most assiduous in his attentions now, it will not last once I accept his proposal and there is no more sport. He says he loves me, but I can see his true nature. His eyes change in an instant as soon as one thwarts him." Philippa gave a grim smile. "And heaven only knows that I would be forever doing *that*."

Selena laughed. "It is what I like best about you. But I suppose you will need a husband whose pride is not too great to tolerate such a tendency."

"And that is not he." Philippa absently braided the fringe of the red wool blanket draped over her. "But Maria applies such pressure she practically insists I marry him and has gone so far as to accept him on my behalf. I gave an unequivocal no to Mr. Thackery just now and left before anything further could be said. I needed to make it clear, but I also require someone with authority to take up my cause."

"Your mother?" Selena proffered.

Philippa shook her head firmly. "No, not her. You must see she has not the capacity to invest in anything that infringes upon her comfort. George had promised to be my champion, but he does not stay with Maria, and he has not come as often as he'd promised. Apparently, one of his friends was injured, and George is spending all of his time with him. Of course, I shall take him to task the next time I see him, but I believe only Lucius will do. I need his help."

Selena nodded. "And you shall have it." She looked up when the footman arrived, carrying the platter with tea and lemon cakes and gestured for him to put it on the low table in front of them. He set the tea down and left.

"Lucius is expected home in an hour. We shall lay the case before him. No—" Selena bit her lip. "*I* shall speak to him first, and I will tell him exactly what I want, which is for you to stay with us, and then we will meet him together. Now, let me prepare you a cup of tea. Then I will have a maid ready a room for you, where you can wash up or rest—whatever you need. I will send somebody for your clothes, for you are too petite to fit into anything of mine."

"I am sure we will have to wrestle them out of Maria's grasping fingers." Philippa accepted the cup gratefully and took a sip. The warm, sweet tea did much to restore her hope. "She will say she bought the clothes, which is not far from the truth. Perhaps she will not allow me to have them."

"*Hm.*" Selena pursed her lips as she sipped the tea, a smile lurking in her eyes. "I shall simply send a nice note around, requesting that the trunk of clothes be made up, and if Maria should desire my assistance, I will be happy to oblige. She need only tell me when it is convenient and I will come. Anything to avoid me darkening her doorstep should do the trick."

Philippa laughed, and some of the tea spurted through her lips in a most unladylike manner. The corner of Selena's mouth curled up, and she handed Philippa a napkin.

Selena was being so kind, but after the brief spell of amusement, Philippa's spirits sank again. She had not planned on burdening Lucius and Selena with her presence while they were in London. They had their baby to care for and surely did not wish for a little sister to hinder their lives. But she was desperate enough to hope Lucius would say yes.

***

A maid came to her room to summon Philippa at the end of the afternoon, and she found Lucius and Selena sitting in the drawing room before a small fire. Lucius had a white cloth thrown over his coat and was holding his son up to his chest. Philippa wanted to tease him about presenting such a paternal picture but did not dare. Marriage had brought a positive change over him, and there was no need to remind him of what he had been before.

"Come in. Have a seat." Lucius directed her to a chair. His tone was kind rather than admonitory, so Philippa did not think she was about to be scolded or thrown out. She also had confidence in what Selena could accomplish where Lucius was concerned.

"Maria is pestering you to marry Mr. Thackery, is she? I had thought the matter quite settled last Season when you declared yourself determined not to have him." Lucius narrowed his eyes, but Philippa did not sense the irritation directed toward herself.

"You only had my opinion on the matter through my letters." Having taken a small nap, Philippa was rested and less distraught than she had been when she arrived. But the memory of the whole affair threatened to darken her mood. "It was apparently not settled in Maria's mind, nor in Mr. Thackery's. The assault began almost as soon as I arrived in London."

Lucius shared a glance with Selena, and Philippa wondered if he was remembering how Maria had tried to keep her brother and Selena apart. Perhaps so, for his next words gave her courage. "Well, it will not do. And I shall have something to say to that."

"I wish you would. It is not just Maria, although she is the messenger. It's Charles. I believe he hopes to gain more influence by boasting of a relationship through marriage with a man who drives Parliament. Nothing can get Maria or him to see it any other way." Philippa kept her eyes trained on Lucius. He was her only hope, but she trusted him.

He began a small bouncing movement with Hugh who gave off a lusty burp. Lucius raised his brows. "Not bad, little fellow." He transferred his gaze to Philippa. "Of course you may stay here. I will not have my little sister bullied by Maria or Charles about whom she should marry. Why did you not come to me before?"

A sudden surge of tears threatened to overcome Philippa again, and she swallowed quickly. She'd thought she had mastered all desire for tears.

"I thought I could manage it, but I did not realize how far Maria would go in her aim. I was able to bear the hints, the threats, and even the tedious parties where she continually threw me in Mr. Thackery's path when I would rather have been anywhere else." Philippa lifted her head and found her brother looking at her in concern.

"I truly thought if I made it clear I would under no circumstances marry Mr. Thackery, she would see how futile it was to insist. But Maria is so stubborn she promised me to him against my will. She seems to think that with a little pressure on her side, I will see reason."

Lucius let out a wry chuckle. "Maria is not well acquainted with reason."

Selena stood and tucked a fresh cloth under their contented baby's chin, then kissed Lucius's cheek. "Let us discuss how you might enjoy the remainder of the Season, Philippa. I make a very poor chaperone. Even if I could leave Hugh to accompany you, my presence would not exactly endear you to the Society matrons."

Lucius scowled her way. "If anybody has anything to say to my wife, I will make sure it is said to me—and not repeated."

"As much as I am thankful to have a champion in my quarter, I do not wish to take on Society." Selena smiled at him fondly. "I just wish to raise children and be a wife."

Philippa stared out the window at the darkening sky and longed for something unnamed. Perhaps it was that brief connection she'd shared with Mr. Blythefield. It was as if her heart presented him to her mind in just such a cozy context. It was the first time she could imagine saying similar words about another person. What a strange thing, too, because they were scarcely acquainted. All they had done was to bicker and bandy about words. That was—until today, when he had declared himself her friend.

There was a knock on the door, and Philippa's heart leapt. It was completely irrational, but she hoped it might be Mr. Blythefield. Briggs entered.

"Mrs. Maria Holbeck."

Lucius shared a look with Philippa. Maria bustled into the room, speaking before she had fully entered. "I told Briggs to bring Philippa's trunk up to the room where she is staying, although I don't know why she should stay here with you. Mother left her in my charge."

"Mother did not leave Philippa in your charge to compel her into a forced marriage. She is not without protectors, Maria. How could you attempt something so harebrained?"

Maria took immediate umbrage to his words. "I most certainly do have the authority to arrange such things for her. Mother wrote me a letter, which you can see for yourself right here. I've brought it with me." She attempted to pull it out of her reticule, but Lucius stopped her by raising a weary hand.

"Enough. It does not matter what Mother said. She may have left Philippa in your care, but I am head of the Clavering household. I tell you now that our sister will not marry Mr. Thackery—or anyone else she does not wish to marry."

Philippa stayed very still so as not to attract notice to herself. Despite Lucius's position as head of the household, she had an irrational fear that somehow Maria would win and her future would be decided. The sooner her sister left—and without her—the better.

Maria appeared to be wrestling with the impotence of having the control whisked away from her for she sucked in a breath, attempting to calm her agitation. "Lucius, you are holding the baby wrong. He would be better suited cradled in your arms rather than against your chest."

Philippa thought Lucius handled his sister with great forbearance, considering his sister had never been able to become a mother and had no idea how to hold the baby.

"I am very sure you are right, but he is comfortable for now." Lucius looked down at Hugh with infinite tenderness. "I still will not give you permission to marry off Philippa."

"Charles will be most displeased, and you do not want to cross him. He is a man with a formidable career ahead of him. And he knows better than you ever could—because you refuse to enter into politics—what a man of influence Mr. Thackery is. Philippa has a brilliant future ahead of her if she would only align herself to him. I cannot imagine you would not want that for her."

"No, Maria. I don't want that for her, and if Charles wishes to express his discontent—have him come himself." Lucius gave a weary sigh and handed Hugh into the arms of his mother. He then leaned forward.

"I want Philippa to enter into a love match if that is what she should wish for. I am sorry if this is beyond your comprehension, but I tell you now that Mr. Thackery's suit has been declined. Philippa will be staying here, where she is free to receive or reject whichever suitor should happen to make her the object of his attention. If you are very cordial, Maria, I will ensure that she does not go the rest of the Season without seeing you. Sisters should never be separated, especially when bound with ties so dear." Lucius pronounced these last words with his heaviest irony.

"Well." Maria stood, her jaw clenched. "I will not stay for tea. Charles will be expecting me. How unfortunate that you have chosen this path, Philippa. Do not expect me to console you when at last you realize what you have lost."

Maria picked up her cloak and whirled around to leave. She grasped the doorknob, but it opened before she could exit. George walked in, his eyebrows raised in surprise when he caught sight of her. Maria took one glance at him and huffed before exiting without saying a word.

George swiveled to look at her with a blank expression, then glanced at the party seated in the drawing room. "What did I miss?"

Philippa leaned back into the sofa. It was over, and she was safe. This was good news, and yet ... she could not explain to herself why she still felt so empty.

CHAPTER EIGHTEEN

*J*ack arrived at Westminster just before two o'clock—his mind, for once, not on the business and debates that lay before him. *It should be*, he tried to admonish himself, but his thoughts had drifted again and again to Miss Clavering, and he felt as though he could not rest until he knew how she was. He had not seen her in three days. And although he was beginning to know Sir Lucius somewhat better through their joint committee, they had not met this week and Jack could not presume to go to his house unannounced. Of course, just when he *wished* to see Miss Clavering was precisely when she was not making those almost daily visits to Susan.

It was time to focus on business. Jack needed no reminder that he had his work cut out for him. He needed to show the more senior Whigs he was able to lead the party by pulling enough weight to his side for reform. Mr. Whitmore the elder had impressed upon him how intrinsically linked the position and the bill's success were. If Jack could not gather enough votes—from both political parties—to show how essential repealing the Corn Laws was to the English government, he would have difficulty proving to anyone he was fit to be Leader of the Opposition.

Despite his long-held ambition, it seemed a new dream was edging into his old one, and it was taking over his thoughts: the idea of having a wife beyond a compliant woman who stayed at home, bore heirs, and possessed no opinion. Jack had not been able to rid himself of the image of Miss Clavering when he had come upon her that afternoon. He had not thought to see such distress on a face that was usually filled with mischief, plans, delight—a face that was ... completely desirable.

How Jack longed to have the right to remove her from her source of distress, but he had no right at all. He did not even have the right to know what it was. He could no longer deny to himself that he felt none of the passion with Miss Sommers that he felt with Miss Clavering. Miss Sommers was admirable; she would look fine on the arm of a politician, but she did not stir his soul. And Jack was beginning to realize that Miss Clavering did.

A realization was not enough, though. He needed to begin pursuing her—to find out if she felt the same. He had some small hope that Mr. Thackery had not harmed her in any way if she *had* had feelings for him, though Jack suspected she did not. Her eyes did not rest on Mr. Thackery or follow him around the room when they were together. And without wishing to give over to pride, Jack thought that when Miss Clavering looked at *him,* she did feel something.

Could he imagine her in his life? *Yes!* She loved his sister. She made no disparaging comments about his mother, though she knew his mother's charity bordered on folly. She reminded him of his father's proper place as head of the household, something Jack had slowly been losing sight of over the years. His father, once a source of fun, gentle guidance and a fount of useful information, had become a person Jack had begun to regard as foolish. But he did not wish to behave so abominably to his own father, and Miss Clavering was helping him see that. She seemed to fit so naturally at his side. Miss Clavering was wholly unfazed by his eccentric family.

He wondered when he might be permitted to call her Philippa.

"Jack, here you are." Mr. Whitmore motioned to him from outside the Parliament chamber, and Jack came at once. "There are some men I want you to meet, who are seated at the corner table there. Their boroughs in Manchester and Yorkshire don't carry as much weight as the counties with more seats. However, as small in number as they might be, they are sympathetic to the cause."

"Of course, sir. I must say I have not succeeded in gaining quite the number of votes for repeal that I had hoped. Mr. Cummings and Lord Bailey are not to be persuaded. But I am hoping my dinner will fix the interests of those who are wavering. If some of the more influential landowners see what it is to allow for free trade, they might convince some of the others that having a healthy England will be—even in the short run—more prosperous for our country than protecting the interests of few."

"It is a fine thing that you organized this party. To own the truth, I was not sure you would follow through." Mr. Whitmore gave him a knowing grin. "And if the stories I hear are true, Lord Palmer will be attending as well."

This was a gratifying win for Jack. "Yes, I received his acceptance two days ago. He will add to the consequence of the dinner, and those who are on the fence must surely be brought over."

"Fine job." Mr. Whitmore put his hand on Jack's arm and led him to a table where two men sat. "Here let me introduce you to Mr. Gibson and Mr. Atkinson, whom I have told you about. They are ready to discuss the bill. Mr. Atkinson is in London with his wife, whom I've heard is the real enthusiast behind repealing the bill."

On leaving Westminster, Jack felt more hopeful than he had done in a while. The two members that had arrived were both Tories, but they were clearly keen on reform. This gave him hope that his deep desire would be realized—a majority vote to abolish the Corn Laws and an appointment to the lead position in his party by having been the man to bring it about. With any luck, the more intimate and informal dinner at his house would be the trick to prompt such a result.

***

The next day, Jack returned home from a few hours at the club, where he had gone early enough to drink his coffee and read in peace. It was quickly dawning on him that he needed to set up his own establishment if he were going to have peace at home. Whether it was his sister or mother needing someone to escort them or his father wishing to discuss investments, the Blythefield house was too chaotic to be a refuge.

As had become his custom, Jack went first into the dining room to see how the refurbishments he had ordered were progressing. The rug, curtains, and sideboard had been replaced, and even the table had been polished. Someone—*Miss Clavering?*—had changed the dusty centerpiece to something they'd had stashed away in the library: an orange Ming Dynasty vase that had scroll handles on each side and was filled with dried Cape gooseberry. At the windows beyond, white draperies hung—

parted and held with tassels—and sheer curtains underneath hid the view of the buildings behind. The room was light and airy.

He crossed over to the drawing room and knew from the sounds within, as soon as he put his hand on the doorknob, that Miss Clavering was there. *Philippa*. He tasted her Christian name silently on his lips.

Jack opened the door, unsure of what he would find inside. Would she still be tear-stained or would she be glad? Perhaps glad to see him? He stepped into the room, and Philippa turned a smiling face to him. At the sight of it, something in him relaxed.

Jack stepped forward and bowed deeply before her, joy springing him back upright again. "Miss Clavering, how happy I am to see you here. I hope you are settled?" He glanced at his sister, unsure how much she knew about Philippa's distress.

She answered his unspoken question. "Yes, Susan is aware that my sister and I have had something of a falling out. I am now residing in my brother Lucius's house. And I must say, I am happier for it. Susan has shown me the dining room." She arched a brow. "Well done, Mr. Blythefield."

Jack's emotions tumbled together. On one hand, he was gratified by her praise—it was worth more than the praise of anyone else. On the other hand, it grated to hear her call him Mr. Blythefield when he had already begun calling her Philippa in his head. It planted a seed of doubt that she did not share the same attachment.

Then again, she could hardly call him Jack without them having reached an agreement.

"Jack, the dining room really is lovely. I was so proud to show it to Philippa. Think how fine it will be for the dinner you are to host." Susan got to her feet and walked over to arrange one of the curtains, which had been snagged on the chair near the window, marring its smooth fall.

Jack clasped his hands behind his back and turned to Philippa. "Yes, indeed. As I alluded to in Hyde Park, I was inspired to host a dinner to try to bring about the votes that are more elusive in the formal setting of Parliament. Now that the drawing room is done, and the dining room with it, I dare attempt it."

Philippa was about to respond, but Susan gave a small gasp and headed for the door. "I'd nearly forgotten. Will you please excuse me? I must speak to the cook about dinner tonight or we will not have it on time." She left the room.

"Your sister seems to do the work of matron of the house at times. Who will be the hostess at your dinner?"

Jack walked over and took the closest chair to her he could without risking impropriety. He wanted to be next to her but did not wish to force upon her an unwelcome advance or embarrass her should anyone enter the room.

"I have not quite decided. I must say I have no experience in the matter of hosting a dinner, but Miss Sommers has been helping me. She is well-versed in such matters. It would not be proper for her to play the role of hostess, as she is unrelated, but she is willing to share her knowledge."

Philippa's gaze on him was unnerving. She seemed to want to ask what he wished he could blurt out. *Miss Sommers means nothing to me.* Of course, she could not ask and he could not answer. At last, Philippa dropped her gaze. "Should you not have your mother act as hostess? It seems the most fitting choice since you are unmarried."

Jack could not entirely hide his horror at the thought. He opened his mouth to speak, but then … how did one actually say there was no way his mother could possibly be an appropriate choice for hostess? He could not explain it. Philippa was waiting for an answer, so he needed to try.

"I am not sure about the suitability of my mother in this role. She has ideas that are not common to Society. The party I'm hosting is one that requires finesse, for it is bringing men of vastly different views together to try to get them to agree on this one crucial bill. I cannot risk anything going amiss at this dinner, for it would kill the motion before it even made it to the vote."

Philippa clasped her fingers together and knit her brows. "I do understand your reticence on the matter. But surely your mother can be brought to understand the importance of this issue and respond in the manner you should require?"

This seemed unanswerable, and as Philippa looked as though she wished to say more, Jack waited. "But I am generally too forthcoming with my views. I am sure you know what is best. Have you then considered Susan for the role?"

Jack was beginning to feel as though the walls were closing in, and he was stuck in some sort of trap. It was not the kind of sensation he had when he was getting unwelcome lures cast out from a young woman, or from her mother. Rather, it was the feeling that he was being asked to do something he knew was correct but didn't dare. Philippa deserved a truthful response.

"I fear Susan is too silly for such a role." He flicked a glance at Philippa to see how she took the news and when she frowned, rushed to explain himself. "I love her dearly. I love my mother—my whole family. But sometimes I think they are not the Blythefield face I want to put forward to Society. Not if I wish to achieve my ambition."

Jack stood suddenly, struck by the sense of selfishness and arrogance he was portraying to a woman he had hoped might form a good opinion of him. "I know my words, unfiltered as they are, must make you think me odious. It can be a struggle to carry the weight of the family alone. I also realize I am speaking to you with more familiarity than I should."

"I do not mind it. In fact, I like this side of you." Philippa laughed, and her cheeks had spots of pink. "This informal side."

Emboldened, Jack came and sat on the sofa with her. "And I confess that winning your good opinion has become an object with me."

Philippa did not pull away—a good sign—and settled her gaze on him. "In that case, allow me to say that Susan has a good heart. In fact, she has one of the purest hearts I know. I do not think she will embarrass you at your party, especially if you give her instructions on exactly what you need from her. And I believe the joy you'll give her by asking her to play hostess will do much for her confidence."

Jack wished to recapture the closeness they'd had in the phaeton. This sofa was much too large. "Yes, I think you are right. I am being made aware of my faults in not having declared a hostess before now. I suppose, as long as Miss Sommers was lending a hand, I was not too focused on the omission. I will have no choice but to ask Susan, for I have no other option."

"I know you said your mother would not do for the role. But does she want it?"

Jack shook his head. "She will not come to the dinner. I asked her, and she declined attending. She said her reforms on the streets are more important to her than any reform I could make in Parliament."

Jack could have stared at Philippa's face all day. Her eyes were so clear, and they crinkled when she found something funny. Her teeth were like pearls when she opened her mouth to speak. And her frame was so petite—not delicate, but compact. The kind of person you wanted to draw in your arms. How had he not noticed from the first time he'd met her that she was not merely pleasing to the eye—she was a dewdrop of perfection?

He had forgotten the train of their conversation.

"I can understand why she might say this. Most women need a purpose in life, and from what I understand, your mother has one. That brings her the satisfaction she needs. At least, in part." At these bright words, Philippa smiled at Jack, then looked at the clock on the mantle. "I believe I should be going home, for it is getting late."

Philippa stood, and Jack shot to his feet. They faced one another, and she seemed as reluctant to go as he was to let her. He kept his arms firmly at his side to resist doing something completely inappropriate, like taking her in his arms.

"Mr. Blythefield, upon meeting you, I had thought you cold—devoid of passion."

"Did you?" One arm lifted of its own accord, and he reached for her hand. When she gave it, he held on. "And what do you think of me now?"

"*Mm.*" Philippa lifted smiling eyes to his. "The verdict is out. Sometimes I think I see a glimpse of a warmer nature underneath the glacial exterior, but it is well buried."

Though she teased, an urgency coursed through Jack to convince her that a warmer heart beat underneath his reserve. "I am not cold."

His voice was gruff, and he cleared his throat, the feelings that had been building inside of him wrenching the words out of his lips before he was fully ready. "Call me Jack. Please."

Philippa's eyes grew wide. "I... I could do so, I suppose. I just—"

The door opened, and Susan reentered. Jack released Philippa's hand and breathed through his nose. If only his sister could have had better timing.

Philippa pulled away before his sister could notice they had been standing so close. "My dear Susan, I must go. But I promise to visit again soon. Was Fernsby in the kitchen?"

"Must you leave already? Yes, Fernsby was sitting with Cook. I'll send Andrew down to fetch her."

Susan opened the door to the corridor but remained visible as she gave the footman instructions to fetch Philippa's maid. Jack could not finish the conversation, or see how Philippa felt. If he had been too forward, or if she was pleased. Would she call him Jack?

With Susan watching, he bowed before Philippa, and she curtsied back. Then she turned to go. It was only after she had taken leave of Susan and had left that he realized he had not yet gained permission of the use of *her* Christian name.

CHAPTER NINETEEN

*P*hilippa sat in peaceful silence with her sister-in-law and nephew. Susan had sent a note around that morning saying Jack had asked her to serve as hostess for his dinner. Of course, Miss Sommers would be there, and she would really be directing things. But Susan would be the *face* as hostess for the dinner, and she was overcome with the honor.

Philippa had confidence in her friend but knew that Susan could easily fall prey to self-doubt and that this would be a challenge for her. She knew how to run her own house, but could she welcome distinguished political figures in a way that set her brother to advantage? Would she be able to keep her emotions secret from Mr. Merrick? What role *exactly* did Miss Sommers have in the affair—in Jack's heart?

She didn't think that Miss Sommers truly had a claim on Jack's heart. Not after he gave Philippa the use of his Christian name ... She froze at the memory. Her heart chugged back to life at the thought of his nearness, the way he'd held on to her hand, the intensity in his voice. No, she no longer thought him cold.

Lucius entered the nursery and leaned down to kiss Selena, who was feeding the baby. He tossed an invitation on to the seat next to her. "My lady, we are invited to a political dinner party."

In between the daydreams that crept over Philippa, she was setting stitches on her embroidery, which had been brought over in the trunk with her dresses. She did not mind embroidery so very much, as long as she had other more exciting occupations to break up the pastime. That had not been the case at Maria's house.

She quirked a brow at her brother. "Attending a political dinner? Lucius, I hardly know you. I find it hard to credit that you are not working to gain a seat with all this industry you have displayed."

"Mills has the seat in my county, and he is welcome to it. As I said, I have a personal interest in abolishing the Corn Laws and can lend my aid in convincing the other MPs." Lucius sat across from Selena and threw one foot over his other leg, letting the tassel on his boot dangle. "I have worked over the figures, and without restrictions on free trade, landowners will be able to sell in manufacturing towns, as well as locally. With the larger market share, they should earn more than they are currently. Right now, the price of grain is too high and the workers in manufacturing towns can't afford to buy bread. It is my goal to prove it if I can, although I must say, I am not as confident as Blythefield that such a thing is easily done."

Philippa turned her face down to her stitches when she heard Jack's name, fearing the blush that accompanied her beating heart would give her away.

Lucius glanced fondly at his wife. "But we will return to Mardley whether or not the new bill is successful. They will have my views and can take it or leave it. I won't have you sitting here, my dear, when you and Hugh can be breathing the fresh air at our estate."

Selena beamed at him and patted the back of her baby gently.

"This dinner might be tedious for the women, but Blythefield was right to invite them. It lends a different, more intimate note than a political debate between men in the Commons. With the right ambiance, we shall win over some of the here-and-there-ians, who vote less on principle and more on who is likely to perform them a service. Shall you accompany me, my dear? It's tomorrow night."

"With such delights as you've described, how can I refuse?" Selena's laughing eyes, directed at Lucius, turned pensive. After a moment, she said, "Can you go without me? It is not that I wish to be parted from you, but if Hugh should be hungry while I'm gone..."

"There is a wet nurse should you need it, as I keep reminding you. But I understand that you should not wish for your son to go hungry." Lucius met Philippa's gaze with a grin that held both mock exasperation and pride.

"Nor should I wish for him to cry without me here to tend to him," Selena added, then kissed Hugh, whose eyes were wide open and his unblinking gaze fixed on his mother. "Why not take Philippa with you? I am not able to accompany her to as many events as she might like. Everybody adores Philippa and will be glad to meet her in company, rather than resigning themselves to her sister-in-law instead, who can make no other conversation beyond how well her son eats. Philippa lights up every event she attends and needs to be seen much more. Besides, the Blythefields are particular friends of yours, are they not?"

Philippa suddenly became aware of her heart when Selena directed the question to her. She would be interested in a dinner where women were invited in some degree into a political discussion, but that such a dinner was in Jack's home complicated the matter. He had not precisely invited her that day in the park. It was only when everyone else had talked of going that he did so. Would he not have extended her an official invitation if he thought her presence essential?

"Would Maria be there?" she asked.

"I doubt it," Lucius answered. "Holbeck is staunch in his position, and if Blythefield is smart, he will only invite the more moderate MPs who can be persuaded."

"And Mr. Thackery?" She did not trust her hands to be steady when she waited for the answer, so she lay the embroidery frame on her lap.

Lucius tightened his lips and shrugged. "I do not know all who have been invited, but I imagine he will be there because he acts as the whip for the Tories. But you can be sure of one thing. He will not speak two words to you or I shall have something to say to him."

Philippa weighed the consequences. She hoped her heart did not deceive her when she thought Jack might like to have her come. She transferred her gaze from Lucius to Selena. "Yes, Susan is a particular friend of mine, and she has told me she will act as hostess for the party."

Selena had been feeling for wet on the cloth under the baby, but she looked up at this. "Susan? Is she not young? It seems odd to me that Mr. Blythefield—he is not engaged, I believe—that he should not request his mother to act as hostess. It is a large role for a girl as young as Susan to assume."

As Lucius was busy inspecting the baby's wraps and ringing for Nurse, Philippa was not pressed to answer right away. She did not wish to betray the disclosures Jack had made to her concerning his family and the shame he'd felt over them. When Nurse had come and taken Hugh away to be changed, Selena turned a questioning gaze to Philippa.

"Mrs. Blythefield is interested in social reform more than politics. I believe she thought herself unsuited to hosting her son's party."

Lucius got up and poured himself a finger of brandy. "So, my wife will not come with me, and I am left escorting my younger sister to a party. Nothing throws the final shovelful of dirt on the coffin of my bachelorhood than such a prospect as this."

"I believe your bachelorhood died when you married, Lucius," Philippa replied in a dry tone.

He sat and gave such a long-suffering look that Selena laughed. "Poor dear. It is a hard trial to bear—you who were once such a catch." She winked and pulled a reluctant grin out of him.

Philippa would go, though the prospect unnerved her, most particularly at the thought of meeting Mr. Thackery. She also had a fluttering sort of nervousness about seeing Jack again, but that was something she needed to bury deep until she could sort out what it meant.

"I shall attend with you if you wish it. I am surprised you are only receiving the invitation now. I am to understand the dinner has been prepared for many weeks."

"Yes, and I have been remiss." Lucius swallowed the rest of his drink. "I had forgotten about the invitation until Blythefield approached me at our meeting to ask whether or not I was coming. I told him I undoubtedly would and that I would be bringing my wife. He will not mind if it is my sister instead."

Philippa hoped that was true. The memory of her brief moment with Jack in his drawing room was an elusive thing. When she had closed her eyes that same night, his face loomed large in her vision. In the cold light of day, she feared it had not happened exactly as she'd remembered it. "Do you think it will accomplish what he hopes?"

Lucius shrugged. "I do not know, but I must go. He mentioned Lord Palmer and one or two other significant people who had been invited. This dinner will be no small affair. What size is Blythefield's house?"

Philippa set her embroidery down. "Oh, rather large. It has the drawing room and dining room on the ground floor. It's bigger than the Holbecks' house. They will be able to fit forty at the dinner table, I believe."

"As many as that?" Lucius gave a soft whistle. "I had not been given to understand that Mr. Blythefield had more than modest means."

"From what I understand—although this is only from things Susan has said—Mr. Blythefield has a separate estate, which would make such a dinner possible. And although the family estate was once grand—and the townhouse with it—it is debt-ridden and not kept up. Susan said the Blythefield estate is little more than a shell of what it once was."

"I suppose I shall see it for myself tomorrow. I'll be out most of the day, but see that you are ready for me at seven o'clock," Lucius warned Philippa. "Being married to a woman who is more prompt than most of her sex has spoilt me. I won't be kept kicking my heels."

"Fear not, Lucius. I have nothing planned tomorrow that will hinder me," Philippa returned.

Lucius and Selena entered into a conversation about one of their servants who was expecting a baby and needed to be replaced, and Philippa was left alone again with her thoughts. Selena and Lucius never let her feel unwanted, but Philippa did entertain some doubts about how welcome her presence could be when they had more important things to think about. Rarely did she let herself dwell on the horrifying marriage proposal she had received a week ago—and at the hands of her own sister! But now she was going to have to face the man once again.

Philippa drew in a deep, fortifying breath.

***

"Phew!" The next day, Selena leaned back against the sofa as another young gentleman left after having come to call upon Philippa. He had followed on the heels of Mrs. Yardmouth and her daughters and had left at the same time. The drawing room was now empty. "I guess the *ton* knows you are living here now. I am not sure my parents' drawing room was half as busy when I was out in Society."

Philippa could only be pleased at the attention, especially without Maria here to spoil it. When she'd come out under the auspices of her sister last year, Philippa had thought the Season would always be full of gaiety such as it was now. And last year, it had been to some degree.

In hindsight, she now understood that Maria had been making an extraordinary effort to launch Philippa for her first Season. However, when Philippa refused two suitors that Maria had found perfectly acceptable, and this year threatened to dissuade Mr. Thackery, Maria had thrown up her hands. Unless there was a particular gentleman that Maria was interested in for Philippa, she allowed her sister to attend only the events that Maria wished to attend. As Maria did not necessarily endear herself to anyone, nor was she at home to any but a very few callers—certainly none that Philippa liked—Philippa's two months in her household had been dull to the point of despair.

Despite Sir Lucius's gruff manner and Selena's complicated past, which, combined, should scare off all but the most determined visitors, there had been a steady stream of callers at the Clavering residence. Matrons came with their daughters, who had exchanged a few words with Philippa at various events, and young men came to pay her court. It was most gratifying.

"I am sorry to bring you so much trouble, Selena. But I must say I have not had so much fun since I first entered Society last year and was too naive to know it could not last with Maria. You do not mind so very much?" Philippa frowned, worried that her sister-in-law might become worn out.

Selena sat upright and cleaned a spot of tea that had spilled on the platter. "Do not fret. It is good for me to remember what it was like to be in Society, and the people who are visiting you are very pleasant. I suppose I cannot hide forever."

"No." Philippa grinned at her. "You are much too charming to hide away—and much too young. Furthermore, your children will one day need to make their own debut in Society—not Hugh, of course. But should you have daughters, you will need connections in London to be able to launch them."

"Do you know, I had not thought of that." Selena looked up. Their conversation was interrupted by the butler, who stepped into the room. They had not heard the knock on the front door.

"A Mr. Lloyd to see you," he announced.

Philippa's gaze flew to Selena's in horror. "Oh, no. I cannot. He is deathly boring. We must not admit him."

"Dearest, we could hardly turn him away. He must have seen the last visitors leaving our house. We cannot say we are not at home to visitors." Selena turned to Briggs. "Show Mr. Lloyd in. But do not feel any need to rush in doing so."

Philippa leaned back against the sofa and groaned. "Now—only *now* do I see the benefit of having spent the Season with Maria. She was too unfriendly for anyone to visit. I am almost tempted to move back there."

Selena laughed. "Such cowardice. I had thought you had more gumption than that." She leaned in with a loud whisper. "Daunted by a mere suitor who happens to be a not-very-great favorite."

Philippa gave Selena a side glance. "You have not met Mr. Lloyd," she grumbled.

Mr. Lloyd was shown into the room, and he bowed deeply—first before Selena. "Lady Clavering. Please allow me to humbly express my gratitude for accepting my visit today. Although we are not yet acquainted, I am hoping this afternoon's visit will remedy that." Mr. Lloyd stood upright, but not until he had grasped Selena's hand and held it, giving her a fulsome gaze.

He then stood before Philippa. Behind him, Selena met her look with wide-eyed mirth. "Miss Clavering, I am at last able to fulfill my heart's desire and visit you. Whenever I attempted to do so at the Holbeck residence, I was always told that the family was not at home to visitors. I was beginning to fear I was unwelcome."

"N—no," Philippa managed. It was nothing short of the truth, but she could not say such a thing.

Selena stepped in. "Mr. Lloyd, won't you please sit down? The pot of tea is still hot. Shall I make you a cup?"

Philippa glared at Selena, trying to impress upon her through a look not to do such a thing or he would never leave. Selena returned a bland smile.

"That would be very kind of you." Mr. Lloyd sat and took the cup she offered. He set it on the table next to him and made a steeple with his fingers, which he opened and closed in contemplation while Selena and Philippa waited for him to speak. "I do not know if you have been in the habit of visiting London's most impressive sights, Miss Clavering."

Every time Mr. Lloyd broached a new topic of conversation, Philippa could never guess in advance what it might be. This did not add to the delight of his conversation, for it was always ponderous and said in such a way that convinced her he had prepared his speech. Any sense of compassion she might feel for someone who was so awkward was rapidly dispelled when his discourse turned into a monologue that was impossible to interrupt.

She shook her head, and he appeared gratified to hear it. "Well. I have brought a guidebook on London's sights—not that I do not know quite a bit about the subject already, but there are those smaller details, you know, the more elusive ones that delight the hearer. You, Miss Clavering, are not from the City, as I am, and I believe you should see all the famous sights in order to be well informed for such topics of conversation that come up in polite Society."

He patted the book he had been holding discreetly in one hand. "I've taken the liberty in the time that I was unable to visit you to reacquaint myself with every significant sight mentioned in the book. And I have jotted down some notes about each place with facts and figures that should enthrall, in hopes that I might persuade you—that is…"

Here Mr. Lloyd looked at her, and his glance made it evident that enthusiastic approval of his suggestion was the only proper reaction. "I've made arrangements for us to be able to visit them all, beginning tomorrow. As there is no event I'm aware of this evening that might fatigue you as one of the gentler sex, and thereby postpone our mission, I am sure you will be well-rested to begin our adventure tomorrow."

"Excuse me." Selena stood and turned suddenly toward the desk, keeping her back toward Philippa and their visitor. "I just remembered I have something I must…" Her voice came out breathlessly, but Philippa detected the tremor of laughter in it.

How dare Selena abandon her?

Fortunately, as Philippa's ability to contain her ire was rapidly dissipating, a dull thud was heard on the front door, which was opened immediately, and was followed by the sound of George's voice. There were other voices she recognized as well, and her shoulders began to relax as she discerned who they were.

Mr. Lloyd turned in his seat, his back stiff, frowning at the noise that was interrupting his proposed plans. The door opened, and her brother stepped in, hair windblown and eyes bright from the outdoors.

"Afternoon, Selena. Philippa. I've brought my friends to bear you company. Well, not Duck, of course. He will be laid up for another month the doctor says—and even then only walking with a cane. But Amos, Evans, and Robert are all here. I knew you would wish to see them."

The three gentlemen came in and bowed before Selena and Philippa. George greeted Mr. Lloyd in a more subdued tone, then turned back to Philippa and grinned. She shot him a scolding look.

The men sat down, and Selena, having composed herself enough to return to their circle, saw that each of them was comfortably settled. George and the three newest visitors took up all the remaining seats in the circle, talking without cease so that Mr. Lloyd was no longer able to get a word in edgewise.

"Lady Clavering," Robert Whitmore said, after Selena had handed him a cup of tea. "I believe you will be attending, if I'm not mistaken, the dinner party held by Mr. Blythefield? I saw your name and Sir Lucius's on the list. Mr. Blythefield apparently decided the party would be more of a success if the ladies were invited, and I'm inclined to agree."

Selena sat and tucked her satin-slippered feet under the chair. "I was invited, but Sir Lucius and I decided I will not attend. Philippa will go in my place."

"You don't say." Whitmore eyed Philippa. "You always seem glum when Mrs. Holbeck brings you to political parties. You don't think this will be a dull affair?"

"I do not see how it can be," Philippa replied. "There will be my friend Susan, Mr. Blythefield's sister. Also, if I am not mistaken, you will be discussing the negative effects of stopping free trade and the motion to repeal. I'd like to hear the conversation and better understand the topic."

"Women should not—" Mr. Lloyd began.

"I can hardly credit my ears," George crowed, popping a meringue into his mouth. He swallowed it. "You, always such a flighty thing. It's hard to imagine such a topic could interest you."

"Well, George, if you would spend a bit more time conversing with me as a woman of sense rather than a flighty little sister, you might have discovered it for yourself."

Matthew turned to her. "Who will be hosting the dinner?"

Philippa smiled at him. He was still under the throes of love. "I believe Mr. Blythefield's sister Susan will be hosting. His mother has some other project she is unable to put aside." When Matthew heard that, he nodded and rested his chin on his hand.

The conversation turned to other Society events in the coming weeks, and they speculated on which ones were likely to be a crush. Mr. Lloyd opened his mouth to speak more than once, but either George or one of his friends was too quick to fill the silence for Mr. Lloyd to take his turn.

Philippa was grateful. George could not have known that Mr. Lloyd had darkened her doorstep at the exact moment he happened to come with his friends, but she thought George was perhaps trying to make it up to her for not having provided sufficient protection from Mr. Thackery. He had already apologized, once he'd learned of her move into Lucius's house, and she had forgiven him. For all that, she was not sure he would have done better had he been given a second chance. He was still young. Philippa suspected he would not truly become attuned to the needs of others until he had been touched by Cupid's arrow himself and could think of nothing else but *one* woman. She was looking forward to the day when she might witness that.

Although Mr. Lloyd far outstayed his welcome, George refused to leave until he was able to escort Mr. Lloyd personally out of the premises. She had had a late start, but Philippa was at last able to begin her toilette for the party, and when Lucius sent her word that he was waiting, she hastened downstairs with only a ten-minute delay.

Inside the carriage, Philippa fidgeted with her hands. She sighed, then leaned back, looking at the darkened streets as they rode through them.

"With such a somber face, I will begin to think you do not wish to come with me," Lucius said. "And here I thought you might enjoy a party given by your friend and her brother."

"I don't know, Lucius." Philippa turned her face slightly to the window when she caught a scent of linden blossoms in the spring breeze. "I know at this party I must meet Mr. Thackery for the first time since I rejected his suit. I cannot look forward to that. If only it were just my friend I were dining with."

"And her brother?" Lucius said with a lift of an eyebrow.

Philippa glanced at him sideways, surprised at his statement. She hadn't thought she had given any clue as to her growing curiosity about Mr. Blythefield, unless Selena had picked up on her feelings and spoken of them to Lucius. As much as Philippa loved her brother, he rarely noticed anything beyond the end of his nose.

"I am very fond of Susan," Philippa replied firmly. Let that set him in his place. She was not about to reveal to Lucius whether her curiosity over Mr. Blythefield had led to a deeper emotion. Although, if she dared to examine her own heart, she would probably have to own that her heart was already lost.

CHAPTER TWENTY

*M*iss Sommers had come, as prearranged, a short while before the party was to begin. She was accompanied by her mother, who'd promised to stay out of the way and let the young people prepare. Mrs. Sommers would be helpful when some of the MPs' wives arrived, as she was skilled at these events, and she would also balance their number since Mr. Gibson had arrived without his wife.

Jack was more nervous than he typically was before even the most challenging parliamentary debate. He had seen to it that his parents were otherwise occupied, so there would be no untoward incident that might derail his plans and embarrass him. That had required a bit of finesse. His father had been working quietly earlier that day, and although his face had seemed a bit exultant and his eyes overly bright, he'd assured Jack once again that he would be perfectly content with a quiet dinner in his study.

Jack's mother had left two hours earlier, a martial light about her as she went forth on one of her missions. He had been too preoccupied when she'd described what it was. He only knew that her friend's latest project had excited his mother's zeal. Jack had not bothered to contact his brother, since he had made it clear that Christopher was not exactly welcome.

Miss Sommers ran her finger down the names, as she had not seen the finalized list. "You have the Morrises here. Lord and Lady Palmer. Sir John is not bringing his wife, which is no surprise. She never attends any event that carries a whiff of politics. Mr. Whitmore the elder— excellent. Edward Zachary and Miss Fairfax. Barely betrothed, and they are attending a political dinner together—I applaud them. Mr. and

Mrs. Grunden. Lord and Lady Harrowden..." Miss Sommers turned a questioning gaze to Jack. "Who are the Harrowdens?"

Jack had invited Lord Harrowden after having met him at Parliament, though not without reservation, knowing Philippa's dislike. Lord Harrowden was a vote after all. And after speaking with him, Jack judged him to be a likely one if he could be persuaded. He seemed to have no firm ideas on the bill yet.

"Lord Harrowden recently won a seat, and he shows interest in the reform. I thought it prudent to invite anyone who might be persuaded to the cause, and even better—vote for it."

"I see." Miss Sommers skimmed the rest of the list before setting it on the escritoire and taking in the hired servants bringing in refreshments.

Jack knew it would not be long before people began to arrive. "Would you like to see the place settings?"

She nodded, and he led her to the dining room. Miss Sommers was attired in a shimmering green gown which suited her complexion, and she looked very fine tonight. She walked over to the table that was laid out with thirty-eight settings and examined the cards one by one, to see who was placed next to whom.

The changes in the dining room gave a more modern touch and created an ambience of conviviality. Jack, looking around, exhaled and willed himself to relax. Susan had told him that Philippa suggested placing near each plate arrangements of flowers that floated in small glass bowls of water. He had to admit Philippa's taste was unerring. Servants had just lit the candles on the table, which reflected off the water, making the table sparkle.

"I can find nothing to fault here," Miss Sommers said. "You have given a great deal of thought to the place settings, for it was not easy determining which MP would be more likely to influence or be influenced. I must say that for some, it is not always a sure thing at a glance. It is perfect. Did your sister help? It is as though you had benefited from a woman's touch."

"Susan did the work, but she took suggestions from her friend, Miss Clavering." Jack had the sudden urge to do something and went to move a chair that had been perfectly placed.

At his revelation, Miss Sommers wore a polite smile and let it pass without comment. The door to the drawing room opened, and Susan stepped in.

"How do you do?" She curtsied in front of Miss Sommers. "I saw your mother seated in the drawing room, and I've offered to have a footman bring her something to drink, but she said she didn't need anything. It is pretty, isn't it? The table and the room?"

"It is, indeed." Miss Sommers examined Susan and appeared to hesitate before saying, "Is this what you are wearing, Miss Blythefield?"

At Miss Sommers's words, Jack directed his gaze to Susan's dress, which she had confided to him had been chosen with Miss Clavering's help. Her dress was modest, but in a brighter color than he had ever seen on her. He wasn't certain whether it was too bright for a girl who had made her debut at such a young age, but he did have to admit it looked well on Susan.

"It is … That is to say, I had thought …" Spots of color had flown to Susan's cheeks as she looked down at her dress.

Miss Sommers stepped forward and laid a hand on Susan's arm, bending her head with gentle condescension. "It *is* lovely, and on someone else, it would suit the occasion perfectly. But as you are yet unmarried and uninitiated in the eyes of the *ton*, it is perhaps a bold choice to make. If you will allow me to make a suggestion, you had better wear something paler so that you don't stand out."

Susan flushed to her roots and darted an apologetic look to Jack. "I see."

At the chagrin on his sister's face, a protective urge rose up in Jack. "Miss Sommers, I thank you for your advice, but as Susan is not merely in attendance but is acting as hostess, I believe the color is perfectly fitting for the event."

Susan sent him a grateful look.

Miss Sommers pressed her lips together before returning a reply. "Of course, you will know best. Forgive my interference."

"It is nothing," Jack said, piqued, but not wishing to be backward in showing his gratitude for her help. "After all, you are here as a guide, and I do value your opinion. But the guests should arrive at any minute, and Susan needs to be here to greet them."

He gestured forward to the drawing room where Mrs. Sommers was seated with all appearances of being content to wait until the party began. Jack brought a small glass of sherry to each of the three women, including his sister, whose eyes widened.

"You are the hostess of this event," he murmured. "As such, you may have a small glass of sherry before the event begins. But none of the champagne or anything stronger—and only a little wine at dinner, mind you."

She shook her head and smiled, looking very young. "Oh, no, Jack."

Jack inhaled deeply and looked to the door. As if on cue, a knock sounded, and Jack signaled to Susan to come stand at his side as the guests began to arrive, with Mr. Whitmore and his wife the first in attendance. Their son Robert arrived separately, but not long afterwards.

Susan greeted the Whitmores and the next couple to arrive with a fluid grace, and he was proud of her. When Mr. Thackery and Mr. Merrick arrived, she greeted them both with equal distinction, though her eyes did light up at the sight of Mr. Merrick. His sister seemed to have put aside her shyness to perform the role of hostess. She was doing it admirably.

Guests came in such a steady stream that the room was full within the half hour. The elder Mr. Whitmore came to the door to greet Lord and Lady Palmer and ushered Lady Palmer to meet his wife. Jack glanced around the room and saw that everyone was talking comfortably and the servants were keeping everyone's glasses filled. Everything was perfect.

Jack told Susan they might leave their station, and he wandered about the room, setting the gentlemen talking—the ones who were passionate about the cause matched with the ones who were still more reticent—greeting the women, and overseeing the servants.

As he listened to some of the discussions, he found that, surprisingly, the issue was not a clear division by party. There were some Tories who were more keen on abolishing the law than Whigs. Lord and Lady Harrowden were in deep conversation with Mr. Thackery and Mr. Merrick, and Jack paused, wondering if that was a group that would benefit the cause or hinder it. He could not be sure of Mr. Thackery's position, since he had changed his opinion from the first time they'd spoken of it. If a man could change once, he could change again.

It was difficult to be the host, Jack discovered, as he looked around the room and tried to discern whether all the guests had arrived and if they had all they needed. It would be easier if he could trust that Susan was up to the task. She was standing somewhat awkwardly near the door, as if she did not dare join any of the conversations. Miss Sommers came and stood at his side, and Jack smiled at her absently. He was too preoccupied to think about making conversation, and they both looked up when the door opened.

Shanks announced, "Sir Lucius Clavering, Miss Philippa Clavering."

Jack's heart stopped when he heard Philippa's name announced and she came in on the heels of her brother. He started forward, the unexpected surprise pulling his lips upward. He greeted Sir Lucius, then turned to Philippa and bowed before her.

"I had not expected the pleasure of having you here tonight."

Her eyes twinkled when she smiled at him. "That is because I had turned down your very kind invitation in Hyde Park, as you well know. I hope you do not mind that I took my sister-in-law's place, for she is not yet ready to reenter Society."

Sir Lucius put his arm around Philippa's shoulders. "I'd hoped she might be a welcome replacement for Lady Clavering. Although I do apologize for not correcting the information earlier."

"Not to worry." Jack smiled at Philippa. "It keeps my numbers even and the evening interesting." This bit of flirtation was actually spoken from his heart, and it slipped out before he could moderate his words.

After giving Jack a curious look, Sir Lucius excused himself to greet Robert Whitmore, and Jack began to lift his arm to escort Philippa over to Susan but thought the better of it. Miss Sommers was watching them, and he'd realized that he had left her standing alone. "Shall I take you to Susan?"

Philippa nodded.

He noticed she had gone a little pale when she spotted Mr. Thackery across the room. Jack was ready to throw the man out if he caused Philippa any trouble, but he could hardly address such a thing when she had not shared the details of her relationship with Mr. Thackery.

Susan kept glancing at Mr. Merrick across the room, who had not noticed Susan at all, apart from their initial greeting. Jack was concerned when he saw his sister's mood turn morose. This would not do. The dinner was on precarious footing, hosted as it was, at his parents' home, which was already one of the more unusual households to be found in London Society. If Susan were to break down while hosting, that would be the end.

"Philippa is here," he said in a rallying tone before realizing he had used her Christian name. He hoped he had not said it loudly enough for the other guests to hear, and thankfully Philippa did not seem to take it amiss.

Philippa slipped her arm through Susan's, and Jack heard Philippa whisper. "Do not let him know you are hoping to be noticed by him. Come. Will you show me how the flowers look in the dining room?"

Jack watched them walk off, and suddenly the success of the party seemed more likely—as if a fresh wind of hope promised victory. That worry taken care of, Jack turned to assess which group would most benefit from his attention and settled on the newcomer, Lord Harrowden. His vote was the least sure, Jack thought.

Lord Harrowden was now speaking to Mr. Atkinson, who was flanked by Robert Whitmore. "Despite my initial enthusiasm for the reform, I am plagued by a suspicion that abolishing free trade will encourage the riffraff of this country to think they can have anything they want whenever they want it. I begin to believe grain prices should remain fixed by the hands of the landowners who can better judge the surplus or deficit."

Jack exchanged a glance with Robert. He knew this did not bode well, and he regretted his impulse to invite the Harrowdens, especially after Lady Harrowden had managed to corner Jack and flirt with him outrageously when he'd gone to instruct the servants to have more candles sent. Now, his gamble that Lord Harrowden would be another vote on the side of repeal was turning against him as Lord Harrowden's ringing voice managed to draw Mr. Thackery and Lord Palmer into the conversation.

"Besides," Lord Harrowden continued, "we cannot allow ourselves to be swayed by some discontented Unionists who want more than just food on the table—they want to be like us. Nor can we bow to the pressure of the factory owners."

Jack narrowed his eyes at Harrowden. The man looked like he was enjoying all the attention being directed his way. And what did he know anyway? He hadn't even attended Parliament the entire session. *Why did I invite him?*

"I have it on good authority," Harrowden continued, "that the owners just want to abolish the law so the bread will be cheaper and the factory owners can pay their workers less." This was met with an outburst of argument. "The majority in Parliament is against the motion for a reason. If we do not keep the laws and decisions in the hands of gentlemen, the country risks being overrun by savages."

You have it on whose *authority?* Jack wondered. Had his dinner been infiltrated by men who'd appeared sympathetic only to show up with the mission to oppose reform?

The elder Mr. Whitmore had been listening quietly but he now raised his voice above the melee. "I understand your reservations, Lord Harrowden. The learned gentlemen gathered tonight"—Mr. Whitmore took a moment to sweep the small crowd with a kindly gaze—"are far from the riffraff you spoke of, as you must be able to see for yourself. Many of them have years of experience in politics, and the ideas we are discussing tonight are for the good of the country. And yet, you find among us many supporters for repealing the bill."

Mr. Whitmore gestured to Jack at his side. "Mr. Blythefield himself is a respected landowner and although he is a Whig, he has many Conservative ideas. He would not propose anything radical or harmful to England or to the civil foundations upon which we stand. On the contrary, he has invited you here—"

A strange noise came from the hallway, interrupting Mr. Whitmore's speech. Jack turned toward it, half in irritation, half in alarm. His servants knew how important this dinner was. He could not quite decipher what the sound could be, and he glanced at the door which was closed. The noise grew louder, and it was not just one voice but several. It was not the moaning he'd first thought it, but singing. Another voice joined in.

"Excuse me, gentlemen. I must see to this disturbance."

Jack started toward the door and crossed gazes with Philippa, who looked as alarmed as he felt. She began to walk toward him. It was not just singing he was hearing, but *inebriated* singing.

Philippa reached the door at the same time he did. "Allow me to assist you," she whispered. Jack barely nodded as he hurried into the corridor with Philippa following, and they pulled the door shut behind them.

The first person who met his astonished gaze was Matthew Evans, who was flanked by three other men of undistinguished appearance. Fuming, Jack reached out to take Evans by the arm, but he halted, hand outstretched, when he saw the man's expression. Mr. Evans did not in the slightest way appear to be under any influence. Rather, he had an apologetic look on his face.

"What in the *deuce?*" Jack muttered.

Mr. Evans was not given a chance to answer, because the three men—whom Jack now perceived wore coarse, patched clothing and reeked of some homemade choice spirit and questionable hygienic habits—stepped around him. The singing fell off when the men gazed at Jack and Philippa in all their finery. Jack's mother came through the door last.

Where was Shanks? Not that he could have done anything against this crowd, old as he was. Jack was bewildered by the unprecedented event and paralyzed by what it meant to his dinner party.

Through the noise of clearing throats and shuffling feet, Philippa's clear voice rang out. "Good evening, Mr. Evans—and everyone. Good evening, Mrs. Blythefield. I propose we step into another room while we decide in what way we may assist."

Jack snapped to attention. The very thing. His father was in his study, but perhaps the library.

"Jack." Mrs. Blythefield grabbed him by the arm. "This is what I have been trying to tell you. I am giving you a chance to see for yourselves the effects that the lack of proper wages can have on a man."

"Yes, Mother. But let us discuss this in the library."

Philippa seemed only to be waiting for his word, because she darted forward to the library—one benefit of her having spent so much time with Susan was that she knew where it was. "Mrs. Blythefield, I see there is a warm fire in here that will surely do you much good. Matthew, will you assist these men to enter?"

To Jack's relief, this was precisely what Mr. Evans did. Jack soon had the satisfaction of closing the door behind them in the library and removing the corridor of all sound, but not of filth. Shanks came out of the dining room, breathless.

"Have someone clean this mess," Jack hissed before stepping into the library.

Inside, his mother gestured to the drunken band with a flourish. "Jack, I present to you Mr. Smith, Mr. Orwell, and Mr. Nebitt."

Silence. He looked at them each in turn, and no one made a sound. Misters Nebitt, Smith and Orwell pulled off their caps, and one of them wavered on his feet. Another put his arm around the man's back to steady him. Jack opened his mouth wordlessly. Of all the scenarios which had crossed his imagination when picturing this evening—including a rogue vision of kissing Philippa when she walked through the door—this scenario was not one he had been prepared for.

Jack whirled around when the door opened, but he saw only Sir Lucius step into the room. "I thought I might be of assistance."

Jack's mother put her hand on one of the men's shoulders. "If this does not persuade you to join The Society for the Suppression of Vice, I do not know what pitiful sight could. With such an influential assembly gathered in one place, their goodness of heart, I am sure, will stir the gentlemen in the drawing room to help in this cause."

Jack sidled up to her. "Mother, this is not the place," he said in low tones.

Philippa stepped forward as well. "Mrs. Blythefield, how right you are to see to their needs." She smiled kindly at the three men, standing foolishly just inside the room. "But shall we not bring them to the kitchen where they might be fed? And I do wonder if the servants might have some excess clothing for them so that they may clean up. Shall I accompany you?"

"No," Jack said, darting forward. He could not let Miss Clavering go in the company of such rough men. "I do not think you understand."

Sir Lucius stepped forward and put his hand on Jack's arm. "I will go. Matthew?"—he gestured to Mr. Evans, who nodded. Jack would have to find out later what Evans had had to do with this whole affair.

Sir Lucius turned to the three men. "Shall we?" he said, as he escorted them out.

Philippa came to Jack's mother and put her arm around Mrs. Blythefield's waist. "You must be exhausted after such a noble effort. Now that the men have your guests well in charge, shall we bring you to where the servants might attend to you? I am sure some tea would do you good."

"Why, I am rather tired," Jack's mother said. "Yes, I do believe that is a good idea."

Now that the worst of her mission was over, his mother appeared to crumple from the effort. Jack held the door open as Philippa brought his mother to the staircase. A servant was wiping the last bit of mud from the corridor, and the only sound was the conversation that came from the drawing room.

Jack stepped up to the door and realized he was trembling. He breathed out slowly, threw back his shoulders and opened the door. Conversation ceased when he entered, and all eyes turned to him.

"My apologies, ladies and gentlemen, Lord and Lady Palmer. It was only some drunken beggars, who entered when my butler was in the dining room. They have been taken care of."

CHAPTER TWENTY-ONE

*P*hilippa accompanied Mrs. Blythefield upstairs, where she took her into her room. Surprisingly, it did not seem odd to be in her private quarters, and since the older woman did not appear to be put out by the sudden familiarity, Philippa decided she would not give it another thought. She allowed Philippa to assist her in removing her cloak and helping her to the chair by the fire.

Mrs. Blythefield sank into the chair with a sigh. "Thank you, my dear." A footman must have notified her maid, who was not long in coming with some hot water.

Philippa moved aside so she could place it near the wash basin. "I am sure you would like some tea, would you not, ma'am?"

Mrs. Blythefield nodded, and Philippa turned to the maid. "Would you be so kind as to bring some tea and sandwiches for your mistress? I will remain here with her until you return."

The maid dipped a curtsy and left, and Philippa sat on the other small chair placed next to the fire, which was not sending off any heat. She had not thought to ask the maid to bank the fire, but there were enough burning embers that Philippa was able to add a log and coax a small flame from it. "Allow me to place this blanket over you. You must be very tired from your efforts."

Mrs. Blythefield permitted her to do so and picked at the wool fringe of the blanket with her fingers. "Tonight was particularly tiresome, it is true. Bringing the men to my home was not something I'd planned to do. I was with Mr. Draper, who is part of the committee, and when I saw how sorely the men needed something warm to eat, I urged him to help.

We thought we might bring them to our kitchen, but I had forgotten the servants would all be occupied this evening." She yawned.

"How did Mr. Evans come to be with you?" Philippa asked. This was something that had been playing on her mind. He was the last face she had expected to encounter that evening, and in such a circumstance.

"Mr. Evans was so kind. Mr. Draper was assisting one of the men, who was a bit … well, that is to say, he'd had too much to drink. The man caused Mr. Draper to fall and hurt his foot. He had to hail a driver to get home, so I was left with the three men. I had no idea how I was going to help them."

Mrs. Blythefield clasped her hands and smiled up at Philippa. "It was quite by chance that Mr. Evans came upon me in this predicament. He said he was coming home from a party, and he stopped because he recognized me. What a gentleman he is! He asked if I was in need of help, and I admit I had quite thought I could manage when we left the gin house, but caring for three gentleman is not easy when you have no support. It was most providential that Mr. Evans should come just at that time."

"I see." Philippa turned to study her. She could see no resemblance to Jack in her features—only in Susan's fair hair and pale complexion. "Do you feel you have accomplished your mission? Where will the men go once they have eaten?"

Mrs. Blythefield sighed, looking weary. "Mr. Draper had planned to take them to a local parish where they could get sober before returning to their homes. You must tell Mr. Evans that that is what he must do. Such a shame Mr. Draper could not see the project through to completion." She met Philippa's gaze, a spark of determination lighting her eyes. "As soon as one takes care of one need, another need crops up. There's so much to do, and so few people to take these things on."

Philippa nodded in sympathy. "You are noble to care so deeply for the disadvantaged. But it is true that it's a difficult job to do on one's own."

"Oh, but I am not on my own. Mrs. Arcot is with me, and we have a committee. Mr. Draper, in particular, is a great service when he has two working feet." Mrs. Blythefield turned a suddenly intent gaze on Philippa. "I don't suppose you would like to join us?"

Philippa concealed how little desire she had for Mrs. Blythefield's proposition. "No. I am more interested in how changing laws can bring about good—the way your son does. Each person must use his talents as he sees fit."

"Do you think my son does much good in Parliament? Are they not simply men debating and arguing over what will most benefit the entitled? I always deplored the fact that Jack works to assist those who already have the advantage."

Philippa turned to Mrs. Blythefield in surprise. "Your son is devoted to reform, Mrs. Blythefield. This is why he has invited all these gentlemen here tonight. It is so he can bring down the price of bread—so the workers will have enough to feed their families."

It was Mrs. Blythefield's turn to look surprised. "I had no idea Jack was involved in such a noble endeavor. My husband is primarily interested in shoring up wealth for our family, and Christopher is bent on seeking pleasure. I had assumed Jack was the same."

Philippa reached out and took Mrs. Blythefield's hand in her own. It was a daring gesture, but she followed the impulse of her heart. Mrs. Blythefield seemed more lonely than she let on, and Philippa wondered if this was why she was so devoted to social causes. "Perhaps you should spend more time with your son. You might find that you have much in common."

Mrs. Blythefield kept Philippa's hand in hers as she sat in contemplation. "Yes, perhaps I should."

The maid returned with the tea, and Philippa had her turn the log so that the fire might burn even brighter. She poured tea for Mrs. Blythefield and handed her a cup, then stood, smoothing the fabric on her dress. "You have had a fatiguing evening, and I shall leave you now, ma'am."

"Thank you, Philippa." Mrs. Blythefield looked down as the maid came to unlace her boots, and she submitted quietly to the ministrations. "Susan is fortunate to have a friend like you."

It had not been until Susan's mother said Philippa's name that she could be sure that Mrs. Blythefield even remembered who she was. She always seemed to live in a world of her own making.

"It is I who am fortunate. This Season would not have been half so pleasant without all the time I've spent here with her. Good night." Philippa curtsied and took her leave.

Downstairs, the guests were already seated at the table in the dining room. The first course had been served, and when she entered, Jack stood quickly and went to meet her at the entrance. "Thank you for caring for my mother," he whispered.

"I was glad to be of assistance," she replied, looking up at him. She could see the worry lines between his eyes. "Is all well? Were you able to bring the conversation back to the topic of repealing the bill?"

Jack gave a slight shake of his head. "I think some of the guests were a bit shocked, but I was able to explain it away. I only hope the rest of the evening is pleasant enough that they will forget the interruption. Sir Lucius and Mr. Evans are still with the men—I am guessing in the confines of the kitchen, for I am not hearing any singing."

Philippa chuckled. "They did appear properly chastened once we brought them to the library and they took in their surroundings. Let us hope they were satisfied to have performed before supper and will not feel the need to thank us with another song."

Jack laughed, smoothing some of the worry lines on his brow. He glanced behind him at the table and said in a near whisper, "I am sorry for your seat placement, as you are next to Lord Harrowden, and I know you are not overly fond of him. It was a last-minute adjustment. One of the guests never showed, and I allowed Miss Sommers to rearrange the table settings—which, perhaps, I ought to have done myself."

Philippa was careful to keep her expression schooled, though she was falling prey to jealousy. *Right. Miss Sommers is his unofficial hostess.* And then there was the disagreeable necessity of sitting beside Lord Harrowden. She summoned a smile. "You could not have been overseeing the table settings when you had more important things to attend to. Thank you for your concern, but it will be fine."

Jack smiled and held out his arm, and she put her hand on it, allowing him to lead her to her place at the table between Mr. Whitmore and Lord Harrowden. At least Whitmore would make a pleasant dinner partner. On the other side of Mr. Whitmore sat Miss Sommers, and her look was difficult to decipher as she watched Jack accompany Philippa.

The first course was finished, and once Philippa had sat, the servants carried in the second course. She quietly filled in Robert Whitmore, who was sitting on her left, on what had happened in the corridor. She made a hearty meal of the fish, as their conversation turned to lighter topics. It was a respite, for she knew Robert well and enjoyed his company. "How do you think Mr. Blythefield is doing in his endeavor?"

Whitmore broke off a piece of bread. He glanced at Jack on the other side of the table in earnest conversation with Mr. Atkinson. "It is too early to say. I can see why Jack was reticent to host at his father's house. I suppose it is not as easy as when you've set up your own establishment. It was my father who thought this would be a good idea. The earlier interruption, though quickly subdued, might not help with those on the fence, but all of us who are pro-reform are working on setting a better tone for the rest of the dinner."

"My brother and Mr. Evans are not returned. I hope the servants in the kitchen will find something for them to eat, since I believe they will miss the dinner entirely."

"Yes, it's not an easy matter to feed and care for three men who are more than a trifle bosky. I'm not sure what they will do with them afterwards."

"Oh," Philippa rubbed her fingers on her napkin. "They're both resourceful. Mrs. Blythefield mentioned the parish. I trust my brother and Mr. Evans to find a way to care for them that is compassionate and effective, and I assume Lucius has already given orders to the servants."

When the dessert was brought, Robert Whitmore turned to Miss Sommers on his other side and began talking to her.

"Miss Clavering." Lord Harrowden was seated to Philippa's right, and he addressed her now that the conversation partners had changed. She had almost hoped she might be able to go the entire meal without having to speak to him, but she was not so lucky. "What an odd coincidence for us to be meeting at this dinner, is it not?"

"Indeed." Philippa stabbed at the orange wedge on her plate and put it in her mouth. "And what was your objective in coming? Are you for the reform?"

Lord Harrowden's face took on an odd smirk—so very much like the man she knew back in Castle Combe, where Lucius's hunting box bordered his estate. "Let us just say that I can be persuaded to vote for repealing the Corn Laws if I can see the benefit to me as a landowner. I was invited to hear more on this topic, and the vote is tight enough that mine could mean something. Then, there are others who depend upon me to shift the balance against the bill. That is what makes this evening so entertaining. Who knows which way the wind will blow?"

Philippa was rapidly losing patience with him. *Entertaining, indeed.* "That is much too cryptic for me, I am afraid. As a mere woman, I cannot be expected to understand how politics works."

"No, I suppose you cannot."

Lady Harrowden laughed loudly on the other side of the table, and many of the older women, who had accompanied their husbands, stared at her. Philippa saw Lord Harrowden shoot his wife a warning look.

The door to the dining room opened, and the guests turned to see who the latest arrival was. Philippa was expecting it to be her brother, but it was Mr. Christopher Blythefield who entered the room. His outfit—a puce waistcoat and yellow jacket—was completely at odds with the sober tones of the other gentleman's clothing in the room.

"I'd forgotten you had your important dinner. Was it tonight?"

Oh no, not again. Philippa glanced at Jack. Although his face appeared severe, she thought she could read the agony that was underneath. It was another stain on his dinner.

"Is this seat for me?" Christopher called out to his brother, and Jack gave the slightest nod and gestured for him to take it. Lucius's seat had remained empty, and Jack had probably thought the evening less likely to turn sour if he let his brother sit rather than throwing him out.

Christopher took the seat, adding, "How perfect. It shall not be cold bread and sausage for me. Ah—" He looked around the table and noticed that they were on dessert. "Nothing but sweets? Where is the proper dinner you had promised?"

Jack looked across the table at Philippa now, and his face was a mix of fury and helplessness. She kept her gaze steady, wordlessly attempting to strengthen him.

He stared at Philippa for a long moment, before addressing Lord Palmer, seated on his right, in a voice loud enough that could be heard by all, signaling that they should resume their conversation. "Lord Palmer, I was heartened to hear that the experiment your steward conducted showed that workers were twice as productive when their spending capacity increased."

On Philippa's left, Robert Whitmore gave Jack his support by praising the cook's plum pudding. Slowly, the conversation picked up until the guests at the table had mostly ignored Christopher Blythefield's interruption. Philippa's heart sped with anxiety when he began to nod off in front of his plate, and she attempted to catch Susan's attention. Susan was ignoring her dinner partner and staring at Mr. Merrick, who carried on an animated conversation with one of the younger wives at the table.

Philippa turned her face to Jack, and he met her gaze, wearing a numb expression. She indicated the drawing room with her eyes and mouthed, *Shall we go?* He was close enough to perceive her meaning and nodded.

Philippa tried in vain to attract Susan's attention as hostess, but she was unable to do so. It was up to Philippa to take matters in hand. "Ladies, if you are all satisfied, Miss Blythefield and I propose to adjourn to the drawing room and let the gentlemen take their port."

Susan looked up in alarm and stood, abashed. The women, some glancing at Christopher, seemed anxious to quit the scene of the second domestic disaster in this evening's dinner. The pitch in conversation rose slightly as they pushed back their chairs.

Philippa and Susan led the way into the drawing room, and Susan leaned in to whisper, "Thank you."

Philippa was unable to answer because Miss Sommers and her mother came up to Susan, wearing severe, tight-lipped faces. With a glance at Philippa, Miss Sommers said, "I am sorry, Miss Blythefield, but my mother and I are unable to stay any longer. Please present my excuses to Mr. Blythefield. I did not wish to disturb him."

"Oh, I … very well. I will tell him." Susan darted forward to have a servant bring the ladies' wraps, and Miss Sommers and her mother left as soon as their effects had been fetched to them.

Philippa's heart sank in dismay, and she was determined that by the time Jack came into the drawing room with the gentlemen, all of the women would be having tea and enjoying perfectly ordinary conversations. She did not regret the loss of Miss Sommers. But Philippa could only hope that it was not too late to salvage what was rapidly turning into the most disastrous party she had ever attended.

CHAPTER TWENTY-TWO

The conversation among gentlemen over port seemed to flow more easily than it had with the women at dinner, despite the fact that Christopher drank his port in a sullen, dazed silence.

Jack was relieved when it came time to lead the men into the drawing room and was further reassured when he saw that Christopher had no intention of leaving the dining room. Jack could barely summon a smile for his guests with his mind so beleaguered by the two interruptions his party had suffered—and both from his own family. It was his worst nightmare come true.

The sound of conversations from men and women echoed in every corner of the room, but Jack hardly knew what to do with himself. In the past, he'd always been able to manage his family and whatever absurdity they were embroiled in while still presenting a conventional face to the public. He knew his family was decent and kind—although he was beginning to wonder about his brother. What had possessed Christopher to show up that way, and half-baked?

His mother had only acted out of the goodness of her heart and a belief that what she was doing was correct—that, he knew full well. It was still a misguided attempt. After all, what gently-bred woman went around bringing drunken laborers home to a London townhouse? Jack needed to keep a better eye on her. He repressed a sigh. But with what extra time?

Alone at the entrance to the drawing room, Jack knew he needed to see to his guests and looked around desperately. His eyes settled on Philippa, who had been watching him. She did not remove her steady gaze when he looked her way. She gave a slight smile and nod of encouragement. Her eyes seemed to say, *You can do this.* Jack took a deep breath and walked the few steps to where Mr. Whitmore was standing next to his wife.

Mr. Whitmore turned to face Jack. "It has been an unusual evening."

"Truly." Jack kept his voice low. "How shall we proceed from here?"

Mr. Whitmore glanced around the room where various groups of men and women congregated. Some of the men appeared to be seriously discussing the merits and disadvantages of the bill, but many of the guests whispered and laughed and seemed more centered on gossip.

"I will bring Lord and Lady Palmer together with Mr. Atkinson and his wife, and my wife and I will join them. It is my understanding that the women are for the reform, and it will help their husbands to hear it. You pull my son and Mr. Thackery into conversation, since he is a principal player and I'm not sure on which side he'll fall. Considering the vote is tomorrow, we must make this last endeavor count."

Jack nodded. "Give me a few moments, and I will do just that. I want to see that Miss Sommers"—he looked around—"Where is she? Or rather, my sister—that the women have all they need."

Jack suspected Mr. Whitmore had proposed the dinner party more for Lady Palmer and Mrs. Atkinson than for any of the men, since they appeared to have a strong influence over their husbands. He assessed the groups gathered in the room, searching for Robert Whitmore. His gaze landed once again on the petite form of Philippa. With a calm grace that made her seem more mature than her years, she led some of the gossiping women to seats, lowering the near calumnious tone in the room to something more stately.

Susan! Jack had had no time to see how his sister had been faring in her role as hostess. He searched for her now and watched in growing alarm as Susan went up to the small party that held Mr. Merrick and Mr. Thackery. She stood at his side, waiting until Mr. Merrick noticed her. When he finally caught a glance at Susan, he turned his back and continued talking as though Jack's sister were not there.

Susan went completely white and stepped back, and Jack could almost feel the blow. He hoped she would not make a fool out of herself, but his hope was in vain.

She tapped Mr. Merrick on the shoulder. "Mr. Merrick, I thought…" Her voice trailed away when Mr. Merrick frowned at her. "I thought I might be able to bring you something."

He looked at her for a long, condescending moment, and Jack took a step forward. Before he could intervene, Mr. Merrick said, "There is nothing at all I need from you, miss." He gave a curt bow and turned his back once again.

It took only a brief moment for understanding to hit before Susan gasped and ran out of the room. Jack looked helplessly at Philippa, who shook her head. She continued to bring Mr. Gibson to a seat nearer to the fire, keeping up a cheerful flow of conversation. Apparently, she did not judge it wise to go after Susan just now, and Jack had to agree. He needed at least one woman present who had her head on her shoulders and was able to lend some air of normalcy. He looked around for Miss Sommers again and was puzzled as to her absence.

After Mr. Gibson was settled, Philippa came up to him and said in a normal tone that was heard by those around them, "Mr. Blythefield, might I assist in pouring the tea for your guests?"

The footman had brought in the tea—and despite the dessert they had consumed—accompanied it with platters of cakes. The beautiful pyramid of sweetmeats, marzipan, and candied fruits was wasted on an unappreciative crowd. He was sure anything he ate would turn to dust in his mouth, but he managed to nod. "Yes, that would be excellent."

Philippa began to pour the tea with graceful hands, and he could not imagine how she was able to keep her calm when there was so much whispering. She acted as though nothing had happened out of the ordinary, whereas Jack could hardly keep his mind from spinning enough to know what to say next. Everything he had feared had all come true. By tomorrow, everyone in London would know about unruly disruptions in the corridor, his brother arriving uninvited and in his cups, and his sister who wore her feelings for all to see. It could not have gone worse.

Robert Whitmore appeared too deep in conversation to be disturbed, so Jack squared his shoulders and went to Mr. Thackery and Mr. Merrick— and now Lord Harrowden, who had joined them. He listened to them for a few moments and—if they had ever been in favor of repealing the Corn Laws—he was now undeceived. It had been a weak consideration on their part. Still, he had to make a push.

"Mr. Thackery, as you know—" Jack began.

The door opened, and with the way the evening had gone, Jack turned with misgiving, cutting off his words to see who it was. His father stood in the doorway, dressed in his day attire and with that feverish look of excitement Jack had come to know and dread.

"Excuse me." Jack walked to the door, just as Sir Lucius and Mr. Evans piled in behind Jack's father. Mr. Blythefield looked as though he wished to address the crowd, but Jack reached his father before he could say a word.

"Father, how delightful. Shall we just step to the side to discuss whatever it is you came to speak about?"

"Investments," his father replied in a ringing voice that surely reached every corner of the room.

Mr. Evans stepped forward and joined their circle as Sir Lucius went to Thackery and Merrick. That was a balm. Sir Lucius would be able to handle that group.

Mr. Evans addressed Jack. "I would be honored if you would introduce me to your father. I have long desired to make his acquaintance."

Jack studied Mr. Evans, wondering if he'd planned to speak to his father about Susan. If so, it was premature. "Of course. Father, this is Mr. Matthew Evans. Mr. Evans, this is my father, Mr. Blythefield."

"A pleasure, sir." Mr. Evans bowed but did not say anything else and appeared to be there to listen.

Jack's father glanced at the men in the room as though he wished to speak to them, but he was cornered. He looked down at the paper he held in his hands, then up at Jack and Mr. Evans, addressing the two of them.

"I know you are assembled here tonight for quite another reason, my son. I do not remember exactly what it was, but I feel this investment opportunity needs our urgent attention. We have a chance to invest in public land in the Americas at only four pounds an acre, and it would be selfish to keep such a thing to ourselves."

Jack was rendered speechless by frustration. Hadn't he warned his father not to look into any investment opportunities? And now to do so and interrupt Jack's dinner!

"Four pounds. Can you imagine?" Mr. Blythefield said. "And this is a most fertile soil that will surely reap a return for the money within months. The best of it all is there are stewards in place who will take charge of the land, and we need only send the money in order to secure it. I thought perhaps your guests would be interested…"

"Father, no—" Jack replied in a low voice.

"Mr. Blythefield, that is a most interesting opportunity. As your son is aware, I count myself skilled at recommending lucrative investments." Mr. Evans sent a meaningful glance to Jack.

Jack deciphered the look, remembering only now that Mr. Evans had promised to assist him and steer his father toward investments that would succeed—and do nothing without Jack's approval. He could trust the man. Jack nodded his encouragement, grateful for this man's help once again.

"Might we discuss this together in your study?" Mr. Evans said. "Perhaps we may clarify the opportunity before presenting it to the others." He gestured out of the drawing room, adding, "I find men are more apt to consider an opportunity when they have the facts."

"Very good, very good." Jack's father followed Mr. Evans without further need for encouragement.

With feelings akin to a weary soldier returning to battle, Jack faced the room. Mr. Thackery had broken off from his group and fixed his eyes on Philippa. Jack saw her look up in alarm at his approach, and he stepped forward to intercede. Sir Lucius arrived first and, with a polite smile to Mr. Thackery, took his sister's arm.

"Evening, Thackery. Philippa, the refreshment table has those marzipan sweets you like so well." He led Philippa away from Mr. Thackery.

Mr. Merrick came and whispered a word in Mr. Thackery's ear. They both came over to Jack. "I believe it is time for us to go."

Jack nodded, not exactly surprised and not at all sorry to see them leave. He only regretted that he had been taken in by their seeming willingness to consider overturning the controversial bill. Lady Harrowden stood as soon as she saw Thackery and Merrick preparing to leave, and her husband joined her. Jack beckoned for the footman to come and bring coats.

It seemed to be the signal for the entire party to leave, beginning with those who were most undecided on abolishing the bill. After such a disastrous dinner, Jack was fairly certain not a single one of them would return a positive vote tomorrow. In fact, he could not even be sure he had a career in politics to look forward to—not with the peculiarities of his family publicly known. Even if the worst had been staved off, there had been a hint of scandal. And that was enough for the *ton*.

Lord and Lady Palmer were some of the last ones to leave. "An unusual dinner, to say the least." Lord Palmer smiled and did not seem at all put out. "Well, we have the final debates tomorrow before the vote. Perhaps those who did not attend the dinner will carry the day."

Jack was ready to sink with shame, and even the usually cheerful Mr. Whitmore looked somber. "Well, it is not the first time a repeal has been shot down and will not be the last. But common sense will eventually prevail. We cannot fix prices indefinitely."

Sir Lucius observed the sudden exodus from the drawing room. He stood, with Philippa at his side, and came to the door of the drawing room, where he folded his arms as the remainder of the guests took their leave. Soon there were only the three of them.

"I had just turned my back, and everyone decided to leave? I assume I missed something significant," Sir Lucius said.

"Only the entirety of the Blythefield family exposing themselves to ridicule," Jack said. He leaned against the cheerful yellow wall nearest to him and lowered his head.

Philippa left her brother's side and came to him. "I will see that Susan is all right tomorrow. I don't believe one night of tears will do her harm, and I have hope in being able to turn her mind in a better direction." She clasped her hands. "Your vote is tomorrow as well, is it not?"

Jack raised his eyes, the vision of tomorrow's debates bleak. "Unfortunately, yes. We have no time to undo tonight's damage."

"Perhaps there was not so much damage as you think. There was no outright scandal. No one knew your mother brought those men in, and I'm sure hardly anyone noticed that Susan was upset."

"Or that both my father and brother showed up, unannounced and informally attired, for reasons known only to them."

"Jack—" Philippa took a step closer, and he noticed that Sir Lucius regarded them with a keen eye. He had not missed the intimacy in her greeting.

"Much of the *ton* is selfish. Your family is not. Your mother is benevolent in wanting to help those who are less fortunate. Your father is generous in wishing to share his investments so that others might benefit." She smiled apologetically. "I'm sorry—I did overhear. Your sister has such a good heart, she has quickly become one of my closest friends. And you work tirelessly for reform." Jack noticed she had not mentioned his brother. "If only more families were like yours, London would be a much less hostile place."

She stepped away and glanced at her brother, who added his pence. "And much less interesting."

Jack accompanied them into the corridor as Mr. Evans exited Mr. Blythefield's study. He gestured Jack aside as Philippa and Lucius moved to take their cloaks from the footman.

"I believe I have talked him out of that particular investment. People have been speculating on American land over the last two years, and it has nearly ruined their economy. Most of the investments are unsound." Mr. Evans put on his hat. "Instead, I have introduced some new opportunities your father appears to be excited about, and these are ones I can trust. I will draw up the papers and have you look through them first."

"Thank you," Jack said simply. He did not have it in him to say any more. Sir Lucius and Mr. Evans went toward the door, discussing what Lucius had heard about the American investments.

Philippa turned back. "You may have noticed, but Miss Sommers and her mother decided to leave early. I think they were displeased. I am sorry."

"I am not," he replied. "By that, Miss Sommers showed that she is a fair-weather friend and therefore not one I am interested in keeping. You, however, are not."

Philippa smiled. "I am not." She held out her hand, and Jack took it in his, placing a kiss directly on it. She curled her fingers into his for a moment and kept her gaze on him.

"Do not lose heart," she said, then slipped her hand from his and left.

Jack walked back into the drawing room to escape the prying eyes of his butler, but the servants were cleaning the drawing room. He went into the dining room, half-expecting to see his brother fast asleep with his head on the table, but it was empty. Christopher must have gone to the room that was his when he stayed the night.

Jack sat at the dining table and stared at the dark sky through the sheer curtains. If anything had gone right tonight, it had been because Philippa was here. She cared for his mother, knew when to support his sister and when to let her go. She'd spoken to his guests with ease—to both men and women, and regardless of their age and station.

What a man could become with a woman like her at his side.

CHAPTER TWENTY-THREE

*P*hilippa leaned back in the reclining sofa with Hugh on her lap and tucked a finger into her sleeping nephew's fist. "It was a near disaster, although I think we were able to patch some of the worst things up."

Selena sat on the chair nearby and listened without saying anything.

"First, his mother brings home three men—the kind neither you nor I are in the habit of meeting, I daresay—directly from the gin house, from what I could understand. Everyone in the drawing room could hear their drunken singing, though I believe the disruption was explained away. Then Jack's—"

Philippa was silenced by Selena's surprised look at her informal use of Jack's name, and she flushed. "He asked me to call him Jack, although please don't ask me any questions, because we do not have an understanding."

"Of course not." Selena rested her perceptive gaze on Philippa, and there was a smile in her eyes. "Go on. Then what happened?"

"Then his brother walked in, which would not have been a bad thing. I understand Mr. Blythefield attends Society gatherings on a regular basis. But I fear he was a bit on the go, for he could not stand straight. He spoke with heavy sarcasm in front of his brother's guests, then kept nodding off. I was afraid he was going to fall asleep with his head on the plate."

Selena sucked in her breath through her teeth. "It sounds like a most unfortunate gathering." She reached over to pull the blanket more securely over Hugh's legs.

"That's not even all. When we had finished dinner and returned to the drawing room, Mr. Merrick gave Susan the cut direct, and she ran off crying to her room. Then, Jack's father entered, and it looked as though he was ready to give a speech about some investment opportunity—clearly inappropriate for the occasion. I begin to wonder if Jack's father is not beginning to … I don't know, beginning to age in his mind?"

Philippa caressed Hugh's tiny hand. "Poor Susan. Mr. Merrick made his distaste for her family quite clear after they exposed themselves. He won't be offering for her hand."

"She will do better with a man who is not so fickle," Selena answered quietly. "Better she find out before she is irrevocably tied."

It was only now that Philippa made the connection. Selena had gone through just such a humiliation. It was more drastic in Selena's case, with her father gambling away their family fortune then drinking himself into an early grave, but the consequences were the same. Her fiancé had ended their betrothal, and Society quickly made her feel unwelcome.

"Fortunately for Lucius, you found out in time, too."

"*Mm.*" Selena glanced at Philippa and smiled. "Fortunately for us both."

Philippa sighed. "I would like to go to the Blythefields, but I hesitate. I am sure today must be difficult, but I don't dare find out. Would they want me after having suffered such a thing?"

"Why would they not? You are on such easy terms with Susan, one might think you live there. You have never before hesitated to visit Susan on a moment's notice, and if you don't go, she might feel you are rejecting her." Selena creased her brows. "You must not let her feel that. I know it all too well."

"No." Philippa looked down and gently caressed Hugh's head. "I don't fear seeing Susan. Of course, I want to put her at ease—she should not fear my rejection, no matter what anyone else might say. But what if Jack…" Philippa did not know how to express the rest of what she felt—what she feared.

"You are beginning to have feelings for Jack that makes it more complicated to arrive at his house without worrying you are being too forward," Selena guessed.

"Yes," Philippa exclaimed. "That is exactly it. Something has shifted between us, and I no longer feel like I am merely visiting Susan. The pull to see Jack is even stronger." She risked a glance at Selena. "I am not sure that I've admitted it even to myself before now. When Susan ran off, it was I who stepped into the role of hostess, and it felt like the most natural thing. There was no one else to perform the duty, for even Miss Sommers had made her distaste evident and left the party early."

"Do you have reason to believe Mr. Blythefield has a *tendre* for you?" Selena's gaze was fixed on Philippa, who looked down, unable to meet it. For the first time in her life—that she could remember—Philippa felt shy.

"I believe he might, but he has never said so, apart from asking me to call him Jack and pressing a kiss on my hand." Philippa listened to the baby's soft breath, comforted by his warmth on her lap.

"Here," Selena said, standing. "Hand over Hugh. It is time for you to visit Susan, for she needs you. I cannot say whether Mr. Blythefield is in love with you, since I have not seen how he is with you for myself. But if he does have feelings, he will not rest until he declares himself. That is a separate issue entirely. In the meantime, there is the matter of Susan. It is not like you to be sitting here when you could be over there comforting your friend."

Philippa lifted her nephew to his mother and got reluctantly to her feet. Selena set Hugh in his cot, and he shifted in his sleep, then fell into an even deeper slumber. Selena walked over to Philippa and turned her around, pushing her toward the door with her hands on both of Philippa's arms.

"Go, dearest. Then come back and tell me how it went."

Philippa smiled and let herself be led—or rather *pushed*—out the door of the nursery. The sudden realization that Jack had spoken of there being a vote today brought her a rush of consolation. She would not have to meet him there. One thing she knew for certain, something had altered between her and Jack, and she would no longer be able to meet him without this new, charged undercurrent coursing through her. And now that she was aware that the tug of feelings was probably love, there was only one thing to do.

She would take care not to cross paths with him when she went to Susan's. She would wait until Jack came to see her.

***

When Philippa arrived at the Blythefield home, Fernsby left her to go to the kitchen and join the servants, and Shanks shuffled over to the drawing room to announce Philippa's arrival. The room was empty, and he ushered Philippa into it to wait. She sincerely hoped he was not going to climb the steps himself to fetch Susan, but from the sounds of it, he was.

Philippa stood suddenly, wondering if it would be completely inexcusable to offer to go up to Susan without being announced. She could not imagine how long it would take him and what sort of shape he would be in when he arrived.

There was another knock on the door, and Philippa walked over to the doorknob of the drawing room, hesitating. She heard nothing without and at last opened the door and stepped into the corridor. It was still empty of servants. Making a sudden bold decision, Philippa walked forward and opened the door herself.

"Philippa!" Matthew Evans was standing on the doorstep with a bouquet of flowers. "You are the very last person I expected to open the door."

"Come in, come in." Philippa quickly shut the door behind him. "I know it is most unusual. In fact I can't believe I dared attempt it, but it appears there is no footman to assist the butler, and—I don't know if you've noticed, but he is quite aged." Matthew nodded, and she went on, "Come into the drawing room quickly. I believe Susan is going to come down."

"I see." Matthew followed her into the drawing room, and they turned to face each other. He bit his lip and stared at Philippa without really appearing to see her, then turned and set his flowers on the table in front of him. "How is she?"

"Susan?" Philippa gestured at a chair and took the seat across from him. "I don't know. I haven't seen her since last night. She ran off when Mr. Merrick turned from her without acknowledging her presence."

A deep crease appeared on Matthew's brow. "He hurt her, the cur. He deserves to be horsewhipped."

"It is good news, though. He can no longer dangle her on a string," Philippa said. "She will have to admit the feelings did not run deep with him. That means her heart is clear for you to capture."

"If I can do such a thing." Matthew sighed.

"You can hardly do it if you are to fall into a deep decline," Philippa said severely. "You will simply have to apply yourself."

"I don't think you can understand." Matthew looked at Philippa. "Have you never been in love?"

The question shot through her like a bolt, and she was unable to answer. He did not allow her to evade the question, however; he kept his gaze fixed on her until she was forced to reply.

"I am not sure if I have ever been in love," she said, honestly. "But can one truly be in love when there is not a shared understanding? Anything else is only an infatuation."

Matthew frowned and picked up the bouquet from the table at his side and put it on his lap. The door opened, and both Matthew and Philippa stood. The butler stepped aside for Susan to enter, and when he saw Matthew, his brows drew together in surprise. Philippa was too embarrassed to explain Matthew's presence and was thankful when the butler stepped back without waiting for an explanation.

Susan came directly to Matthew. "I must thank you, Mr. Evans. I learned from my father about your care for him last night in proposing an investment scheme that he might like. I believe I can trust you to lead him into something that will not ruin our family?"

Matthew set the bouquet back in its place and took both of Susan's hands in his, bowing over them. "You most certainly can trust me for that."

Susan slid her hands from his grasp, then glanced at Philippa. Her eyes were red from crying, but her face was resolute—stronger than Philippa was accustomed to seeing.

She went over to Philippa. "Thank you for coming today and for stepping in to host in my place. Jack was already gone when I left my room this morning, but one of the footmen told my maid that you had carried on with the duties, and that all was well." She bit her lip. "I fear I made a fool out of myself yesterday. No one was ignorant of my sentiments."

"Sit," Philippa encouraged her. "You look fatigued." Philippa took Susan's usual chair so that Susan was forced to sit closer to Matthew.

"That is what vexes me most," Susan said. She glanced at Matthew. "I am speaking freely, but after what you did for my father, I believe I may call you a friend."

"You certainly may," Matthew answered gravely. In his concern, he leaned so far forward that Philippa thought it took all he had not to leap up and take Susan in his arms.

"What vexed me," Susan continued, "is that I wore my heart on my sleeve for Mr. Merrick, who did not deserve it in the slightest. I gave away a piece of myself to someone unworthy, and in the process, exposed myself to ridicule."

Philippa was about to say that the guests had scarcely noticed when she left—which would have been consoling, yet not quite truthful—but Matthew spoke first.

"You could never expose yourself to ridicule. To do so, you would have to act without sensibility. I believe you incapable of such a thing."

He spoke so earnestly that Philippa could see Susan relaxing. Philippa needed to give them more time together without leaving her friend entirely unchaperoned. Goodness, it was complicated in this household—to keep the necessary protocol for a virtuous maiden without a family structure in place to see to it. Philippa wasn't sure how Susan had managed to stay so innocent. Her friend had been born to it, apparently.

"I will ring for tea, if you grant me leave," Philippa said to Susan, who nodded. She went to pull the bell, then stayed by the door waiting for the servant to come, before giving the instructions. When the servant left, she walked over to a small bookshelf that contained only the most basic collection of books fit for a drawing room. There was a more standard collection in the small library, she knew. Philippa skimmed the titles, listening to the sounds of murmured conversation from the couple.

The tea arrived, and Philippa prepared it under Susan's direction, then expressed a wish to drink her tea nearer to the window so she could read. There she attempted to tune out the details of a conversation that was budding in intimacy. But she could not have summarized a single line of what she read.

After a suitable amount of time, Matthew stood and announced his leave, and Philippa came to join Susan in bidding him farewell. She remained standing after he had gone and turned to Susan.

"I cannot remain much longer, myself." Philippa had begun to grow too restless at the thought of meeting Jack here. It had been a stroke of luck that he had not come, but if she stayed it would appear as though she were waiting for him.

Susan's face showed calm, and all traces of tears had disappeared. "I am so glad you came to see me. Thank you for everything."

Philippa clasped Susan's hands. "I only want what's best for you." She paused. She could not pry for information, but how she longed to know if Matthew's suit would prosper. "It was good of Mr. Evans to come..."

"Mr. Evans is a most noble man. I do not deserve him," Susan replied, dropping her gaze to her feet.

"Why?" Philippa gave Susan's hand a little shake to get her friend to look at her. "Is it because of some silly notion that you are not his equal in some way?"

"Because I am too foolish," Susan replied, her eyes welling with tears. "He deserves someone with more sense."

"The only sense he requires is for you to see that he is desperately in love with you and for you to accept his proposal should you return his regard." Philippa gave Susan's hand another squeeze. "And only the biggest simpleton could fail to do that."

CHAPTER TWENTY-FOUR

*I*t seemed to Jack that the volume of noise in the Commons grew when he walked into the chamber. He did not attempt to speak to anyone, but some of his friends who were respected members of the party still came forward to greet him. They must have known about—but decided they would overlook—last night's debacle.

Robert Whitmore took his usual place at Jack's side. They were not intimate friends but saw eye to eye on nearly every issue. Well … on every issue when Whitmore wasn't dancing with Philippa.

"It should not surprise you, after their behavior at last night's dinner, that Thackery, Merrick, and Lord Harrowden are doing damage to our efforts at repealing the bill," Whitmore said. "They have pulled a few people to their side, saying that no one with such an odd family as yours should have any say in the future of England. They even called into question your status as a gentleman, I am sorry to say. I believe they are in the minority in their prejudice, however."

Jack shook his head. "It does not surprise me at all. It's a disappointment, but Merrick and Thackery always did seem rather changeable on this and other issues."

The room was called to order, and the vote on the Corn Laws was the first business of the day. As soon as the speeches opened, Jack took the floor. He had decided in advance he would attempt to disarm his opponents by bringing up the topic that was on everyone's mind—his disastrous dinner. Hopefully, by doing so, he would bring them back to the true issue at hand.

"Some of you were at the dinner in my family home last night. Those of you who did not attend have heard all about it by now, I am sure. I am not here to talk about that, however, as it is fitting that only matters of the *law*"—he lent heavy significance to the word—"should influence what is decided in Parliament." Jack had prepared what he would say before coming today, but even as he spoke, his convictions—and confidence—began to take root.

"We have debated numerous times on the subject of repealing the Corn Laws. We men of Parliament may be passionate in our convictions, but we are not given over to emotions and impetuous decisions. We now have a choice before us. We have seen the damage that restricting free trade has done to England's economy and its poorest members. Do we continue to allow this bill to stand and invite years more of economic distress?"

Jack looked up and met Sir Lucius's gaze in the front row of the spectator's balcony. Unlike last night's dinner, when Jack was out of his depth, before the Commons, he was in perfect command of himself. He detailed the facts Sir Lucius had provided him with in the committee meetings, proving a repeal would be beneficial for both landowners and laborers.

He concluded by summarizing his arguments. "I am here today to urge you to vote on repealing the bill so landowners might export their product and thereby reach a wider base of people to purchase it; so laborers might feed their family and not turn to vice—or revolt—out of despair; so the health of the economy and the supply and demand might determine the price of bread, not a small quorum of men who do not represent the interests of the entire country."

Jack looked around the room, catching the eyes of those men who would meet his gaze. "Do we decide to hold on to the Corn Laws for personal gain or Parliamentary factions that do not call into consideration the good of England? Or do we decide to open up His Majesty's country to free trade because we have made an informed decision that this is what will most benefit us all? This is what we must decide today, and I cannot do so in your place."

Jack sat to a smattering of applause and shouts of "*Hear! Hear!*" and some of the men around him grasped his shoulder. Opponents of the motion leapt to their feet and presented their own arguments in equally passionate—and longer—speeches. No one publicly discredited Jack because of his family's eccentricities, as he had almost feared when he was coming to Westminster that day. Jack began to think he might be able to pull through this embarrassment with his career intact.

This was the only bill on the table for the day, and at the end of the speeches, the Speaker announced it was time to vote. "All in favor of repealing the Corn Laws, raise your hands and say, 'aye'." Then, "All those against repealing the bill say 'nay'."

The MPs did so, but the vote was too close a count to see at a glance which side had won. Jack tried desperately to count, but there were too many 'ayes' mixed with 'nays', and he was not fast enough.

The Speaker changed his tactic. "Those of you who are for repealing the bill, stand on the left side of the chamber. And those of you who are against, stand on the right."

The House did so, and the clerk began to count those in favor of the vote. Jack stood on the left side, studying the faces of those who were on the right. He was unsurprised to see Thackery, Merrick, and Lord Harrowden on the opposing side. On his own side, he noticed Mr. Atkinson and was gratified that not everyone who had attended his dinner had turned away from supporting the motion to repeal.

The clerk handed a paper to the Speaker, who read out the numbers. "We have the final tally. Two-hundred and forty-eight in favor of repealing the Corn Laws, and two-hundred and sixty-nine against."

The law had failed by twenty-one votes. Everything Jack had pinned his hopes on had failed—and possibly his future position as Leader of the Opposition with it.

The room erupted in speech, and Jack walked over to the bench and picked up his hat, ignoring the sounds around him. Both Whitmores came to speak with him, and he answered them numbly, responding to a few others as he made his way out the door.

He needed time to digest what had just happened. It was only the first large bill he had attempted to overturn in his political career, and he was still young. Perhaps the consequences of his failure to bring it about would not be as bleak as he feared. There was even a chance his career would not be destroyed, despite the devastating loss. Still.

**

Jack walked. At first, he was not really sure where he was going as he marched down the paved sidewalk on Parliament Street, ignoring the pedestrians around him and remaining insensible to the carriages that bowled by at a brisk trot on the street. He kept his eyes straight ahead as he tried to process the vote, his future in Parliament—his own personal future and where he was headed.

It was when Parliament Street turned into Whitehall that he began to doubt that his direction was aimless and his walk idle. Sir Lucius lived on Whitehall Court, and that was where Philippa was. When he came to the narrow lane that was Whitehall Yard, which led to the river, he paused. Did he dare see Philippa now when he was fresh from his defeat? Could he face her?

His feet moved forward, and he turned right, walking past Lord Carrington's house until he came to Whitehall Court. Now that he had come this far, he couldn't think about turning back.

"I am here to see Sir Lucius," he told the butler as he presented his card. In truth, he was fairly certain Sir Lucius would not yet have arrived from the Commons, although Jack had not stayed to find out.

"I am sorry to inform you that Sir Lucius is out," the butler said. He paused, and when Jack did not answer right away, he began to close the door.

"And Miss Clavering? Miss Philippa Clavering?" Jack clarified, in case there were any other sisters he was unaware of. It was entirely possible. "Here is my card."

The butler allowed him to step in. "I will see if she is at home to visitors," he said.

The door to the drawing room opened, and Philippa came out of it with Lady Clavering. Philippa was in outdoor attire, except for her bonnet. When she saw Jack, she stopped short and broke off from conversation. She opened her mouth to speak but was interrupted by the front door opening. Jack whirled around to see Sir Lucius enter the house.

"Blythefield. It was good of you to come. I didn't see you after the vote." Sir Lucius took off his beaver hat and handed it to the butler.

"I couldn't stay." Jack turned to face him. "I didn't have the heart for it."

"I don't blame you," Sir Lucius said. He divested himself of his coat and handed that to the butler before gesturing forward. "Come into the library, and I can have some brandy brought."

"Lucius." Lady Clavering was standing at the entrance to the drawing room. "Shall we not invite Mr. Blythefield into the drawing room for tea, so that we might hear about the debate as well?"

Jack glanced at Philippa, whose color was heightened as she dropped her gaze. He could have kissed Lady Clavering's hand for proposing it. Sir Lucius stared at his wife and there seemed to be an unspoken conversation between them before he turned to Jack.

"If you are not opposed to the idea, shall we join the ladies? I am sure they would prefer to have your thoughts on the matter rather than hearing it only from me. I can have some brandy sent here, if you'd like."

Jack smiled. "Tea will suit me very well."

Sir Lucius and Lady Clavering led the way into the drawing room, and Jack approached Philippa, allowing her to step through the door before him.

"I take it your vote was not successful," she said, sympathetically. She slowed her steps, and he treasured their brief moment of intimacy.

"It was not."

With Lady Clavering chatting to her husband about some household affair, Jack had almost the sensation of having Philippa to himself. She stopped some feet away from the sofa and armchairs in the middle of the drawing room.

"I am so glad you came here first. You will find sympathetic ears among us." Philippa smiled then turned to join her brother and sister-in-law, and Jack followed.

Sir Lucius sat on the sofa next to his wife and put his arm around the back of it. "As you must have guessed, the motion to repeal the Corn Laws did not pass."

"I am sorry to hear it," Lady Clavering said.

"As am I," Philippa replied. She sat on the chair, and her look was one of such sweet sympathy that Jack had to wrench his gaze away.

"Yes, well…" Jack could not complete his thought.

As the tea was brought in and served, Jack summarized the debates and what he thought had gone wrong. Sir Lucius added his point of view on the matter as well—both keeping their thoughts brief with respect to the ladies. Philippa participated more actively in the conversation than Lady Clavering, and Jack was impressed with her grasp of the nuances of the law and the motion they were trying to pass.

Apparently, Sir Lucius was too, for he turned to his sister. "If you were a man, you might make the Clavering family proud by taking a seat in the Commons and actually doing some good there. You have a better understanding than some of the men."

Philippa smiled at his unexpected praise but lifted her chin. "If men had more understanding, they would allow women to participate in Parliament *without* having to become a man!"

"I, for one, would not have you be a man for the world," Jack said— then grew hot up through the roots of his hair. He could not believe the inanity he had just uttered in front of Philippa, and her family too! Lady Clavering laughed in what sounded like a cough over her sip of tea, and Sir Lucius merely raised both brows. Jack did not dare look at Philippa. If only the ground would swallow him whole.

Lady Clavering glanced toward the window. "It is such a fine day, is it not? Perhaps we ought to take advantage of the weather and go for a walk in the park if Hugh is content with Nurse."

Sir Lucius looked at his wife, as if trying to read her intentions. "Yes. A fine idea." He turned to Jack. "Would you like to join us? Philippa?"

At last, Jack dared to glance at Philippa again. She had taken off her pelisse and had laid it next to her, along with her bonnet. Her cheeks still held two spots of color that must have been from the embarrassment he had caused her. If she said yes to the walk, despite having just returned from another outing, then he would be sure of her regard.

"It is a splendid day. A walk would be nice," Philippa said, with a flirty look that thrilled Jack to his toes.

"A walk it is," Sir Lucius said, getting to his feet.

"I will go and see that Nurse has everything she needs." Lady Clavering stood and left the room at a brisk pace, and Sir Lucius followed her into the corridor, leaving the drawing room door open. Jack and Philippa both stood more slowly, and Philippa lifted her pelisse from the chair.

"Please. Allow me," Jack said, stepping over to assist her. When she had her coat on and turned to face him, he dropped his hands rather than succumb to the temptation of buttoning it for her, or taking her into his arms. He did not step away. Philippa stood immobile, looking up at him with a questioning gaze.

Sir Lucius entered the room. "Why don't the two of you walk to St. James Park, and we will meet you there. Knowing my wife, she will want to see that the baby is fed and changed before we leave. It will take us at least a half hour to get everything ready."

Philippa moved forward. "Very well. Near the cherry trees?"

Sir Lucius nodded and went up the stairs, and Jack offered his arm once they were outdoors. His heart beat quickly from excitement. As if by mutual agreement to save their intimate conversation for a more private setting, they spoke only of the most mundane subjects on their ten-minute walk to the park. Jack listened to the warmth in her voice, so very different from the "bull-headed" description he had once used to refer to her. He wondered if she had changed because of him, or if he had been completely wrong about her from the start. He suspected he hadn't really allowed himself to see her for who she was.

They entered the park, and Philippa drew in a deep breath and smiled up at him. She seemed to be waiting for him to say something, but he hardly knew where to begin. How did a man propose marriage when he had not prepared a speech?

Jack steered her gently toward a lane that led in the direction of the cherry trees and was less frequented than the broad path they had been on, though it was not a fashionable hour to walk, and it was not Hyde Park. There appeared to be only a handful of couples walking and some nannies with their charges.

He moved over to let an older couple cross their path, whom he acknowledged with a bow, all the while aware of how nervous he was. He cleared his throat.

"I cannot thank you enough for your help at my dinner party last night. It was good to have you there." Jack blew out his breath. "The dinner might have cost me my hoped-for position of Leader of the Opposition, although I'm not sure the vote failed to pass because of it. I suspect some of the men, like Thackery, Merrick, and Harrowden were always against the repeal and were just causing trouble."

Philippa shook her head. "Lord Harrowden finds trouble wherever he goes, and I cannot imagine Mr. Thackery looking out for anything other than his own interests. I am sorry they ruined your party and undermined your attempts at reform."

Jack looked down and was briefly mesmerized by Philippa's pink kid boots that peeped out from her pale day dress as she walked. "I don't think they ruined the party," he said, drawing his eyes upwards and exhaling. "Everyone knows my family did that on its own."

Philippa shrugged at his side. "Your family might fall a tad on the eccentric side, but they live passionately. They are honorable." She turned and met his gaze. "I like them."

Jack drew her arm into his and pulled her near—as close to a hug as he dared. *She liked his family.* Never had he thought to meet a woman who would say such a thing. "Well, in any case, I shudder to think how it would have gone had you, Sir Lucius, and Mr. Evans not been there."

"I hope that means you will favor Mr. Evans's suit? I do seem to remember telling you when we first met that I thought he would be an ideal match."

"I do remember. Because of his fortune, if I am not mistaken." Jack smiled down at her.

"No…" She drew the word out. "I merely said that because I thought it would be the only thing to tempt you to consider it." Though Philippa quickly turned to look ahead, he caught a glimpse of her upturned lips.

"Because you thought me abominably mercenary, I suppose," Jack said.

"I could not be sure, but all signs pointed to it," Philippa replied primly. He could hear the teasing in her voice.

"Philippa, you wretch," Jack replied without heat, and she giggled. They walked in silence for some paces, and he furrowed his brows. "But I don't believe Susan is any closer to accepting your Matthew, no matter how noble a gentleman he may be. Last night she ran off because Mr. Merrick snubbed her. Surely she will not switch her affection so quickly."

"Well, when I was with the two of them today in the drawing room, they seemed to be well on their way to reaching an understanding." Philippa slowed and pointed ahead. "The cherry trees. I cannot wait until the blossoms rain down whenever a breeze shakes them. It's the prettiest sight."

Jack tucked away a determination to bring her here later in the spring. "You were at my house today? With Mr. Evans?"

"We did not arrive together, but yes. And I drank my tea near the window, so he and Susan might clear the air between the two of them. You really need to improve your library collection in the drawing room."

"Have you not finished making changes in the Blythefield home?" Jack teased, stopping her progress as he turned to face her. His smile fell when he saw she returned his regard with a look of uncertainty.

"If I have overstepped my bounds, Jack, you must tell me. I will not suggest another improvement." Philippa had dropped her hand from his elbow, and her arms hung loosely at her side.

"You have not. Philippa, don't you see? I came to you straight from my defeat without planning on such a course. For once in my life, I did something completely without planning it. It was as though my heart led me straight to you."

Jack lifted her two hands and pulled them to his chest, holding them in his, and she came without resistance. Her enchanting face broke into a smile that he could wake up to every day of his life, especially when it came with such dancing eyes.

And right now, that smile was close enough to kiss. "Will you marry me, my wonderful Philippa? And live with me? And exasperate and delight me—and suggest improvements in my home until death do us part?"

Philippa laughed and assumed an artful expression. "A marriage proposal! And here I had not planned to get married in London at all."

"Where do you plan to go next? Off to the country? I will simply move there, and then I will ask you, 'Will you marry me? And live with me? And exasperate and delight me until death do us part?'"

"You forgot about improving the home," she reminded him.

"Nothing escapes you, my little beauty. I will move to the country and propose to you and include home renovations in the marriage contract." Jack pulled her hands to his lips and planted a kiss on them.

"I suppose I shall not make you go to all the trouble of moving." Philippa's smile, which reached her eyes, blinded him. Or maybe it was his joy that did that.

"Yes, Jack. To all of it."

"Good. Because I could not bear it if you had returned any other answer." Jack smiled, a bubble of hope expanding in his chest until he thought it might burst. Their eyes met, and Jack lowered his gaze, intent on her lips. His heart thudded at her nearness and her intoxicating scent. Every sense tingled at the realization that he was going to kiss his betrothed for the first time—

"Blythefield!"

Jack pulled away and turned in time to see Sir Lucius and Lady Clavering. As Sir Lucius closed in on Jack, he leapt away from Philippa.

CHAPTER TWENTY-FIVE

"Lucius, don't!" Philippa put up her arm to stop her brother, who had left Selena's side and marched toward Jack. Philippa could see from his expression that he had only one purpose in mind, and it was not a friendly one. "Jack has asked me to marry him, and I have accepted. So please lower your fist and stop making such a scene."

Lucius stopped and jerked his head up as two couples strolled around the bend, flirting and laughing. He dropped his arm. "Is this true, Blythefield?"

"Yes." Jack pulled back to face Lucius squarely. "My feelings for your sister, which have been growing over the last weeks, became very apparent to me last night. I would like to make Philippa my wife—with your approval."

Selena hurried forward. "I offer you my heartfelt congratulations." She smiled at Lucius. "They will suit very well, will they not?"

Philippa watched Lucius's initial outrage taper off and reason set in. "Then I suppose there is nothing to do but invite you over tomorrow to discuss terms."

Jack smiled, and a hint of relief shone in his eyes. "Thank you. It would be my honor. I may not gain the position I was angling for after the less-than-hopeful outcome of the dinner and vote, but I am very well able to support a wife, which I will willingly go into with you tomorrow, sir."

"Well, since we have come for a walk, we may as well take it," Lucius said. "But this time, we walk together, and there will be no kissing or any other displays of sentiment in a public setting."

"Lucius, there was not a soul around," Philippa protested. She slipped her hand back into Jack's arm where it fit so comfortably.

Lucius glowered at her. "And that is precisely the problem."

Philippa rolled her eyes. "And do you mean to tell me you and Selena never kissed before you were married? *Hm*? Especially after spending an entire day alone in the carriage together and marrying her at night by special license?"

Jack squeezed Philippa's hand.

Selena laughed. "Lucius, one must not be a hypocrite. Let us walk." She took her husband firmly by the arm and began moving forward.

"Yes, but it's my *sister*," Lucius grumbled.

As Philippa and Jack followed Lucius and Selena, Jack leaned down to whisper, "I would very much like that kiss, and if I get another opportunity, I warn you I'm going to take it."

"I consider myself warned." Philippa's cheeks hurt from the effort of trying to refrain from laughing out of sheer joy. She attempted instead to turn the conversation to something more mundane. "Have you had a chance to find out from your brother why he came to your dinner?"

"I have not seen him. I had gone riding this morning before heading to Parliament. But I was surprised upon my return to find a note he had penned before leaving. In it, he apologized for his behavior, blaming it on a heavy loss at the card table. He assured me it would not happen again, although I don't know if I can believe him."

"Well, it is a start," Philippa replied. "Perhaps his life will take a more serious turn, especially if Matthew does indeed guide your father toward more profitable investments. Your brother might end up inheriting a solvent estate."

"He might," Jack conceded. "I only hope my father will not botch the opportunity Mr. Evans is giving him, and that he will see the matter through."

"Perhaps your brother might be prevailed upon to assist your father. Their working together on the good of the estate might give your brother a purpose—and his guiding presence would prevent your father from making an unwise decision."

"It is possible." Jack put his hand on her waist to steer her around a rock that was as small as her fist. He did not let her go as he added, "You might very well be right, my wise darling. I will speak with both of them on the matter."

They finished their walk at an easy rhythm, discussing such diverse topics as family, politics, and weddings. Jack told Philippa more about his estate and promised her that he would whisk her off to live there should his political ambitions come to nothing. It was both wonderfully ordinary and thrilling to think she was setting out on such an adventure.

When he left her at her brother's house and promised to come the next day, their time had felt too short. She wished they'd had just another minute or two to themselves.

The next day, Jack came as promised, and in view of both Lucius and Selena, bent down to kiss Philippa's hand before going off to the library to speak with Lucius. Selena sat with Philippa in the drawing room while they waited, and for some inexplicable reason, Philippa was nervous. She had no reason to be. She knew Jack was perfectly acceptable as a suitor and that Lucius already had a favorable opinion of him. She just hoped her brother would go easy on Jack. After what seemed like hours, they came out of the study and joined the ladies in the drawing room.

"Congratulations, Philippa," Lucius said and went over to stand near Selena. "Or perhaps I should be congratulating myself, because you will no longer be my responsibility. You are to be married."

Philippa leapt to her feet and went over to Jack with her hands outstretched. Grinning broadly, he took them in his own.

"We must celebrate the happy news." Selena knit her brows as if she had just remembered something. "But, Lucius, I think we should check on Hugh before we do. He might be missing us."

Lucius had been about to sit down, but at his wife's words, he took on a look of resignation and held out his hand to help her rise. He lifted his finger at Jack. "But I will return. We will not be above five minutes."

Jack gave a nod. "Yes, sir."

He faced Philippa with a smile that she returned. They were two feet from each other, and they stayed perfectly still until the sound of the door closing behind her could be heard.

Then Jack walked forward and threw his arms around Philippa and pulled her against him until she could feel the buttons of his jacket against her chest. His eyes flicked to hers, and her breath suspended. In a second, he leaned down and his lips were on hers. Then he was kissing her. He kissed her hungrily—again and again in his fervor—and Philippa could only wonder that such forceful passion could come with such soft lips. He kissed her until her knees threatened to buckle under her.

As if he sensed her unsteadiness, Jack finally slowed and put his hands on her cheeks then kissed her again, more deeply until Philippa's heartbeat reverberated throughout her body and there was not a thought left in her head.

At last, Jack released her from his mesmerizing grip. He let his hands slide down from her face to her shoulders, then he trailed them down her arms. He looked into Philippa's eyes, attempting to smile while catching his breath. "Perhaps it was a blessing that Lucius interrupted us yesterday. I'm not sure *that* would have been quite the thing in a public park."

Philippa put her hands on Jack's arms to regain her balance. She had never known herself to be so giddy—or her stomach to feel as though a flock of birds had taken flight inside it. Neither had she known what it was to be truly happy until this moment.

"It appears Jack Blythefield is not a cold man," Philippa proclaimed. "In fact, I have it on the very best authority that a much warmer nature beats under that austere face he likes to show the world."

"Your sources are correct," Jack replied. "But then, I cannot say I ever knew just *how* warm a nature I possessed until you sparked it to life, my darling."

***

Jack led Philippa to the sofa and took a seat next to her to wait for Lucius and Selena's return and to celebrate the upcoming nuptials. He wondered what his own family would think once he'd announced the news, although he had a pretty fair idea of what Susan would say. As for his position in the Commons, only time would tell if he was chosen to be Leader of the Opposition or if he would continue as a simple Member of Parliament—or move to his estate and raise a family with the captivating woman next to him who had said yes. He only knew that what he'd considered to be the smallest priority in his life was now the most vital and that everything else would somehow shift and settle and find its place as well.

Sounds of Lucius and Selena descending the stairs from the nursery reached Jack's ears, and he looked at Philippa, who smiled up at him. He interlaced their fingers, bringing her hand up to his lips to place a kiss on her knuckles. Her face was close to his, and her eyes did not leave his face. He could stare into them forever.

"Just think, my love, what the two of us will accomplish together," Jack said. Philippa returned no answer, but a mischievous glint in her eye accompanied her smile. He couldn't resist giving her a quick kiss before the approaching footsteps invaded their intimacy.

As the drawing room door opened, he leaned in to murmur, "There will be a Mrs. Jack Blythefield in the world, and the world will never be the same."

"That sounds ominous," Philippa whispered back with a soft chuckle.

"Not ominous," Jack replied. "Marvelous!"

***

ACKNOWLDGEMENTS

Philippa Holds Court was a difficult book for me to write because I had decided to present a snapshot of life in British Parliament without knowing anything about the subject beforehand. I spent more hours on research for this book than I have for any other element of life in Regency England to date. I beg your indulgence for the creative license I took to bend historical facts to fit my story.

The Corn Laws, established in 1773, were not abolished until 1846, although they were up for repeal numerous times. I'd read somewhere that the bill was debated in Parliament in 1819 when my book is set; however, I could not find any debates on the topic recorded in Hansard for that year. The other laws mentioned in passing did come up for debate in the Commons that Session, and the parliamentary positions and processes were as close as I could bring them to the era. I could not have written this without the help of the Historymakers group, particularly Nancy Mayer and Karen Pierotti. Any historical errors I made are my own.

And because this is a historical *romance* book, I am thankful for friends who helped bring the romantic element back to life when I had fallen down the pit of dry research and had lost my way. This is a shout out to my wonderful critique partners—Anneka Walker, Julie Christianson, Jess Heileman, Emma Le Noan—and also to my editors, Jolene Perry, Ranée Clark and Arielle Bailey. You were all essential in bringing my book to life, and you are fabulous.

Last but not least, it is my pleasure to write alongside the authors of the Sweet Regency Romance Fans group: Sally Britton, Deborah Hathaway, Jess Heileman, Martha Keyes, Ashtyn Newbold, Kasey Stockton & Mindy Strunk. Come and find our group on Facebook. We have lots of fun!

Memorable Proposals

A Regrettable Proposal
A Faithful Proposal
A Daring Proposal

***

Clavering Chronicles

A Fall from Grace
Philippa Holds Court
The Sport of Matchmaking

***

Multi-Author Series

His Disinclined Bride
A Yorkshire Carol

***

Contemporary & Memoir

A Noble Affair
A Sweetheart in Paris
*Stars Upside Down - a memoir of travel, grief,
and an incandescent God*

*J*ennie Goutet is an American-born Anglophile, who lives with her French husband and their three children in a small town outside Paris. Her imagination resides in Regency England, where her Regency romances are set. Jennie is also author of the award-winning memoir, *Stars Upside Down*, and the modern romances, *A Sweetheart in Paris* and *A Noble Affair*. A Christian, a cook, and an inveterate klutz, Jennie writes about faith, food, and life—even the clumsy moments—on her blog, aladyinfrance.com. You can learn more about Jennie and her books, and sign up for her newsletter, on her author website: jenniegoutet.com.

Photo credit goes to Caroline Aoustin

CPSIA information can be obtained
at www.ICGtesting.com
Printed in the USA
LVHW102015080422
715703LV00001B/2